THE BACKUP PLAN

JIM RYKER THRILLERS
BOOK 1

KEVIN TUMLINSON

NICK THACKER

ONE

Of all the things Mark Adams had been taught during his military days and especially during both military and CIA training, 'Never run while being American' was one lesson he'd always hoped he wouldn't have to put to the test.

Tongue in cheek as it was, it was good survival advice. Nothing was more conspicuous than a runner—and an *American* runner, darting and diving through the streets of a Katakstan border town, was just about as conspicuous as you could get. He could set his head on fire in a Starbucks and get less attention.

Of course, the men chasing him were probably more than happy to set his head on fire for him, if they caught him.

They were *definitely* going to catch him.

Ducking through stalls, trampling over slow-moving pedestrians, and leaping through narrow cracks between cars, Mark was starting to hope—a thin, wispy, gossamer thread of hope—that he *might just make it.* He might just get to the extraction point. He might just be able to get to the other side of the wall. He might just reach the American Forward Operating Base, and get the hell out of this country.

He might just live through this.

And then there was the shot.

He didn't hear it. You don't hear a shot like that—not with the crowds of hawkers and vendors yelling in *Pashto* and half a dozen other languages to sell their wares, the screams of frightened and angry pedestrians alarmed at the white American sprinting past and shoving people aside, the incessant honking and loud music coming from the tsunami of cars on the street. You might think that even among all that racket there'd be some pause in the air, some narrow window through which the sound of a gunshot could ring.

But in all that racket, any shot fired was just more of the same, one more note in the symphony of white noise. You didn't hear it.

You *felt it.*

Mark didn't need to hear that shot in order for it to do its job. He took the hit, right in the back of the thigh, a thud to the meaty part of his leg that suddenly burned like it was filled with fire ants and kerosene, taking everything out of his run but the forward momentum.

And down he went.

He had been in mid-stride when he was hit, and the loss of a stable leg to absorb the impact of motion was the end of the line.

His momentum crashed him into and carried him over the wobbly cart of a man selling ancient-looking American products— phone cases and cables and other accessories that were covered in a scrim of dust and grime, in packaging that had been exposed to all manner of weather and pollution and God only knew what else as it had made its way from wherever it had been stolen to the here and now. The cart's owner screamed in *Pashto* as another filthy American byproduct came crashing into his livelihood, rolling through it to land in a heap of rubble and debris and blood on the street.

Mark was so distracted by the searing pain in the back of his leg that he barely noticed the impact with the cart, nor the feeling of the skin on his palms, forearms, and chin being scraped away by the rough pavement. His momentum carried him in an obscene cartwheel, a gangly and awkward forward flip and roll, right off of the lip of the chipped sidewalk and into the street itself. Cars swerved, there was a crash, more honking, more screaming. Some of the screaming was his.

Mark lay on the filthy street amidst a spreading puddle of his own blood, his chest heaving, the wound in his leg demanding his attention. And it got all of it, every scrap, until his training kicked in. He was mentally checking himself, running his mind over to the places it didn't want to go, assessing the injuries, his current state, his chances and choices.

And then there was the realization that he was *done*. Or close to it. There was no getting up, no running, with his leg in that condition. There was no path to escape for him. It was all over but the dying.

The hard drive was in his back pocket.

Should he destroy it?

He was already feeling weak, his mind thick and slow—shock, maybe. Or maybe the loss of blood was already getting to him. But whatever it was that was generating his growing brain fog, it was causing him to fumble. He could only sort of half-monkey-paw at his back pocket, to pull the hard drive out with fingers that were slicked with his own blood. He held the little rectangle tight—a small solid state drive about the size of a deck of playing cards. He had liberated it from a stolen laptop just a couple of hours earlier, in an effort to complete his mission, to keep the world safe from the drive's contents.

He'd been ordered to bring it home. But if that failed, he was to destroy it.

He raised his hand high, and was preparing to bring the drive down hard on the pavement, as hard as the last of his strength could manage. If he could muster enough energy, he'd do it again. Maybe toss it under the wheels of one of the cars zipping past.

A hand gripped his wrist—a sudden, undeniable grip that squeezed so hard that it felt like it was on the verge of snapping Mark's forearm in two.

He looked up into the face of the man who held his fate literally in his hands.

The man, Faraz. The leader of the *Kharif*. The highest-level target in the region.

Mark was trained, and the training ran deep. He could deal with pain. He didn't react to that grip, didn't even cry out from the crushing pressure of it. But it did stop him. His plans to destroy the drive were as done as he was. And in the next second the man holding his wrist pried the hard drive free and let Mark's arm drop.

Three more men swept in, dragging Mark roughly to his feet, and the pain in his thigh screamed at him in raging protest as he was violently shoved forward, directed off of the street and into a battered and filthy SUV that had just screeched to a stop in front of them. The others, including the man who had taken the hard drive, climbed in beside Mark, and began conversing with the driver, speaking in *Pashto*.

Mark understood all of it. He'd had nearly every language from this region hammered into his head during his training. A full year of intensive, immersive language study was just part of the gig, and he'd actually taken to it quite well. It was a lot easier to sweet talk local women when you could be clever in their language, and so he'd had incentive to become fluent.

He also understood that he was *meant* to know what these men were saying. Meant to hear the words for *torture*, for *slow*, for *capture video*.

They would video the whole thing and broadcast it over the internet, making sure that every news outlet on the planet got it, all at once. They'd make an example of Mark Adams, as they had so many other American swine who dared to set foot in Katakstan. His head would fall from his shoulders as their people cheered. He'd be an example. A warning that these men secretly hoped the Americans never heeded.

Americans losing their heads was good for morale. It was the best recruitment tool the *Kharif* had.

"It's no good!" Mark shouted, his *Pashto* and his accent perfect. *"The hard drive has a CIA encryption. You will never crack it."*

There was a pause in the conversation, a dip to silence. He knew he had them. He saw the man—the one who had grabbed him— hesitate, then hold up a hand, signaling his comrades to stay quiet.

Maybe they hadn't meant for him to understand them after all.

Faraz was facing Mark, as if waiting for him to continue.

This was the only card. This was Mark's only chance. This worked, or nothing worked.

"Without me you'll never get in," he said in *Pashto*. Then, to emphasize his point, he repeated in English. "You will never unlock that hard drive without me. I'm the only one who can figure out the key."

This was a half-truth.

There were hundreds of Americans in Katakstan who could work out the encryption key. Mark wasn't even the best from among them, when it came down to it. He had enough knowledge and intel to *maybe* get this sussed out, to unlock the drive before someone among these men got impatient and put a blade through his neck. He had a slim chance.

He also had some intel in his back pocket. The kind that made him sick to even think about. But if it came down to it, he'd use it. That was part of his training, too.

It was a long shot. They might not believe him. But they should. Because he was telling them the truth. That hard drive *was* encrypted. Finding the right key would take them months, possibly years. Even if they somehow managed to grab and torture every CIA operative in the country, their chances were very slim.

They needed Mark's help. He knew it. *They* knew it.

Faraz signaled and they drove, leaving the noise of the street behind, along with the puddle of Mark's blood soaking into the packages of a pile of junk and the grime of the street. American pop music played on the SUV's stereo, and Mark was allowed to use his belt to painfully tourniquet his leg.

At least he wouldn't bleed out before the torture started.

If he played this right, he might actually survive long enough to be labeled a traitor to his country.

TWO

Fort Larlan, West Texas

Jim Ryker had done some grimy, dirty work in some very hot places across the globe—from Middle Eastern deserts to the dense jungles of the Amazon. In that work he'd had to contend with IEDs and snipers, with Taliban extremists and suicide bombers, with toxic plants, poisonous wildlife, and guerrilla mercenaries. And none of it was more blatantly and oppressively grueling and uncomfortable as digging this fence line in the East Texas heat and humidity.

Drenched in sweat, baked from the sun overhead, Ryker just kept going. His hands, sheathed in a borrowed set of rough leather work gloves as thick and stiff as cow hide, were nevertheless feeling the strain of repeatedly jamming the old fashioned post hole diggers into the tough Texas soil, wrenching a plug of rock-hard dirt free, and then jamming a post into place as the next in nearly a hundred miles of fence posts. He filled around the post with the removed soil, wetting it from a plastic milk jug to soften it, then tamping it down, packing it tight. It would dry harder than cement by nightfall.

He moved on to the next post.

He'd been doing this work for nearly six hours before an aging Chevy pickup appeared on the horizon, rumbling over the distant ridge and trailing a plume of dust as it navigated the barely graded "road" that led to where Ryker was working.

Ryker checked his watch. He wasn't due to be picked up for another four hours. Often, he would walk most of the way back on his own steam, all of the gear and equipment stowed in a makeshift cart that rolled with all the ease of a square block over the rough terrain.

He was used to hikes like that. Or had become used to it again. Training like that died hard in the body, and only with years of letting it fade. Ryker had only been away from all those deserts and jungles for a little over a year, and in that time he'd done work like this—hard labor in uncomfortable places. Work that opened up his pores and let out not only the sweat but the time, the memories, the betrayals from friends and the things left unsaid.

Penance, maybe. What little penance he could hope for, after the things he'd done in all those deserts and jungles. But no matter how much he sweated, no matter how often he tore muscles and broke blisters on his hands, all that was still in there, inside him. It couldn't bleed out, no matter how deep of a wound he cut into himself.

So, maybe not penance, after all. But punishment. He could see that.

The truck pulled up slowly, its windows down because it had no air conditioning. Not that any level of air conditioning could compete with this God forsaken Texas heat.

"You planning to just keep goin' 'til you die from heat stroke out here?" the driver asked.

Ryker stood up straight, stretching his aching back before leaning on the post hole digger. He gave a weary smile, and pulled the canteen from his belt, taking a long swig before pouring some over his face and neck. The water was probably lukewarm, in reality, but it felt and tasted as cool as ice in comparison to the day. He shook his head, huffed, sighed. "Just trying to get as much finished as I can before I have to move on."

The man in the truck—Avery Clemmons—was somewhere north of 85 years old, and his face and arms showed Ryker that the bulk of those years were spent right on this ranch, with a short break to go serve his country in a war that took three of the four Clemmons boys. Avery was the only one left out of four brothers, and he had come home to scratch a living out of the dirt, keeping a herd of cattle alive for the past sixty years on not much more than a patch of grass and the grace of God. One of those two had run out more than once, leaving Avery to scramble and dig and gouge at the earth for whatever he could pull from it.

Avery was too much of a Christian to blame God directly. And instead was the kind of soul that thanked Him anyway, even for the meager amount of food he could grow and the money he was forced to stretch until it threatened to snap like a rubber band.

Ryker admired men like Avery for their persistence, and for their faith. Ryker had a bit of faith himself, despite the attempts of both the military and the CIA to burn it out of him. If Avery, and men like him, could hold on to some sliver of faith in the face of drought and struggle, who was Ryker to let it slip? He might have a hard time reconciling his past with any hope for a reward in heaven, but that didn't mean he was devoid of hope altogether.

Avery was the reason Ryker was here.

Penance and punishment, Ryker thought, as he had thought a thousand times before.

These were words that came to mind in odd and quiet moments, usually while Ryker was doing hard labor, but just as often when he was contemplating someone who was good and worthy. Service and honor were the words his family lived by. But penance and punishment were the words that shaped and defined him more than any other, these days.

They were words that even Ryker thought was a little unfair, though.

Penance and punishment for... *what*, exactly? For serving his country, just like his grandfather and uncles had done? Like his father had? Like men such as Avery had? Should Ryker suffer for doing his job? For following orders?

For mistakes that were made and wrongs that were done, under my watch.

Ryker knew that not all of those wrongs were on his ledger, but he was keeping record of them anyway. Because he'd been there. Done things. Given orders himself. And *just following orders* had long ago stopped being enough to keep his stomach from turning at the thought of it all. The only thing letting him sleep through the night these days was work like this. Blistering, mind-numbing, back-breaking work, done without complaint.

Penance and punishment.

Avery waved one weathered hand at the post hole digger. "Toss that in the back and get in. Ya got visitors, back at the house."

Ryker felt a spike of ice go through him, straight through his guts, running his blood cold despite the hot Texas sun. "Visitors? I don't know anybody here."

"They know you, though," Avery said. "Government types. Serious. Suits."

Suits. The word triggered something in Ryker that he had hoped to leave behind for good. Memories of sitting in small rooms, blinded by lights aimed directly into his eyes. Emotionless voices hounding him, questioning him, accusing him. Days, weeks, months of answering questions that didn't have answers. And then answering them again. And answering them again. Until finally someone must have come to agree with Ryker, that he knew nothing useful. And at that point, they hadn't so much let him go as told him to go away, and stay gone.

"Avery…" Ryker started, then shook his head.

"You in trouble, Jim?" Avery asked. "Maybe I tell 'em I couldn't find you? That you lit out, took off, maybe headed for the river?" Avery nodded in the direction of the anemic thread of water that ran through one end of his property, five miles up the fence line.

Ryker shook his head again, laughing lightly. "*That* river? I'd get maybe twenty feet before I'd just be walking through bone dry desert again."

"Dried up a bit these days, for sure," Avery nodded. "But I didn't say you should actually *go* there."

Ryker nodded as well. "I hear you. But… no, thanks. I appreciate it. But if these people thought you were covering for me to escape, they'd make things pretty hard on you."

"Lived my whole life hard," Avery shrugged. "What's a couple of government types going to do that life ain't done worse?"

"I'd rather we not test it and find out," Ryker said.

Avery studied him for a moment, saying nothing, and Ryker tossed the post hole diggers and gloves into the back of the pickup, then stooped and hoisted the little cart with the water bladder and hose, placing it in the back as well. Leave nothing out here that Avery would have to come back for—that was Ryker's rule. The old man had no business out on this fence these days. He should be kicked back in a recliner watching whatever football game he could pick up out here in the absolute middle of nothing. He'd more than earned it.

Ryker took another slug from the canteen, draining it, and then climbed into the cab of the Chevy. In a moment the two of them were rattling along, taking the road at the only pace it would allow, which was *slow* and *jarring*.

Slow was good. Slow gave Ryker a minute to think.

He'd really believed he'd shaken them this time. He'd known, when he'd left that room with the lights and the questions, that when they said, "Make yourself scarce," the thing they left unsaid was "we'll be tracking you."

He'd decided he wanted a life that didn't involve pop-ins from his former employer. But he'd never fully let himself be fooled. They had means of tracking him—eyes in the sky that could read the text on a dime from orbit. There was nowhere he could go where they wouldn't eventually track him down. It was the reason he'd never bothered using a different name. "Jim Ryker" wasn't his real one, anyway, but there was really no point in switching pseudonyms in an effort to give the CIA the slip. They were the experts at that sort of thing.

They would find him. That was what he knew.

So this... it really shouldn't have come as any surprise.

"You came out here to get away from somethin'," Avery said as they bounced along. He had to speak up, nearly shouting to be heard over the cacophony of rattling, squeaking and rumbling from the Chevy as it protested their route. "I don't need to know your business, Jim. Don't *want* to know. But... hell, I think you're a good one. You helped me out here. Didn't even ask me to pay you, which I couldn't've done anyway. Best I ever could offer ya was a pot full of mustard greens and a kettle full of coffee. But I ain't ever seen anybody work so hard for so little. Workin' like someone as had a whip on yer back. I knew you had to be runnin' from something."

"I'm sorry, Avery. I never meant to bring any of it here. I should have told you."

Avery laughed, loud and sharp. "You damn well should *not* have told me *nothin'*, Jim. I'm twice old enough to know how this works. And I know people when I see them, right down to who they are. You? I knew you was runnin', and I knew you was hidin'. But I also knew you was a good one, and still are. I just... whatever happens, when we get back to the house, I want you to know that I see that about ya."

Ryker pursed his lips, inhaled and exhaled through his nose, nodded. "I'm sorry I won't be able to get the fence finished," he said.

Avery waved this off like foolishness, and they rode along in silence for a long while. Then...

"What was it you did?" Avery asked suddenly.

Ryker laughed. "I thought you didn't want me to tell you?"

The old man shrugged. "I'm pushin' 90 and got nothin' to worry about losin'. TV only gets one channel and that's mostly religion. Already read all the books twice, and won't be able to get any more for a bit. So tell an old man a story."

Ryker smiled. "I'll leave you some new books. I have a few in my bag. I was done with them anyway." He looked over and saw that Avery had a stern look on his face, even as he stared ahead at the rough terrain.

Ryker sighed. "Would you believe me if I said I'm ex-CIA?"

Avery barked a laugh. "You? Pull the other one," he said, then shook his head. "It's ok, Jim. I don't need to know. Every man is entitled to his secrets. And you more than earned the right to keep quiet."

Ryker smiled and settled back. Might as well relax, get some kind of rest before they got back to the house. He'd been telling the truth, about being ex-CIA.

Well, except for the 'ex' part. You never really got to retire from the Company.

The men waiting for him—they were CIA, too.

They'd found him.

He had hoped, or had started to hope, that they would just leave him be. Let him vanish in the seams and folds of America. He was only *slightly* breaking the rules, after all. He was staying put, not leaving the country, not causing trouble. He'd dropped off the grid a bit, but not so much that they couldn't find him. A couple of suits showing up at Avery's place proved that. So what else did they want from him?

Wasn't it enough to accuse him, to brand him a mass murderer, to take everything from him? To basically excommunicate him, after he'd spent years of his life doing every dirty deed they ever ordered him to do?

He knew the answer to that.

It would never be enough. And it would never be over. Not while he was still alive.

He knew too much. And that meant that they would never, ever be done with Jim Ryker.

THREE

A black SUV was parked out front as Avery's pickup rattled into the yard. The truck sputtered to a stop, the engine telling the world that it might be old, and might be on its last legs, but it still had some fight in it. A bit too much of a metaphor for its owner, in Ryker's opinion, but he was impressed by the longevity of both truck and driver.

Ryker looked at Avery as the old man exited the truck, slamming the door behind him. Still kicking and ticking, but the guy was too old for this life. Too old to be out here all on his own.

He got a visit from his daughter about once a week, but it was pretty clear she was just doing what she thought was her familial duty—bringing Avery some provisions, bags of coffee and a tin of peanut brittle, some books bought at a local used book store. She would fuss and clean the kitchen, wash whatever meager pile of dishes Avery had left for her, do the laundry in the aging old washer and dryer. And then she'd be on her way, leaving Avery to the empty house, alone, until she swung by a week later.

Ryker had watched all this from the barn, when she was there.

He was sleeping in the loft—which wasn't as bad as it might sound. The old man had converted it into a small apartment decades ago, for his son to live in when he was home from Afghanistan.

Back when his son could still come home from Afghanistan.

War kept leaving indelible marks on Avery's life.

The space above the barn had gone unused for almost twenty years now, Avery had said. Since his son stopped being able to come home from anywhere, the space might as well be a place for a world-roaming ex-solider, ex-operative to lay his head. Room and board in exchange for some chores, that was all Avery had offered. It was all Ryker had needed, or wanted. And he'd paid for it all with a level of back-breaking labor that wasn't even asked of him.

They hadn't talked much about Avery's boy, or about Avery's own experience in the war. Ryker could see that Avery wasn't much for wanting to share either story. Too much pain, too much grief.

Ryker climbed out of Avery's aging Chevy and gave the passenger door a good slam, then moved up the decrepit brick walkway to the front door. Just two days ago he'd been on his hands and knees, pulling weeds from between those bricks. Just one of a thousand little chores that had gone undone for years as Avery slipped deeper into the role of an elderly rancher, too poor and too tired to do anything but watch his life's work fall down around him, with no one to pass it to. No one who cared to take it, when he was gone. The daughter was waiting to sell the place, Ryker suspected. She would take whatever meager inheritance this ranch afforded her—this patch of dry dirt that had soaked up so much of Avery's life and given back only the bare minimum of what was required of it.

Ryker had found out about Avery as he'd been passing through town, as he was *always* passing through towns and villages and middles-of-nowhere. He'd asked if anyone in the area needed a hand, someone to help out for a couple of months. All he wanted was a roof and a couple of meals per day, he'd said. Pay was optional. That was the thing that got him the most bites, Ryker had come to realize.

One of the locals put him in touch with Avery's daughter, and he'd met with her out at the ranch, and that was that. Avery hadn't protested. He wasn't too proud to take some help. And he had later confided in Ryker—after a few beers, after Ryker had shown he was serious about working for his supper—he'd told Ryker that he didn't mind having someone in his boy's old room. "It needs some life in there," he'd said. "And I could see right off that you were like him, in some way."

"What way?" Ryker had asked.

Avery had paused, thought, rocked in his chair and sipped his beer. "Running to somethin'," the old man had finally said.

Running *to* something, Ryker had thought, not running *from* something. That was a strange way to put it. But the more he considered it, the more it had rung true, and so he'd never bothered correcting it.

Avery's ranch had been a good place to hide out, Ryker thought. Quiet. Three squares per day. Hard work, and plenty of it. But that just meant keeping his mind off of things it shouldn't dwell on— which he greatly appreciated. And, of course, there was the *penance and punishment.* Breaking his back, blistering his hands, straining every muscle in his body day after day was the least Ryker could offer the world.

Two men in suits emerged from Avery's front porch, stepping out through the creaking screen door and into the bright Texas sun. If they were uncomfortable in the heat and humidity, they hid it well. Which was no surprise.

They were operators. Trained. Just like Ryker.

"Avery," Ryker said, and the old man turned around. "This... I'm probably going to be leaving."

Avery nodded. "I knew that the minute these boys pulled up."

The old man paused, shook his head, and walked up to Ryker. Advanced age had stooped the man a bit, but he straightened now, a soldier's resolve putting iron in his spine, and he extended a hand.

Ryker took it, and despite Avery's age the handshake was firm and strong.

"You brought some good here," Avery said, his voice husky and strained. Ryker saw moisture in the corners of the man's eyes.

He nodded. "There was already good here," he said. "Tell your daughter to find someone to help finish that fence."

Avery squeezed Rykers hand, then turned and walked straight past the two spooks, up onto the porch, and in through the creaking screen door, which slammed behind him.

It would be the last time Ryker ever saw Avery Clemmens, he knew. Whatever it was these men had come for, it meant that this particular door was being closed.

Ryker turned to the officers, shoving his hands into the pockets of his soiled jeans. "I don't suppose you'd let me catch a shower first?"

"Sorry," one of the men replied. "We're on a schedule. You have just enough time to grab your things and put them in the trunk."

Ryker shook his head. "No sense taking anything. I'm leaving all the books for Avery, and the rest... I have a feeling I'm going to get a whole new kit as part of this."

They said nothing to that, but directed him to the SUV. As one CIA man slipped behind the wheel, the other joined Ryker in the back seat. In moments they were on the move, and Ryker watched the old ranch slide by.

"Ok, you found me," he said, not looking at the man beside him. "I had kind of hoped you weren't even looking for me anymore."

"You should have known better than that," he said.

Ryker looked over to see the man half smiling, a knowing

expression on his face.

"Who are you?" Ryker asked. "Not just a field operative."

The man inhaled deeply, shaking his head. "Who can say these days? Spend a lifetime on the move, wearing whatever identity you need, and you can get to a point where you don't even remember who you were. Am I right, 'Jim Ryker?' Or should I say 'Jack Brody?' Or is it 'Samuel Beckett?' That was a good one. Was that a reference to the Irish novelist or to the character on *Quantum Leap?*"

"Can't it be both?"

The man smiled, nodding. "Of course. Double meanings are part of the fun in this trade, after all."

Ryker was growing annoyed with the game this guy was playing, but he kept himself in check. It wouldn't help him to let his emotions take over. This guy would be trained to keep as much information to himself as possible, to never answer a question directly, and do whatever he could to goad his target into revealing more than they intended.

Ryker had the same training.

So this would be a game of inference and observation, misdirection and diversion. If Ryker was going to learn anything, it was going to come from piecing things together based on practically nothing. And the same went for whoever this man was. Ryker's self discipline made him a tough read.

"You've seen my whole file, then," Ryker said, giving a little ground to see what the man might give back. "Which means you're not just a spook."

"I dabble," the man said, then shook his head, chuckling. "I was retired, actually. Until circumstances brought me back in. Hard to leave the life behind, isn't it?"

Ryker said nothing to this, but he couldn't help but agree. Leaving 'the life' behind was proving to be damn near impossible, despite his best efforts. Despite running and hiding for the past couple of years. Despite slamming himself repeatedly against the hardest labor he could find, hoping it would break him enough that he would no longer remember who he was. No such luck, so far.

With the apparent non-answer, however, the man had essentially confirmed Ryker's guess. He wasn't *just* a case officer. He was from somewhere higher up. He was *in charge*, with enough access to see Ryker's *very* classified file, letting him look deep, right down to some of Ryker's earliest assumed names. That meant he'd know about Ryker's former job under the Directorate of Operations. With the Special Activities Center, SOG, as part of a crack tactical force of paramilitary operatives.

And before that, Ryker's work with the 75th. He'd know Ryker's skills. He'd know what Ryker was capable of.

"So you need me to recover an asset," Ryker said.

For once there was the slightest register of surprise in the man's features, which faded quickly, buried behind the mask of the man's training.

He's good, Ryker thought. *He's maybe a little out of practice, but he's good.*

"We have a... *situation*," the man nodded. "I'll get you briefed once we've gotten you to the safe house."

"Safe house?" Ryker asked.

"Temporary," the man replied, waving. "Mostly it's a waystation. A chance for you to clean up, rest, and be debriefed. It's just for the night, so don't get your hopes up. You're going to have a long flight tomorrow, and I need you alert."

Ryker nodded at this and settled back. He'd gotten all he was going to get out of this man. For now, at least.

As they passed by the outer edge of Avery's property, Ryker silently blessed the man and the land. He wasn't sure if God listened to someone like him, but he hoped that for Avery's sake the blessing would stick anyway.

FOUR

K*harif* **Hidden Headquarters, Somewhere in Katakstan**
Americans, Faraz scoffed.

The makeshift interrogation room was dark and claustrophobic in its proportions. The ceiling was built purposefully low, so though one was fully able to stand upright there was a constant sense that things were about to come down on them, that they were constantly in danger of hitting their head. It was just another way to exert subtle psychological pressure on the people within the room—the interrogated and interrogators alike.

An agitated interrogator was more aggressive, more willing to do the grim work before him.

Faraz knew this, understood it, had even been the one to suggest it, and he hated it all the same. He accepted his own discomfort, however, as a good sign. If *he* was uncomfortable, then the man standing in the center of the room had to be feeling great distress.

The American was swaying, weak and injured, stripped to his soiled undergarment. There was a burlap bag over his head, tied around his throat, the cord just tight enough to cause the sensation of impending strangulation. Like a noose not yet cinched. Waiting.

Anticipation, in situations such as these, was every bit as effective as physical torture. More so, perhaps. Not knowing what was coming next, nor when, was sometimes enough to make even the toughest men crack. Waiting was almost as excruciating as torture.

Though there was plenty of torture as well.

The room was dark, nearly pitch black, except for the three very bright lights aimed directly at the American's face. The burlap hood did allow for light to leak in through the woven material, and Faraz and his men wanted to ensure the American saw nothing in the room.

This was not to hide anything from the man—they had nothing to hide. It was simply another pressure they could exert on his psyche. The exhaustion, the claustrophobia, the feeling that he might be strangled at any second—*anticipation*.

Faraz had let his men do some truly painful things to the American, but he had been incredibly strict about the limits of the torture. Some physical injury was acceptable. But nothing that would cause him to lose any more blood, for now. They needed him lucid, able to answer questions. Blood loss meant weakening the man, increasing his need for food and water, which Faraz intended to deny to him for some time, to certain physical limits.

It was amazing what transferable skills Faraz had learned during his Western education. Though he hadn't exactly taken "Torture 101," there were paths of learning that were palatable to the Western psyche, yet still yielded useful insight into the art of "enhanced interrogation." Psychology and physiology, for example, were clean and respectable disciplines that illustrated core principles that could be leveraged in ways that were quite useful in Faraz's line of work. Knowing how the mind and the body worked—

understanding the connection between them—opened many doors. And eventually, many mouths.

Faraz's education in these areas had been excellent—the very best the West had to offer—and he had learned his craft well. He could read and understand the subtle current of signals from the human body, and he knew when to apply pressure, and where. He knew when the breaking point would be. He knew what physical pains could be pushed *that much further*, and which would take things too far. And all of this had come mostly as inference from the so-called "clean" sciences Faraz had studied. With a little imagination, it wasn't difficult to carry those studies further than Western ethics would have allowed.

Faraz stood before the American, observing telltale signs of weakness and suffering, noting that the process was working. The man—so schooled in self control, so capable of managing pain and keeping secrets—was on the verge of breaking. It was time.

"You have something we need," Faraz said after long minutes of waiting and watching, his voice low and quiet. There was barely any other sound in the room, nothing to compete with Faraz's voice, beyond the rasping and labored breaths of the American, and this sudden speech, after a long period of unbroken silence, was startling to the man. "You are keeping me from my work," Faraz said.

The American said nothing, which was to be expected. He was trained. He had skills, including methods for withstanding torture.

Faraz moved closer, and sighed audibly. "I... don't like using these methods," he said. "*Torture.* It's simply not civilized. I know that my brothers—*they* believe it is the most effective means of dealing with... well, with people like *you.* And I can certainly see where they're coming from. You Americans. Your arrogance. Your assumptions. You make it impossible to co-exist."

He was moving around the American, leaning closer as he spoke. The man's hands and feet were bound, and a chain rose from the bindings at the man's wrists to a pulley in the ceiling. It drooped before the man, offering no support at all, its weight straining the man's arms. An hour ago this chain was taut enough that the American had to support himself on only the tips of his toes, barely able to keep from swaying, but never supported enough to actually *rest*. Now it was just more weight the man had to strain against.

Faraz was behind the American now. "Tell me how I can unlock it, and I can make sure this all ends for you."

For once there was a sound from the American that was not ragged breath. It was the dry, pained bark of a laugh.

"You…" the man started, his voice raw and hoarse from hours of screaming. "You're just… going to kill me anyway."

Faraz sighed again, loud enough for the American to hear. "Yes," he said, nodding. "That's true. But if I get what I want, then I can have things ended much faster. A sudden darkness, rather than… well, our last American guest was with us for nearly six months before his body stopped betraying him by trying to live. You… it seems you are better trained than he was. Better able to deal with pain. Better able to survive. I give you a year. It will be a very eventful year."

The man made no sound at that, and Faraz simply stood, watching.

He hated this.

He hated all of it.

He had a family, a wife and a daughter. And this… it kept him from them. It kept him from being certain they were *safe*.

Since pledging his loyalty to the *Kharif*, this had been the way. The call of his duty to God and his oath to his brothers beckoned him at all hours, it kept him from being by his wife's side, from holding his young daughter. It kept him bathed in the blood of the enemy, it kept his ears filled with their screams, his nose filled with the acrid smell of burning flesh and cordite smoke and the fumes of burning gasoline. And burning flesh.

But all of this was for *them*. It was the only way he knew of to really and truly protect his family. And of course, it was the only way to bring the *Winter* to their adversaries, to the dogs of the West. It was the only way to defeat them—to not only drive them from this, their homeland, but to chase them right back to their den and burn them where they slept. This was the *only way*.

But it sickened him.

He knew what was right. He knew he had a duty to God, as an agent of the Second Harvest. But he was... he was...

Weak.

The word kept occurring to him in moments when he was the most full of doubt, or when he was most prideful, or when he was most apt to forget *why* this work was necessary. He was serving *God*, he reminded himself. He was being *obedient*. But he felt keenly the influence of a different era of his existence, a different part of his life.

His education had been in the UK, attending University under a different name. Not quite a *Western* name—he was not sure if he could have maintained such a disgusting burden. But certainly a false Katakstan name. A mingled name, the surname of a tribe from hundreds of miles away from his own village. Names were so intimately tied to regions, here. The only way to keep anyone from guessing the plans of his people, for sending him for a Western education, was to lie. But the name itself, that had to be real. It had to be tied to a real village, and it had to lead back to a real boy of Faraz's age. That was why his people had driven to that far village, and chosen a boy who resembled Faraz, and slit his throat. The boy's body was burned that very night, as close to the time of his death as possible, as far from where he had lived as they could get. The ashes and bones were buried in the desert, and a stone was placed for him.

Alms were sent to his family, anonymously. A very large amount —much more than that family would see in many years.

As closely as was possible, all of the customs were observed. His sacrifice—for the *Kharif*, for Katakstan, for God—was honored. He would receive his reward in heaven.

The act of murder was as evil for Faraz's people as it was for the Americans and their Christian god. But this was a death in *service* to God. The boy had been given a *reward*. His death sent him on to paradise, and enabled Faraz's people to continue on in God's service.

With that boy's name, with his history worn like a mask, Faraz attended University.

He had spent some of his most impressionable years among the Westerners and their blasphemous traditions. He had learned from them all the ways they could be defeated, learned from their own texts and traditions exactly what could be used to destroy them. And then, unexpectedly he had...

Well, as he had said to his uncle, his father's brother, he had seen their *perspective*.

As he'd thought of it, he had come to *understand* them, as they understood themselves. And that had done something to Faraz. It had changed him. Perhaps weakened his fervor, even causing him to waiver from his oath to the *Kharif*. To God.

When he had spoken of this to his uncle, he had expected outrage. He had expected to feel the sting of his uncle's hand. He had expected that his uncle would spit in his face, excommunicate him, turn him over to the others for punishment.

Instead, his uncle had placed each of his hands on either side of Faraz's head. He had looked his nephew in the eyes, and leaned in until their foreheads touched. And then he had tilted his head back and kissed Faraz on he forehead.

"To know one's enemy is to love one's enemy," his uncle said. "You will never defeat the enemy *unless* you love them."

That had confused Faraz. For a time. But gradually, as he thought about it during long and sleepless nights, as he prayed, as he heard his uncle speak to the men of the tribe, Faraz had eventually come to understand. He had been sent for this Western eduction not simply to gain intelligence about the enemy, but to gain that very understanding. He'd been sent to see their perspective, even to love them, because with that love he could understand how they thought, how they would act. He could better understand these people, enough to bring their destruction.

For a moment, a brief and dark moment in his life, Faraz had been tempted to forgive the Western dogs. But that had been a long time ago. And from his uncle's kiss, Faraz had learned that even when you love someone, they can still be the enemy of God. And the enemy of God must die.

Faraz had joined his uncle in the *Kharif* only a few months later —following in the footsteps of Faraz's father, whom God had taken many years earlier. And like his father, Faraz began to rise in status among the brothers, until eventually he surpassed even his beloved uncle, taking a position of leadership among the *Kharif*.

All the knowledge he'd gained from his time in the UK now served his brothers as they all served God. This was as it should be, as it should always have been.

And still, Faraz could not help the thoughts that wove through his mind in quiet hours, in moments of solitary reflection. He could not help the understanding that had arisen as he'd spoken and broken bread with so many Westerners, as he'd studied their philosophy and learned their thoughts, as he'd seen with his own eyes their families and their traditions and their values, the tenderness and goodness that could exist even among the Western dogs.

He was committed to God and to the *Kharif*, being the Second Autumn and ushering in the Winter for their enemies. He was committed to bring the Spring for his people. But he could not help hearing the quiet voice within, whispering from his heart and into his burning mind... *There could be another way.*

He could not help the voice, but he did not have to listen to it. And would not. He knew *this* way. The way of his father and his uncle. The way of the *Kharif*. The way of his *oath*.

He wanted to see his wife and daughter to safety. He wanted them out of this place, away from the constant threat of war.

And he could only do that if the American talked.

He nodded to the others, hidden as they were behind the three lights, and he exited the room to the sound of the American screaming.

FIVE

Fort Larlan, West Texas

The safe house turned out to be a riverside bungalow on a twelve-acre lot, surrounded by lush tree growth that kept the home hidden from all sides, even above. It was a valley between two rivers—one dwindling to nearly dry, the other running as a robust stream to the Gulf of Mexico, its waters giving life to miles of trees and grass and crops.

Compared to Avery Clemmons' parched and dried-up dirt bed ranch, this was like a big, green slap in the face. A testament to the unfairness of life, maybe. Though Ryker knew that concepts like "fairness" were relative and subjective, at best, and that life wasn't listening anyway. What was fair, when time wore away mountains and turned lush valleys into lifeless deserts, if you just waited long enough? A hundred years from now Avery's farm might be one big grassy meadow, and this place might be a sewer.

For now, though, Avery's place was a hellish landscape, and this was paradise by comparison.

Ryker felt dubious about the safe house, and the fact that such a well-kept place in such a nice area was just standing empty. It looked too lived-in to be a property that had been on hold. And the furniture and decorations marked it as something seized by the government, rather than a home someone had put on the market.

"Who used to live here?" Ryker asked.

The man—who still had not given Ryker a name—merely shrugged. "A retired couple who can now live out the rest of their days in Florida, taking the grandkids to Disney World whenever they visit."

Ryker arched his eyebrows. It was a much more pleasant answer than he had expected. It revealed very little useful information, but at least it didn't imply that something dark and sinister had happened here.

"You seem surprised," the man said.

"I was expecting to do a mental body count."

The man smiled. "Not yet. They probably have at least twenty more years, if they watch the carbs and cholesterol."

Ryker let that go, satisfied to accept the man's story at face value. He stepped deeper into the home, taking in the furnishings, the art on the walls, the complete lack of a television or phone or any other means of hearing from or communicating with the outside world.

It was to be total isolation, then.

"There's a duffle on the bed in the master bedroom," the man said. "Couple of changes of clothes, some toiletries. You can use the shower in there to get cleaned up. I'm having an agent bring some food in from town. There aren't many options, but it should be hot and have plenty of grease and salt. I'll brief you over dinner."

Ryker didn't bother responding to any of that, and instead slipped into the bedroom without a word, closed the door behind him, and stripped. He left his dirty clothes in a pile on the floor at the end of the bed and fished through the duffel to find the toiletries.

Pretty basic set. Deodorant, toothbrush, toothpaste, a small container of floss. There was a hair brush and a container of molding wax—the same brand he preferred.

No razor, though.

They're sending me to the Middle East, then, Ryker thought.

He slipped into the bathroom and started the shower, testing the water to see when it was hot. He looked into the mirror over the sink, examining his features.

Most of his career, as an Asset Recovery Specialist for the CIA, Ryker had worn some sort of beard. It was the easiest of urban camouflage—allowing him to blend in when he was in certain regions, and letting him make a dramatic and fast change of appearance by simply shaving it off, if that was necessary.

If they were keeping him from shaving, he could only think of one reason. Most regions in the world, being clean-shaven would make him less noticeable. But he would blend in better in the Middle East, with his dark hair and tanned skin, if he had a beard.

Simple math.

He climbed into the shower and allowed himself to relax and take his time, letting the steamy water wash over him from head to heel. There had been a shower in the hayloft apartment in Avery's barn, but the pipes had been rusted nearly solid, leaving only an anemic stream, with nothing identifiable as even warm water, much less hot.

He soaped up three times, rinsing and repeating until finally the West Texas dirt that had been baked into his every pore started loosening and running down the drain.

He hadn't had a decent shower in months. Avery's place was on a well and had a septic tank, and it was pretty easy to strain the capabilities of both. For Avery on his own it was fine, but Ryker didn't want to cause any undue burdens on the system. He'd had it on his mental list to give Avery's setup an upgrade, but hadn't gotten to it in time.

Maybe, when this was over, he could circle back.

It seemed like a ludicrous thought, once he'd had it. Something about the series of events so far told him that circling back was the least likely outcome of all of this. If he survived whatever the CIA had in mind for him, he'd be lucky if he didn't find himself staring at four gray walls somewhere for the remainder of his life. He had expected that to be the trajectory of his life, while sitting through various interrogations and interviews a year go. No reason to doubt that he couldn't be put right back on that track. No reason to assume he had actually managed to *escape*.

He wasn't exactly a fugitive. But he'd been explicitly told not to go anywhere. To stay local. To stay on the grid and out of trouble.

He'd ditched that plan the second he was out of sight, and he'd been ditching it ever since. He'd gotten to a point where he thought *just maybe* they were letting it go. Turned out he was wrong. And now it was time to deal with the consequences.

Ryker finished up the shower and spent some time toweling himself dry and getting dressed. He was in no hurry for whatever the anonymous guy in the other room had in mind for him. Besides, this could be the last bit of luxury he got before being dumped somewhere in the Middle East, where he was sure to be welcomed by live fire and throngs of people willing to die just to kill him faster. He was soaking up what slivers of freedom and liberty and comfort he had while he had them.

SIX

The smell of food wafted into the bedroom, and Ryker finally zipped the duffel closed and went out into the living room. Agent Anonymous was in the kitchen, and Ryker could see that he'd removed his suit jacket, loosened his tie and rolled up his shirt sleeves. He was preparing plates of food, and looked happy to do it.

He's gaming me, Ryker thought. *Putting me at ease so he can keep me off my guard.*

The smell of food was real, though, and Ryker realized he was actually pretty hungry.

"Have a seat," Anonymous said, nodding to the little breakfast table in a nook by the window.

Ryker sat, and in a moment the agent placed a plate of food in front of him that had all the trimmings of heaven. Steak, potatoes, veggies. An ear of corn with a pat of butter. A soft roll, still hot enough that a waft of steam rose from it.

"Better fare than I'd hoped for," Agent Anonymous smiled wryly, sitting in front of his own plate.

It was a hearty meal. Ryker couldn't help wondering if it might be his last. He silently said grace and then dove in, shoveling forkfuls of potatoes and veggies fast, as if the plate might be taken away any second.

"Worked up an appetite on the ranch?" Anonymous asked, taking a bite of his roll.

Ryker peered up at him over a forkful of potatoes. "Breakfast was twelve hours ago. Dug a lot of fence posts since then."

The agent nodded. "I'll fill you in while you eat. Good?"

Ryker nodded.

The agent turned and picked up a digital tablet from the counter, made a few motions, then placed it on the table between them, turning it so Ryker could look it over.

On the screen was a surveillance photo of a Middle Eastern man chatting with a group of other men on the street. The setting looked urban.

"Syed Shanyar Faraz," Anonymous said. "Faction head for the local *Kharif* insurgents, operating out of Katakstan. You remember Katakstan?"

Ryker looked up from the tablet to see Anonymous smiling in a familiar and knowing way that made him want to punch the guy. "It rings certain bells."

"I bet," Anonymous smirked, nodding. "Last time you were there, you practically set the whole country on fire on your way out. It was those events that led to the charges against you, right?"

"I followed my orders," Ryker said, his jaw tight. "And the Company screwed me for it."

Anonymous laughed. "Yeah, we do that," he said. "It's kind of our thing. And listen, many an agent and soldier has gone down under the flag of 'just following orders.' That's never been much of a shield. Somebody will always have to pay for the decisions made up top, and it's almost always going to be the guy on the bottom. Don't take it too personal."

Ryker nodded. Then, thoughtfully, said, "I suppose if I were to break your jaw right now there are a handful of operatives waiting to shoot me, right?"

Anonymous smiled and shrugged. "About ten total. With orders to wound but not kill. So if you're going to do it, you'd better enjoy it."

Ryker studied the agent for a moment, then looked back to the tablet, studying it as he crammed mashed potatoes into one of the rolls, and took a bite of what he and his buddies referred to as a "carb bomb."

"When I was extracted from Katakstan," Ryker said around a mouthful, "the local government had the *Kharif* pushed back to the border. They were practically extinct."

"Times change," Anoymous said, reaching to pick up a carafe of coffee from the counter behind him. He filled a cup and motioned with the carafe, offering. Ryker shook his head.

Anonymous put the carafe back on the counter then leaned back in his chair a bit, gingerly sipping hot coffee. "Faraz's men are just one group in a long line of *Kharif* insurgents to swarm back into the area. They got a personnel upgrade about two years ago, with a wave of recruiting fueled by anti-US sentiment. That little snafu with one of your men turned out to be a great recruiting tool, actually."

Ryker let this pass.

"Since the US pulled half our troops a few months ago, the *Kharif* have been pressing their advantage. We're holding them back from the interior, but they're starting to spread along the border, gaining strength as they go."

Ryker swiped at the file on the tablet, reading through a series of redacted documents on Pentagon letterhead. He shook his head. "Typical. We create the problem, undermining the local government so we can put the people we want in charge, and then when things go south we pull out and leave everyone to fend for themselves. What happened, not enough bribes or defense contracts to keep things going?"

Anonymous shrugged. "In part. You know how this works. But it's mostly that the current administration saw a withdrawal from Katakstan as an easy win at the polls. Pull troops out, get our boys back home, disengage from foreign wars that have nothing to do with us, *yada yada*. And then leak only what's safe for the public to know, of course. Keep the real scary stuff hidden under some black ink. We live in a redacted nation."

"So what went wrong?" Ryker asked, though he thought he might already know the answer.

When he looked up, Anonymous was studying him. "You know what went wrong. It's all about those things the public *wasn't* allowed to know. It's a case of doing the popular thing instead of doing the right thing. Same as always."

It was such a candid answer that it took Ryker by surprise. And it made him reassess Agent Anonymous a little. But *only* a little.

"Ok, that's what's changed for the country. What's changed for the CIA?"

"In other words, why did we pluck you out of the West Texas dirt, with plans to drop you into some *Middle Eastern* dirt?" Anonymous shook his head and laughed lightly as he sipped his coffee. He smacked his lips a bit before lowering the cup to the table. "That would be thanks to that old friend of yours. Your man in Katakstan. Mark Adams."

Ryker had taken another bite of his dinner, and paused in chewing for a moment. He swallowed. "Mark? What happened?"

"Your boy went and got himself caught, is what happened," Anonymous said. "He was picked up in *Kharif* controlled territory, in violation of a temporary treaty between the *Kharif* and the current Katakstan government. It's big trouble. Officially he was breaking international law just by being there. But since we were the ones who put him on the ground, we felt it was the least we could do to mount some sort of rescue. And we thought, who better to bring him back in than his old friend and one of our best recovery specialists, Jim Ryker?"

"That's a load of crap," Ryker said, shaking his head. "You and I both know the rules. If Mark was captured while over the fence, he's burned. Disavowed." Ryker leaned forward. "The CIA isn't exactly known for 'leave no man behind.' I know that better than anyone. So what did he have on him? What is it you really want me to retrieve?"

Anonymous chuckled. "I'm impressed. You haven't lost your edge, at least. That's good."

Ryker waited, watching the man's face.

Anonymous shrugged, picked up the tablet, and brought up a new set of files and images. Fewer of these were redacted. All were marked *classified* and *eyes only*.

Ryker looked slowly from Anonymous to the tablet, then studied what he saw there. After a moment he shot a glance back to the other man, startled. "What is this?"

"It's a weapon," Anonymous said. "Pretty nasty one, too, if the wrong people use it in the right way. Our people didn't make it, but we did fund it. And we're very keen on keeping it out of the hands of the bad guys."

"There's no way Mark could have been smuggling something like this out of a hot zone," Ryker said.

Anonymous shook his head. "No, not the weapon itself. It was being developed in a Ukraine facility, and someone used the situation there as cover to steal the designs and smuggle them out. They delivered them into the hands of the highest bidder, who happened to be a *Kharif* acolyte in Katakstan. Agent Adams was sent in to retrieve a hard drive from a base near the Katakstan border. Mark's mission was supposed to be a quick in and out, but you know how these things go. He was intercepted *en route* to the extraction point, taken into custody by Faraz and his men."

"Is he still alive?" Ryker asked.

"As far as our intel indicates, yes," Anonymous nodded. "For now, anyway. Which is part what worries us, frankly."

Ryker instantly knew what he meant.

"You think Mark's turned." Ryker shook his head. "No way."

"Oh come on," Anonymous said, issuing a scornful laugh. "You're not *that* out of touch. You know Mark Adams better than almost anyone. He was burned, and he knows it. He would have cut a deal because it was the only way he was keeping his head on his shoulders. There's no way Faraz and his men would have kept Adams alive this long unless he was cooperating with them. Once they had the hard drive, they had no need of a CIA operative anymore. He'd just be a liability."

"He's running them, then," Ryker said. "Playing them. Buying time."

Anonymous nodded. "Some of the people above me agree with you. I don't."

"So what is this, then?" Ryker asked. "Why bring me in on this? It's not a rescue."

"It *is* a rescue, actually," Anonymous said. "Of a sort. It's an extraction. We're willing to consider that Adams is playing a game, just like you said. Buying time, trying to work out how to get out of this mess with something still at the top of his neck. We're going to run on the assumption that he's dragging heel, keeping that hard drive locked until the last possible second, waiting for someone —*you*—to go in and get it. We want you to go in and make sure Adams gets out, along with that drive. And if Faraz and his people have managed to crack it, we want anything they've learned to be... well, *eliminated*."

"Eliminated," Ryker nodded. "Sure. You want me, all by myself, to drop into Katakstan, into a hot zone controlled by the *Kharif*, to infiltrate whatever stronghold they're operating, so I can extract an agent you *think* may have turned traitor to his country, all while stealing data and making sure the bad guys don't have a copy of it. Do I have all of that right?"

"It's the sort of thing you've done before, in your time serving your country," Anonymous said, a small smile on his lips.

"It's the sort of thing that got me nearly killed before getting me discharged and threatened with life in prison," Ryker replied. "As a big *thank you* from my country, and from the CIA."

"Bygones," Anonymous said, waving. "This is a new slate, Jim. An opportunity not only for you but for Mark. Both of you could use a chance at redemption, right? A chance to show the Company that you're still team players."

Ryker shook his head. "That's not enough," he said. "That isn't enough carrot to get me to face this much stick, not even for Mark. I loved the guy like a brother, but we haven't talked since..." Ryker halted, hesitating. He didn't like thinking about the events that had happened, in that last mission in Katakstan. He didn't like thinking about the role Mark Adams had played in putting Ryker in hot water. He'd spent the past year trying to work hard enough to crush that all out of him. "Maybe I don't care much whether Mark makes it out of this one."

Again Anonymous nodded. "I told them you'd say that. Well, I mean, not *that*, exactly. Such a colorful metaphor, with the carrot and the stick thing. But I told them you'd need more than redemption and second chances to motivate you, and that you might not be Mark's biggest fan these days. That's why we picked up Jill."

Ryker felt his blood go cold.

"You remember Jill, I take it?"

Jill Adams. Mark's sister.

And for Ryker... more.

It had been a few years. The last time he'd seen her...

"Picked her up," Ryker said, his throat feeling dry, tight.

"To keep her safe," Anonymous said.

"Right. *Safe*. Where is she?" Ryker asked.

"She's trying to find her brother, trying to figure a way to help him out of the mess he's in. She's very hopeful. And she has all that political clout to help her get her way. We could hardly stop her from going."

Ryker shook his head and glanced back at the tablet. There were photos of Faraz, of military vehicles and weapons controlled by the *Kharif*, and schematics for the weapon that Mark had jumped the fence to retrieve.

It was the most dangerous place in the world for a woman who was frantic about finding her brother and bringing him home. It was getting more dangerous by the minute.

"You took her to Katakstan," Ryker said.

"She could hardly wait to get there," Anonymous smiled.

"Into a war zone," Ryker said.

"It gets worse," Anonymous replied, and now the smile faded from his lips. "When she went in, we had control of the region. We took her to the forward operating base, right at the edge of the red zone. We were holding the line there, until..." he hesitated.

"Until what?" Ryker asked.

"Two days ago Faraz activated a sleeper cell on our side of the line. They took some strategic strikes, knocked out communications, heavy transports, basically collapsed all the exits. They used a prototype of the weapon," he said, nodding to the schematics. "An EMP. Not terribly powerful. Limited range. Very targeted. But it was enough to shut things down and disrupt communication. The base, and everyone in it, is cut off. No way in or out."

Ryker shook his head, the dinner forming a hard lump in his guts.

Anonymous took another sip of his coffee then reached back for the carafe, refilling his cup and placing the pot on the table. "You're our last play to get them out. Our backup plan."

"And what happens if I can't? What if I say no?"

Anonymous didn't blink as he threw back the entire cup of scalding coffee. "The whole place burns," he said with a shrug. "Along with everyone in it."

The language was deliberate, Ryker knew. The imagery was the point. And with that, he knew something else.

He was going to Katakstan. He's was going to retrieve Mark Adams and those schematics. And he was going to bring Jill Adams home.

"When do we leave?" Ryker asked.

"First thing in the morning," Anonymous smiled.

SEVEN

Katakstan

Three long hops and 48 hours later, Ryker was standing in the open bay of a Boeing C-17 Globemaster III as it glided through the night sky over Katakstan. A warm wind whipped around him as he steadied himself with one hand gripping a pneumatic strut. The slanted deck of the plane's cargo ramp vibrated beneath his boots.

Even at night, looking out using the night vision HUD molded into his dive helmet, the darkened landscape below was exactly what Ryker remembered—dry, barren, dotted with life, but only of the kind that was hostile toward everything Ryker was. Even from this height he could sense the message of that landscape: *You're not welcome here. Die American dog.*

He checked the straps of his chute one more time, tightening, adjusting. He checked his sidearm, his knife, the pockets crammed with bits and bobs he might be able to use for survival, if it came to it. Not a lot. Nothing heavy. Nothing really *useful*. He'd have to improvise when he was on the ground, to gear up from whatever he could find down there. That was what he'd been trained to do. Go in light, fast, and hot. Find what you need on the ground. Take what you need from the corpse of your enemy.

"We're nearing drop point," a voice said in his ear. The radio in Ryker's helmet was dual band, and he'd be on the C-17's comms until he jumped. The plane would almost instantly be too far away for him to communicate with anyone onboard, after that. Too far away to give him any protection or help as he plummeted toward the war-torn landscape below.

The satellite band would kick on the second the radio detected that he was digitally untethered. And once he was on the ground he'd lose that, too. Radio silence from landing to extraction, that was the order. He could turn the sat link back on when he reached the FOB. That was a big part of his mission, after all. Ever since the *Kharif* knocked out comms, the FOB had been in a dark zone. Ryker was the plan to get them back online.

He felt the sore spot at the base of his throat, the injection point where they'd inserted the tracker. He couldn't talk to them, but they'd know where he was at all times. No comfort there. And when this was over he intended to cut the thing out even if he ended up bleeding to death for it. If they planned to keep tabs on him for the rest of his life, they'd have to work for it.

He acknowledged the update from the pilot, rolled his neck and shook his arms and legs to loosen himself up a bit, then took a couple of deep breaths, trying to relax that twist in his gut, the tightness in his chest that always came before a jump. It had been over a year since he'd last done this. He had hoped he'd left it behind for good. He should have known better.

He jumped the second he was given his cue.

He'd been warned that he was going in dark, both literally and strategically. He'd been warned that the area had recently been overtaken by *Kharif* extremists, surrounding the US-Katakstan forward operating base on all sides. He'd been warned that the base was about twenty klicks from the drop zone, and that the C-17 couldn't get him any closer with *Kharif* anti-air artillery flying hot in the area. That was a lot of warnings, as if he had any choice in this. As if he could just decide not to risk it.

He would have to go in on foot, across miles of hostile desert. With not much more than a pistol and a knife for protection. It was almost guaranteed he was going to be killed before he could get to the base. First he had to get to the ground.

His chute deployed, jerking him out of his free fall momentum, and he drifted in a sort of surreal peace for a few minutes. As he cut through the night air, the wind created a white noise that enveloped him. It was almost comforting. He could *almost* forget that he was dropping feet first into enemy territory.

Then he started hearing the piercing whine of rounds whizzing by, and all feelings of peace were shattered.

The Katakstan sky was clear of both light pollution and nighttime clouds, and against the panoply of stars the bulbous and ballooning fabric of the chute stood out stark and obvious to anyone who happened to be looking up. Apparently someone was looking up.

It was no wonder someone had seen him—they had probably spotted the running lights of the C-17 and simply waited. Despite the darkness, someone down there had made out the silhouette of a parachute, blotting out the stars, and was doing their best to help Ryker get to the ground at great speed, perhaps by disintegrating his parachute and liberating him of as much blood and as many internal organs as possible.

Ryker was still too high up. His options were limited. He couldn't cut the straps and survive the drop from this altitude. He had no choice but to continue the leisurely descent.

He was a sitting duck up here. It would only take one of those

50-caliber rounds to end him and the mission alike. Which meant Mark and Jill would be dead as well, along with everyone still in that base.

Out of any other options, Ryker prayed, and kept his legs and body straight as an arrow, presenting the smallest possible aspect of himself to the fighters below. They seemed to be firing straight up, for the most part, and so his best chance of staying unperforated was to be as small a target as possible. From their vantage point, with his body straight as an arrow, he should be about the size of a large cowboy hat at a hundred feet away.

Yee-haw!

That might—*might*—keep him from taking a slug on his way down. But he couldn't do anything about the size of the chute.

As the whine of rounds screamed by him they started shredding the chute, punching holes through it big enough that Ryker could now see those stars he'd been blotting out. The compromised material was doing less and less to regulate his descent, and he realized the ground was coming up at a much faster clip than he would have preferred.

Too high or not, it was time to cut himself loose.

Ryker took several quick breaths, and loosened up, preparing for impact. He drew his fixed-blade from its sheath and, reaching above his shoulders, he cut one of the straps. He dropped, tilted at an angle, dangling and spinning as he reached back up, prepared to cut the second strap.

He'd need the chute off of him for what came next.

Three quick breaths and he slashed at the strap, and fell like a stone though the night air.

Impact came an instant later, just seconds after the cut. He dropped and rolled like a sack of potatoes on the desert soil, and allowed his legs and torso to fold on contact, absorbing the impact before he rolled forward to burn off the momentum.

It was not a graceful landing, and he felt his knee twist followed by a parade of bruises, scrapes, and cuts as he rolled down the hill with all the grace of a Sumo wrestler doing ballet. By the time he skidded to a stop he flopped onto this back, breathing heavy, taking mental account of his arms, legs, ribs.

Everything was still there.

Everything hurt.

But everything worked.

He didn't have time to dwell on his luck.

The source of the 50-cal air onslaught was barreling toward him on the ground now—he could see headlights from vehicles racing across the desert.

Ryker had to move.

He managed to find the knife he had dropped on impact, and shucked off the remains of the pack, leaving it and the chute to tell whatever story they were going to tell. He sheathed the knife as he ran as fast as his twisted knee would allow, taking cover behind rocks and dunes. There wasn't much for cover, but he tried to keep low, to sink into the sand as much as possible.

He heard the sound of engines roaring, closer by than he was comfortable with. Shouts in *Pashto* echoed over the landscape. Ryker recognized what they were saying—it wasn't good.

He was down. He had successfully dropped behind enemy lines, under heavy fire, and had suffered only a twisted knee and some cuts and bruises as the cost. A bargain, and now he needed to make sure he kept that overhead low.

Well done, he thought, allowing himself a bit of congratulations. *Take your wins where you can get them*, as one of his former commanding officers used to say.

Of course, that same officer had another saying: *Celebrate on the move.*

Ryker got moving.

Now that he was on the ground, free of bullet holes, he just had to make his way to the FOB, through a wall of enemy operatives, and somehow get inside without being shot by either the bad guys, who were now on the alert for him, or the good guys, who would have no idea he was coming.

He paused for a moment, leaning with his back against a boulder, flexing and stretching his knee a few times before gritting his teeth and making a limping run in the general direction of the base.

He never thought he'd say it, but he was really missing the Texas heat and humidity back at Avery's ranch. He'd give anything to be digging a hundred miles of post holes right about.

EIGHT

Ryker had managed to limp his way to within five klicks of the base, and at least he could tell that the injury to his knee wasn't serious. The pain was a lot less than when he'd started, and his progress had picked up with time.

But time was the problem.

Getting this far had already eaten up close to four hours. Morning would be breaking soon, and with the light of dawn he'd find himself a whole lot more visible, and possibly hosting many more holes in his body, once the enemy could see him coming.

He needed to pick up the pace.

The twisted knee had really only slowed him down a little, at first, and now he was used to it, able to push through it. There'd be hell to pay later, but nothing some ibuprofen and a decent bourbon wouldn't cure. Eventually the knee was no longer the thing putting him so far behind schedule.

The real delay came from dodging all the damned *Kharif* patrols.

Every mile had been hard won, crawling over dunes and rocks, huddling for cover using not much more than the night itself as a kind of gossamer camouflage, as trucks and Jeeps full of armed insurgents rolled past, casting cones of light over the sand. They were looking for him, and they weren't giving up. These last five klicks would be the most dangerous.

He stopped to catch his breath and to try to plan a route.

With the helmet's goggles flipped upward, Ryker could see the emergency lights of the base, on the other side of a vast ocean of night-blackened desert. It looked like an oasis, especially after a full night of dodging patrols of bad guys and avoiding whatever nasty, venomous critters might be hiding among the rocks and sand here. The FOB looked as inviting as an oasis, but that was the most treacherous part.

Agent Anonymous had broken the really bad news just as Ryker was getting on the plane.

"Everything's being jammed," he said. "Faraz's people used an EM pulse to knock out all technology. Radio is down. Cellular is down. We had some brief contact from a sat phone, but that went silent after a couple of hours."

"So you're saying you haven't been able to brief them on my arrival," Ryker said.

"We could try smoke signals," Anonymous offered.

Ryker might have gone for that, right about now. Because even five klicks out he could see and hear the volley of weapons fire going back and forth at the base. The Americans were holding back *Kharif* fighters, taking shots at anyone who came within range, conserving ammunition by letting the bad guys get *close*. Which had the undesirable effect of letting those bad guys get within range to take some pretty nasty shots of their own.

So far the Americans had the advantage of superior firepower. For as long as that lasted.

They were also getting some backup, Ryker knew. There was a drone strike planned, but it was still more than a day out.

Ryker's job, at least as far as the base was concerned, was to get them intel on the approaching cavalry, and to deliver the sat phone he was carrying, complete with its own power source and directed antenna array. All they needed was a clear shot at the sky and they'd be back in touch with the free world. That would let them coordinate with a mobile operations base several klicks away, and arrange details for an evac prior to the incoming drone strike. In a situation as dire as this, any ray of hope was enough to turn the tide, and that was Objective 1 for Ryker—deliver at least the tiniest sliver of hope.

While that Hail Mary was in play, Ryker's Objective 2 was to use the imminent chaos of the rallying at the base as a diversion, so he could make a run for Faraz's compound—or at least to the general area of where they thought that compound was located—and hopefully extract Mark and the hard drive.

Ryker had some general intel of the *Kharif* home base. Nothing specific enough to give him any real confidence. But it was all he had to work with.

As plans went... this *almost* was one. But options were limited, especially with no intel from the forward operation base. The folks coordinating the drone strike and evacuation were running entirely on satellite data and scant communication from a few embedded assets in the region. Not quite enough to build a *reliable* plan. But then, that's what Ryker was for. His training as an asset recovery specialist was all about *being* the plan, when all other options were gone, or at best, murky.

Ryker was the backup plan.

The first step was to get to that base without being shot by either side. Get his sat phone to the base commander, and get them the info about the incoming strike. It might not be much, but it was a direction.

He'd rested enough. Time to get moving.

Ryker rose from where he'd taken cover, pulling the goggles back down to activate night vision. He was moving at a brisk pace through the Katakstan night, when he suddenly halted.

The sound of an engine roared to life not far from where he was standing—mere feet, from the sound of it.

Headlights turned on, casting so much light in Ryker's direction that the goggles blinded him temporarily. He cursed under his breath as he whipped them up and off of his eyes while leaping to the ground, blindly hoping for cover.

He glanced up and saw that the headlights were aimed slightly off to his left, two piercing cones reaching out into the darkened desert.

"We are ordered to move to a position near the base," a man said in Pashto, his voice echoing across the sand. *"The infidel is surely going there."*

There was a response from another man that Ryker couldn't quite make out.

The first man had started the truck and stood aside to talk to his partner, shouting back over the sound of the engine. Ryker pulled on the goggles once again, disabling night vision and adjusting the lenses to zoom in.

The scene revealed by the helmet cam indicated that these two men had been squatting in this spot for at least the night, manning a makeshift camp in the lee of a jut of rock rising out of the dunes. Now they were gathering some of their things, probably intending to return here after helping to kill "the infidel." They would board the truck in a moment, and roll for the American base.

This presented Ryker with an opportunity.

He moved, keeping himself concealed in the darkness, skirting the edge of the cones of headlights. He got to the camp just as the second man was loading something into the back of the truck.

Ryker sprang on him, putting a hand over the man's mouth as he drove his knife into the guy's throat. He heard a gurgled cry, and shifted his weigh to carry the man off to the side of the truck, putting the vehicle between him and first man.

"*Ahktar?*" the first man called.

Ryker moved again, staying low. From his position he was forced to risk sliding along the truck's front bumper, passing through both headlights, one by one. He worried that the first man would see the pulse of shadow and light from Ryker's passing.

There was no outcry, no alarm.

Ryker moved along the left side of the truck until he was nearly back to where he started. The first man was stepping slowly, cautiously toward the truck. He had an M16 leveled, ready.

American issue, Ryker thought. The withdrawal of US military support in the region had resulted in their enemies getting their hands on millions of pounds of US arsenal. A free gift from the US taxpayers, so that the *Kharif* could go on killing innocent people in the most efficient way possible.

Bitch about it later, Ryker reminded himself. *Write a letter to your congressman.*

He had another grim job to do in service to his country.

Ryker waited until the man was carefully peering around the edge of the truck, and then pounced before the man could react to what he found there.

Ryker drove his knife into the base of the man's skull, and in the throes of death the man's hand spasmed, firing a few quick rounds from the M16 into the dirt and dust of the desert.

Ryker pulled the weapon free as he let the man's body drop to the soil, and paused, listening. There was only the sound of distant gunfire across the desert, toward the perimeter of the American FOB. Anyone still out in this part of the wilderness likely wouldn't notice a few additional rounds echoing through the night, even if they might seem closer than those at the battlefront. *Kharif* had been taking shots at Ryker all night anyway, so this would sound like more of the same.

Ryker searched both men, taking magazines of ammunition, radios, even a couple of pieces of wrapped hard candy. All of these could come in handy. He made use of one piece of the candy right there and then. It had been a long night, and his last meal had been thousands of miles from here. Sugar was fuel.

With its engine warmed up, Ryker slipped inside the truck, put it in gear, and raced toward the base, south of his current position. He'd have to ditch the truck when he got closer, unfortunately. There was zero chance he'd be able to simply drive in.

Either the Americans would shoot him or the *Kharif* would.

But at least he would make better time. He'd figure out how to get inside the base without getting killed once he got there.

For now he sucked on the candy and thought about what he was going to say to Jill, when he saw her.

NINE

Kharif Stronghold, Somewhere in Katakstan

Faraz was watching the faces of each man as they reported on the situation at the American base. The intel they'd gotten from the CIA spy had proven useful, at least. Acting on that information had given them everything they needed to move *Kharif* operatives into position, to route the Americans out of town and force them to take refuge in the base. The very base that, as of now, was the last stronghold before Faraz and his men reclaimed Katakstan for its rightful people.

No, Faraz thought. *Not for the people. For God.*

This was, after all, a holy war.

The people would benefit from the service to God, however, and soon this incessant and endless war could all finally be over. Or if not over, then at least the lines of battle might be pushed further away, where other *Kharif* factions could take up the fight. And at that point, perhaps soon, Faraz might find the opportunity to finally see his family again.

It had been months since he'd last held his wife and daughter. The region was under so much strain, Faraz had worried for them constantly. Danger was everywhere. The compound where he and his men had been taking refuge, planning for their next attack, had been raided by the Americans and their Katakstan allies. Faraz and his people—including his family—had barely managed to get out ahead of the raid.

He still thanked God for the early warning. It had been a true miracle. His prayers were filled with gratitude, and his heart was strengthened by the knowledge that this, such a simple act, was proof that God was *with them* in this war.

His wife, however, had not felt such courage and assuredness. Her heart was filled with fear and doubt. She had begged him to move her and their daughter somewhere far from the fight, somewhere that was safe.

Safe, because it was far from *him* as well.

It was not that she feared Faraz. He knew that. She simply knew that as long as he breathed, Faraz would be a target. A servant of God would always be the enemy of the infidel. They would not stop until his blood fed the sands.

He had finally relented to his wife's wishes, sending her to her sister's home, along with their daughter. They would be far from the fight, but not far from his influence. Faraz had ensured that an armed contingent of *Kharif* guards would always be on hand, protecting them.

His wife had not liked it. Her sister had protested. But all such complaints ended when Faraz had informed them both that it was either this or they could be locked in the deepest tunnels of the camp, surrounded by guards at all times, in a cave so far removed from the world that neither the enemy nor even sunlight could reach them.

"You may live with the presence of the guards," Faraz had said, "or you may live as our prisoners live." And the women had agreed with no further complaint.

He was not certain he would have put them below ground. He was not at all certain it would be safer for them there than where they were. His threat had not been empty—he would have carried it out if forced to. But it had not been the wish of his heart.

His heart wanted them to be free, to be safe, to be bathed in sunlight, to be far from this fight.

How I miss them, Faraz thought, thinking of his daughter's perfect face. He would give his own life to keep hers safe, if it were ever asked of him. Without pause or hesitation, without regret. But, thankfully, God had not yet asked that of him.

Instead, he would gladly give God the lives and blood of many thousands of Americans and Katakstan infidels.

Only thousands?

Perhaps many *millions*, now that God had given him the means.

The weapon was nearly his.

And with such a weapon Faraz would have the might of God on his side. *Millions* of lives would be his to end, if that was God's demand. At the very least, the weapon gave the *Kharif* the ability to humble the West, to bring all of its idolatry and arrogance to an end. The might of the West would be ended by Faraz's hand.

And he, like his father, would become a legend among their people.

For Faraz this glory would require putting millions to death.

His father had done it with only thirty.

When Faraz was a young boy, he followed his father's every footstep. Their village was poor—the infidels saw to this, taking whatever they wanted, leaving his people nothing but scraps. Despite this, however, Faraz's father had always assured them that they had all they needed. "God provides," he would say. "But one day the infidel will pay."

They raised sheep, sheared for wool, sold milk and anything else they could produce. They did a bit of farming, but much of this was limited, even forbidden by the infidels. Still, they made their way. It was a busy life, and his father was well respected, a leader in the village.

When the time of trouble came, his father was among the first to take up arms.

"It is the will of God," he said. "The infidel would take all we have, would desecrate this land and our people. But we will fight. And with God's will to strengthen us, we will win."

The fight with the infidels meant that his father was gone much of the time, to places where Faraz was not allowed to follow. There were secret meetings with the other elders, lasting deep into the night. And father would sometimes return to their home with dirt and oil and blood staining his clothes and his skin. Mother would wash both, and learned never to express her worry or concern for him.

It was not long after the troubles started, and father began spending time away, that the Americans came to the village. They were not there to cause trouble, they said. They were merely looking for *information*. They were hunting "bad people."

They were looking for the *Kharif,* they said.

Faraz, at that time, had never heard the term used the way the Americans said it. *Kharif,* as he knew it, was just the name of the autumn crops—the millet and sorghum that he and his siblings sometimes helped to harvest, in exchange for a bale or bushel or a few stalks to take home, to help feed his family.

Kharif was also what they called the autumn season, the time of reaping. It was a common word, one Faraz had not thought of much.

But *Kharif*, as the Americans used it, meant something else.

Young Faraz could sense it instinctively, and it made him curious. It made him afraid.

"What do they mean, father?" he asked. His father was home for once, had been home since the Americans arrived, except for the occasional late-night meeting with the other elders and men of the village. But the long periods of being away had suddenly stopped. "What is it the Americans seek?" Faraz asked.

"They seek the men of the village, and me with them," his father replied. "They seek to stop what we are doing, to imprison us or perhaps to kill us."

Faraz was shocked, and overcome with fear. He was young, and fear hits hardest in the hearts of boys who love their fathers and follow them all day, through the desert and the fields, doing the work of feeding the family. Faraz cried, out of this fear.

His father slapped him when he saw the tears, then knelt, putting a hand on both of Faraz's shoulders. "You do not cry over the work of God," his father said, his voice hard. Then, gently, he continued. "These men have come to find me, but they will find only God's anger and vengeance. Do not cry."

Faraz—believing his father, still afraid and now feeling the sting of rebuke on his cheek—nodded. He accepted his father's words. He knew that God sometimes required blood. And in obedience to God, and to his father, Faraz stopped crying.

And started *watching*.

His father had him cling close to the American soldiers, to listen to everything they said, to repeat it back to him and the elders word for word, even if Faraz didn't understand the words themselves.

Faraz understood English, the language of the American dogs. He had tutors in the village, teachers who his father paid with wool and milk and sometimes actual kharif—a bit of millet and sorghum, to fill their bellies. He was ensuring that his son got the foundation of an education, because as he put it, "God has a plan for you, my son. And so do I."

Faraz would eventually learn all about that plan, which would entail leaving their village and his family, traveling to the United Kingdom, attending University, learning all the ways of the West, so that he could return here and put his knowledge to work in service to God, in opposition to the infidel.

The entire village would provide the funds for that plan, obligating Faraz to serve them and repay them by leading the fight against the infidel. That plan led Faraz to become everything he was now.

But all of that was still many years away. In this moment, as a small Katakstan boy living in a poor village, young Faraz was a *spy*.

And he was very good at it.

He learned that if he brought the other boys of the village, and if they played ball near the soldiers, and laughed and sang, and smiled and waved, God would perform a miracle—he would make Faraz *invisible*.

Whenever Faraz and the other boys came close to the soldiers, they would notice him and the others at first, would cheer for them as they played their game, would sometimes throw them pieces of American candy, which were greedily scooped up and consumed on the spot. But at some moment, eventually, the Americans would *stop* noticing Faraz and his playmates. And in particular, they no longer noticed Faraz himself, as he crept closer, as he sat in the shade of their trucks, as he sipped water and pretended to rest.

They would talk only with each other, as if he were not there, and their conversation would be filled with information that his father and the elders could use.

Faraz understood very little of the details. He only parroted back the words they used. He would hear them say something, and he would pinch his eyes shut, repeating the sounds and syllables for the terms he did not know until he could mimic them exactly. And he would repeat these to his father. He might not understand the words, but he did understand his father's grin, the look of pride and approval in his eyes. He understood the hand that his father placed on his shoulder. He understood the joy in his father's expression.

Faraz was doing good work, and he was doing it for God. And for father.

One night, when Faraz and his siblings were asleep on the mats, the cool air blowing in through the windows of their home, he was suddenly awakened by a tremendous roar. He and the others stood, blankets falling to the floor at their feet, and stared out of the window at the enormous pillar of fire and smoke rising in the distance, making the night sky as bright as dawn. The explosion was far outside of town, many kilometers, but even at this distance its light illuminated the entire village.

As the fires died down there were screams and shouting, there was the sound of gunfire, and many smaller explosions. The sound of *fighting*, Faraz knew. He turned, scanning the room, looking for father. But father was nowhere to be found.

The fighting continued through the night, and Faraz's mother and aunts chastised him and his siblings, ordering them to lay down, to sleep. As if anyone could sleep with such noise!

But eventually they did sleep, even through the sounds of battle, even through the sounds of screams of agony and the wails of grief and sorrow.

And by morning it was done. By morning the world became quiet once again, and the light through the window was that of the sun, rather than the pillar of smoke and fire that rose above the desert like something from the scriptures.

Faraz awoke to the sound of his mother crying. She was surrounded by her sisters and some of the other women of the village, and they were touching her, stroking her hair, comforting her. Faraz went to her and stood. He did not speak, but only watched. Waited.

She looked up at him, her eyes red and brimming with tears. She smiled, and it was tender. Her sorrow was plain, but so was her determination.

"Your father has been lifted away by God," she said to him. "He has died in the fight with the infidels. But he was brave, and God was his strength. He served as the wrathful hand of God. The others who returned—your uncle and the others—they reported that your father, alone, killed thirty of the American *dogs!*"

Faraz had listened to his mother's speech, and though the news of his father's death had torn a hole in his heart, had shredded his very soul, he also felt the rise of pride. He heard what his mother was saying, and saw how she and the other women became firm, proud. He saw the honor they held for his father.

And though he wanted to scream and weep over the horror of losing his father, he did not cry. For the men—*the American dogs*—had come to this village to find his father, but had found only the anger and vengeance of God.

Faraz remembered his father's words. They singed his heart, branding it, giving it a mark, a sigil that represented a new purpose for him. It was in that moment, learning of his father's sacrifice, that Faraz became a man of God.

His uncle, his father's brother, had become the new head of the *Kharif*. But Faraz became the new head of his family's household. Both were sacred duties. His uncle told him, often, how proud he was of Faraz. But in Faraz's heart, he felt his place was really with the *Kharif*. He felt that his duty was to take up his father's role with the *Kharif*, to lead them in destroying the Americans.

He would one day succeed his father in that role. His uncle would hold it for him, he said, until he was ready. One day, Faraz would avenge his father—it was father's plan for him from the start.

As Faraz took over the duties of feeding the family, he studied harder than ever. He learned everything his village teachers could teach him. He became obsessed with studying the things his father would have wanted him to know. And when it came time for him to fulfill God's plan for him, his *father's* plan for him, and to leave and study in the West, among the infidels, he did this, too.

He suffered during those years. Suffered the anguish of having to pretend. Suffer more the anguish of questioning his own commitment, sometimes even his own faith. He suffered as he came to understand their enemies, because in his study and in answering the call of God and his own father, Faraz had learned a deep and painful lesson, a lesson that burned outward from his scarred and branded heart. It was the lesson his uncle had taught him with a slap and a kiss.

To defeat your enemy you must understand them. And to understand them is to *love them*—if only briefly, if only long enough to know how they see themselves, and where their weaknesses lay.

It was the most painful lesson of his life, second only to the death of his father. It created within him a rent tapestry, a ragged weave that depicted ages of conflict and suffering, that illustrated the growing anger of God, and the wrath owed to the West. And woven within the fibers of that tapestry was something that frightened and sometimes *disgusted* him—his love for his enemy. His knowledge that in defeating them, destroying them, spreading their ashes to the winds, he would also be harming himself in some way.

Such was the price God demanded of Sayed Shanyar Faraz. Such was the price he would gladly pay, in service to God, to his people. In honor of his father.

Each day of his life, every action Faraz took was for God, and for his people. But secretly, it was really *all* for his father.

And now, all these years later, as a father and husband himself, Faraz was finally within reach of the great and terrible power of

God, the weapon that God had revealed to him to be His wrath. Faraz was close. The CIA man had given him the first of the keys to unlock it, and now it was only a matter of time. He was *very close*.

Soon, Faraz would be the instrument of God's anger and vengeance, on a global scale. And this war with the infidels—with the entire Western world—would finally be over, for all time.

TEN

US-Katakstan Forward Operating Base, Katakstan Border

Another round of mortars hit the Southern wall, and Jill Adams was once again huddled under the large table in the center-most conference room of the FOB's admin building. The building was at the center of the base, and therefore the furthest point from the live fire happening all around the perimeter.

The furthest point was the safest point, they'd been told. What went unspoken was the fact that the *safest point* did not necessarily translate to *safe*.

This was not where she had expected to find herself at this point in her life. Though she couldn't rightly say she knew exactly *what* she'd expected, ever, when it came to her brother.

Mark—her brother—somehow always ended up being the reason her life was slightly derailed, slightly off-center, slightly hunkered under a table waiting for a literal bomb to drop.

Ok, to be fair—that one was new, and she had a *bit* to do with it. It *was* a bit outside of normal. But not by much.

Jill loved her brother. She had *always* loved her brother, and she always would. She was his big sister, after all, though they were technically only just shy of a year apart in age. That didn't stop her from being the one to make sure he stayed out of trouble, when they were growing up.

Though she had to admit, *staying out of trouble* was never really how it went. It was more like making sure he *got out* of trouble, once he was in it. And he was *always* in it.

Which meant Jill was always in it, too.

But never like this.

When she'd learned that Mark had been captured, when the CIA had offered to fly her to Katakstan to help find him, there was never any doubt that she'd get on the plane. She'd been getting on planes and driving across state lines and sneaking into mall security offices all their lives, on Mark's behalf. It was their dynamic. Their pattern. Mark got *in* to the trouble, and his big sister Jill played at the biggest role in getting him *out* of the trouble.

You may have gone too far this time, little brother, she thought. *I may not survive long enough to help you out of this one.*

She might not get out of this one herself.

When Mark had first announced he was going into the military, Jill had nearly lost her mind. "You know I can't do anything to keep you safe, if you're ordered to go to war."

"I know," Mark said, nodding, pretending to be somber, resolute. It was a put-on. She could see the tiny play of a smirk at the corners of his mouth.

"I can't do anything to help you if you get in trouble with your commanding officer, either," she'd said.

"You can't?"

She glared at him. "I *won't*."

The grin finally broke, and Mark was all teeth. "Ok, I understand," he said. He held up a hand, as if taking an oath. "I'll do my best to stay on the straight and narrow. And if I slip, it's on me. I deal with my own problems from here out."

Good words. They sounded mature, especially in light of his decision to enter the armed forces. But the grin told her everything.

Or maybe she was just inserting her own bias into it. Maybe she couldn't help but remember all the times Mark Adams had forced himself to be the center of her world, with his troubles becoming her own troubles.

Either way, they both knew there really was no depth of trouble Mark could get into that Jill wouldn't do everything in or even *above* her power to get him out. There was no water she'd let him boil in, no rope she'd be willing to let him dangle from for long.

No matter how much she might want him to writhe for a bit, in the hopes that it might shock some sense into him, she would be there. It was just what she did. Every time.

Although, come to think of it, Mark's recklessness and disregard for caution might be part of what made him a good officer—a truth Jill was reluctant to admit, but ultimately couldn't deny. His record, over the past decade, had proven that he was *born* for this work.

They were eighteen and nineteen, respectively, when they'd had the conversation about Mark going into the military. Jill—always something of a prodigy, first in applied sciences and then in *political science*—had gotten involved with the local political scene at age sixteen. Three years after college, she was a part-time member of staff with Senator Trait, the Republican senator for their state.

Jill may have worked with Trait's offices part-time, as she attended grad school, but she was putting in more hours than most grad students put into a full-time gig *after* graduation. Every minute she wasn't in class or studying, she was in Trait's offices, putting in the time and the work, and learning absolutely everything she could.

And it paid off. It wasn't long before Jill Adams was *noticed*.

She'd gotten her undergrad degrees — double-majoring in poli-sci and physics — at age eighteen, and was working with the Senator in the afternoons and evenings, and full-time during semester breaks, while she pursued a Masters and eventually a PhD. It was a heavy workload, but it came with fringe benefits. One of those was recognition as a rising star, and as a lynchpin on Senator Trait's team. And with that recognition came influence—what was known inside the Belt as "political currency."

From her early twenties on, likely thanks to the fact that she was highly respected and had developed a reputation in a field of actual science, Jill Adams had pull. And every year of her career, that pull evolved and grew, eventually becoming a gravitational force that she could use to grease wheels and open doors. She was a prodigy, for certain. But she was on her way to becoming a political force to be reckoned with. That had its perks.

But her real full-time job had always been dealing with whatever mess Mark created.

The whole experience of her twenties could best be summed up with the phrase, "*Jill Adams is a young political prodigy who is both well-connected and chronically exhausted.*" Tack on "*and her brother Mark is a royal pain the ass, but she helps him anyway,*" and that could serve well enough as the summary statement at the top of her résumé.

Granted, Mark had *always* been a pain in the ass, but she'd had high hopes for him once he'd told her the CIA had reached out to recruit him. Such a remarkable opportunity from such a prestigious agency—surely it meant that Mark had shown great promise and great responsibility.

It was ironically both surprising and inevitable, when she'd thought about it. Mark Adams, her pre-military, trouble-magnet little brother, wasn't someone she thought could *ever* be disciplined enough to attract the interest of the CIA—unless it was to be put on some kind of government watch list. And yet, somehow, serving in the military had managed to change him, had even *matured* him, in profound ways.

He'd managed to have a distinguished and exemplary career in the army at any rate. He was even a decorated combat hero, serving two tours in Afghanistan before being offered some covert ops assignments in places he wasn't allowed to talk about.

Jill's troublesome little brother was actually pretty good at getting *himself* out of tight spots in scary places after all, as it turned out.

It probably helped a great deal that now Mark had entire *teams* of trained soldiers and operatives backing him up and getting him out of whatever jam he got himself into. He was working with men and women whose *jobs* were to come to his rescue, when he got in trouble. He had more people than his big sister to turn to, when it all hit the fan. Which was good—she wanted Mark to be safe. But was also not-so-good—because really, it just encouraged him. He seemed to be comfortable taking more and bigger risks, relying on the safety net of having people watching his six.

In all his years of military service, Mark had only ever reached out to Jill to help him solve more *domestic* trouble. Girls, mostly. Jill would fly to visit them in military towns and bases around the globe, handing them discrete envelopes filled with cash, sympathizing with them over how much of an asshole her brother was for leaving them in this condition, outlining for them the *terms* that came with those wads of money they were clutching.

Every payout came with contracts, and the contracts were airtight. They made all of Mark's domestic troubles go away, so he was free to keep saving the free world from the *very bad people*.

God bless America.

She was proud of him.

Maybe not all the time, and especially not when she was dealing with his more lascivious encounters, but when she heard about the missions he went on, the *very bad people* he helped to take down, the *very good people* he'd managed to save—she couldn't help but feel *proud* of him. She continued to hope that his experience would give him more self discipline and shave off more of his wild burrs, to maybe make him a bit more cautious and conscientious. To make him less of the troublesome little brother he'd been for Jill's whole life, and more of...

Well, more of a *hero,* really. She wanted Mark Adams to be a hero. She believed he could do it. She believed it was in him.

Somehow, though, as she crouched under a table, as mortar fire pounded the walls and dust and other debris rained down from the ceiling, she just wasn't currently certain that Mark was growing out of his tendencies. She was starting to think he was still the kid in the mall security office. Still the guy who couldn't manage to be responsible enough to use a condom.

She was starting to admit that these years of service hadn't changed Mark quite as much as she might have liked. He was still the same troublemaker he'd always been, only now his trouble was spilling over onto her own life in more profound and dangerous ways. These past few years hadn't changed him a bit.

These years had given *her* a boost, though.

Now in her late 20s, edging a little closer to 30 than she cared for, Jill had already served in various government positions as she rose in the ranks, and was currently considered a shoe-in for the same Senate seat she'd served for most of her adult life. Senator Trait had recently announced he was retiring, and Jill had been the party's top pick to run for his seat. She had the background, the experience, the name recognition. She had the funds, and the support of many wealthy and powerful people. And if she lived through *this* experience, she was confident in her shot. And she was going to take it.

She had been only half-decided before getting on that plane to Katakstan, but now she knew, there was never any chance that she *wouldn't* run. It had always been a foregone conclusion. She'd decided to do it all the way back when she was that 16-year-old prodigy working in local politics. It was inevitable.

It was the least she could do, considering she blamed herself for the very fact that her brother was here now. The technology had gotten into the wrong hands, and it had been her fault. The deal looked fine on paper, and would help US allies in the region.

Or so she thought.

Perhaps getting Mark back — with or without the tech — would assuage the fears she had that this was all going to come back on *her*. It was a little consolation, and she would spend the rest of her career trying to undo the mess they were in.

Suddenly, from outside the building the sound of explosions and gunfire dropped off, as it had hundreds of times over the past few days. The quiet, as always, was more deafening and oppressive than the racket of combat. Somehow the quiet was *worse*.

Maybe it was the anticipation, knowing that at any second it could all start up again, as it had over and over for the past several days. A tactic of psychological warfare, she thought. *Keep them on edge, always guessing, never certain.*

Jill's nerves were frayed. The FOB had been under constant onslaught since the *Kharif* had taken out the Northern guard. The insurgents had managed to circle them in, pushing the Americans and their local allies alike back into the base, where they were surrounded and cut off from the rest of the world.

Not long after setting up a perimeter and locking the doors, they'd lost all communication with the outside world. The *Kharif* had somehow gotten their hands on technology that could shut down all incoming and outgoing signals. Cellular was a no-go. Radio was an ocean of static. And the satellite towers were among the first targets taken out by *Kharif* mortar fire.

Power was fading as well, as the massive banks of batteries slowly discharged. The solar panels had taken fire, so there was no trickle charge. They had generators, but fuel was starting to get low, and every drop might be necessary for a last ditch run out of this place. A run that, despite the assurance of base command, Jill knew they'd never survive.

There was simply nowhere to go. The enemy was all around them. They'd be slaughtered right out of the gate.

They were already down to running on emergency lights only. The darkness was all part of the onslaught—making them cower in fear under tables and in doorways wasn't enough. It had to be *dark,* too.

Kharif insurgents had the US forces in the forward operating base surrounded, and even their Katakstan allies on the outside were powerless to help. When the US started pulling troops out of the region, they abandoned tons of weapons and other equipment, all of which was immediately claimed by the *Kharif*. The FOB was surrounded, and the enemy was well armed, with weapons and ammunition stamped "Property of the US Military."

It was a huge mess. And the people *inside* the FOB were looking for answers. Everyone wanted to know what had set this off, and how the *Kharif* had gotten the intel and the tech they'd used to isolate the FOB.

There were rumors of course. Disturbing rumors. Hushed conversations that ended whenever Jill came close. But many lingered long enough, were whispered loud enough, that she knew she was meant to hear. She heard her brother's name, and knew what they were all thinking.

The enemy had a source of intelligence. Someone who knew the ins and outs of the FOB, of US troop movements, of Katakstan's military resources, of weapons and technology stockpiles. The *Kharif* had someone telling them everything they needed to know, in order to exploit the vulnerability created when the US started pulling out of Katakstan.

The unspoken accusations bothered Jill, a lot. But the implications bothered her much more.

If Mark really had given them any of this information, it would have come after something horrible and painful, she knew. The kind of trouble she'd meant, when she'd told him she wouldn't be able to help him. The kind of trouble that might spill over onto her, in a number of ways.

It could be bad for her, politically. It could be worse for her, physically, here in this place. This land that did not respect women in power—or much at all, for that matter.

It seemed that this time Mark's adventures might actually be the death of her. She'd joked about it so often she'd stopped being afraid of it. That was a mistake.

Or maybe not. Maybe this was just one of those situations where all you could do was laugh.

In fact, even now, as she climbed out from under the table along with the rest of the room's occupants, as she thought about this mess, and about the possibility that Mark might be dead, and that she might be running along to join him any minute now, she smiled. And then she laughed.

It was a quick bark of laughter, and she'd clamped down on it immediately. She shifted and turned away from everyone, the entire group of beleaguered administrative and support personnel that had huddled with her here, mostly civilians. They weren't completely unaccustomed to combat, but having it right outside of the walls was a new and jarring experience. Jill didn't want to upset them, and she didn't want them to think anything was wrong with her.

She was mostly hoping there really *wasn't* something wrong with her. She'd dealt with a lot of tension and strain over the past few days. It could be taking its toll.

She moved quickly out of the room, making her way toward the little kitchen where she prayed to God there would be something strong, brown, and harsh on the throat. Preferably whiskey, but she'd take hot coffee as a close second. It had been a week since her last sip of either, and she wasn't picky about which one showed up first.

She'd left the room because she didn't want anyone thinking she was cold or insensitive. Or worse, *cracking up*.

It was just that she'd worried so much about Mark, over all these years, that she'd forgotten to worry about *herself*. And now that she was facing imminent death, she couldn't even remember how she'd gotten here. Not exactly. Not *really*.

That man, the case officer who never identified himself... that was how it had happened. He had popped into her office, with no appointment. He had closed her door, and he had shown her photos and files, had made an offer to put her on a plane, to fly her to Katakstan immediately. Shown her the research — *her* research — that was now in the enemies' hands.

And now, here she was.

Hiding under conference tables as the ceiling rained down.

Wondering if she'd survive another day here.

Wondering when the bad guys would manage to use a mortar or a missile or something to bring the entire base down on top of her.

Looking for the strongest drink she could find.

She'd never even hesitated.

She'd taken that anonymous CIA guy up on his offer without even blinking, because... well, how could she not? It was her fault Mark was here. And she could never turn her back on an opportunity help Mark, if he needed it.

Maybe she should have.

But that had never been her way. From the moment the spook had entered her office she'd known it was about Mark, and she had known she'd go, no matter where he was or what had happened. No matter what mess he'd gotten himself into. No matter what mess he was getting *her* into.

She was mad at herself over it. That unwavering loyalty to her brother—and how had he ever repaid her for it? By getting into even *more* trouble, usually.

But what could she do? She loved him. Always had. Always would. And if there was ever anything she could do to help him, she'd always do it.

The problem was, by coming here, she'd more or less stripped herself of the ability to do anything *useful*. In her haste to get to Mark, to help him, she may have cut off any chance he had, and any chance for herself as well. All her *real* power was back in DC, with its deals and powerbrokers she knew how to play like a fiddle.

Here, she was just one of several people huddling under a conference table, praying to whatever God each of them believed in that they'd be kept safe, kept alive.

If Mark really was the source of intel for the *Kharif*, she would have a much better shot of helping him if she were back in Washington. All her best resources were there. Or were just an email or text message away. She had friends in the State Department. She could pull strings.

But here?

Cut off. Isolated. No communication with the outside world. No *reach*.

Here, she could cower under conference tables. She could sleep in fits and spurts until she was exhausted and her nerves were fried. She could die. But she probably couldn't help Mark get out of this one.

Coming here had been a mistake. One she hadn't hesitated to make, because Mark was her little brother. Her biggest weakness. Her biggest burden.

She entered the kitchen, still hopeful for that drink, and stopped short when she saw a man in full combat fatigues, standing at one of the steel kitchen work surfaces. The emergency lighting in here was limited to one panel of LEDs, and it was directly over the table where the man had made himself a bologna sandwich. He had just taken a bite, and chewed quickly when he saw her standing in the doorway.

"General Clayborne," Jill said, stepping further into the space.

ELEVEN

SOMEWHERE SOUTH OF THE US-KATAKSTAN FORWARD
OPERATING BASE, KATAKSTAN BORDER

The truck rumbled over the night-shrouded Katakstan desert, jarring Ryker to the point where he wondered if his bones might liquify. The suspension on this thing was beyond shot—it might be non-existent, gauging by the grinding, slamming sound that it made with every inch of desert it crossed. Every pebble on the desert floor cost Ryker that much more bone density.

He was also pushing his luck.

His trek on foot across the nighttime desert, after dropping in hot, had taken more time than he'd anticipated. All the dodging and hiding and killing he'd had to do had slowed him down further. And now, as he was just a couple of klicks away from the FOB, daylight was slowly dawning over the horizon, but not slowly enough. He needed it to stay dark *just a little longer*. It was only a matter of time before someone noticed him—even in the dark colored, unmarked combat fatigues, he currently stood out like an American sore thumb driving a junked-out truck too fast and in the wrong direction. Sooner or later, someone was going to get it into their head that he needed more bullets in *his* head.

He'd been running without headlights for most of the drive, depending on the distant glow of the FOB's security lights for direction and the night vision HUD on his helmet to help him avoid obstacles on the dark terrain. As the sky brightened and dawn approached, however, the night vision was becoming more of a liability than an advantage. Soon he'd be able to see better without it. At which point, it would be easier for the enemy to see *him*.

Just two more klicks, Ryker thought, willing the darkness to linger. *Hold out for just two more.*

The FOB loomed ahead of him now, eating an odd sort of barely lit skyline out of the horizon. Between him and the base there was a wasteland of sand and rock that terminated in a perimeter of cement outbuildings, concrete blocks, sand bags, and razor wire fencing. And just beyond that were about two hundred very well-armed and very pissed off US Marines and Katakstan ally soldiers, all of whom had been spending their days and nights firing rounds and projectiles at trucks exactly like the one Ryker was driving, and cheering with each explosive and fiery hit.

Ryker wanted to avoid becoming part of a twisted, molten wreck of metal on the desert floor. Which meant he wasn't getting anywhere near that base. Not yet. Not in this thing. But he wasn't yet close enough to make any kind of reasonable run for it on foot, either. And even if he was, he had no way to readily identify himself to the good guys while hiding himself from the bad guys. That was quite a conundrum.

He'd be shot—maybe by the Marines, maybe by the *Kharif*, maybe by both—before it was all over. It was damn near a certainty.

He needed a plan.

He slowed the truck to a stop at a structure he hoped would be just outside the range of friendly fire. He parked beside a burned-out shell of a building, still smoldering at its base from whatever hit it. The building was on his West side, which would shield him from the eyes of the *Kharif* in that direction. To the East was another structure, in far worse shape. He'd come in from the South, and there was nothing that way to worry about. So far, anyway.

The FOB was North of his position, and from that direction he was still somewhat exposed. But the bad guys were a ways off and a little preoccupied at the moment, sending mortars flying into the FOB in an attempt to open a gap and get inside, to finish this after weeks of fighting.

So far, the Marines and their allies were holding fast and keeping the line. But Ryker knew it would only take one lucky strike to give the enemy the advantage. This was a numbers game, a game of odds and attrition, and the bad guys had more time and more mortars than they needed.

The clock was running out for the FOB. They needed reinforcements. Which *were* coming. But if no one in the base knew, if no one was able to coordinate an evacuation with the drone strike that was on its way, it was all going to go South, and quick. Wasted strike, wasted effort, and everyone dies. So if Ryker couldn't get them the sat phone...

He'd worry about that later. What he really had to worry about *now* was whoever was inside this husk of a building.

Ryker rolled out of the truck, ducking behind it to keep himself hidden, in case anyone peeked outside. He checked one of the M16s taken off of the two *Kharif* he'd left rotting out in the desert. It had a mostly full magazine. He'd collected three more magazines in the scuffle, so he was fairly well armed. His own sidearm was tucked into a holster on his thigh, a quick reach if he needed it. And, of course, there was the knife, in case silence was required.

Silence would come at the cost of being close, however. Close could mean greater risk. Always the balance one had to strike, in this situation.

It had finally gotten too bright out for night vision, so Ryker disengaged that system, keeping the goggles down and the HUD operating. It wouldn't necessarily give him any useful intel—there was no one in contact with him yet, which meant no one to share data or details. The automated systems were geared mostly toward interfacing with specific weaponry, which he did not have, or relaying signals from OPs, which he also did not have. But the goggles would help shield his eyes from debris and other fragments, and there was limited telemetry that could be useful. Anything he focused on would bring up a distance reading, for one thing. That could come in handy in a pinch. He could also snap night vision back on with a quick tap, in case it was too dark inside the building.

Ryker crouched, raised the M16, and pivoted to sweep the area around the building, verifying it was clear. Then he sprinted for the doorway, weapon ready.

There was no door. Not anymore. This building had once served as a guard station with a booth downstairs and some small sleeping quarters upstairs. This would have been manned by a couple of marines on duty, normally. Upstairs in the tiny bunk room were sleeping and living quarters where the next shift would be waiting to take over.

It may have been a small building by most standards, but it was still big enough to house around five Marines at any given time. Plenty big enough that someone could be hiding inside, which meant Ryker had to move as quietly as possible.

Of course, with the bulk of the fighting happening closer in, and US troops pinned within the FBO, this structure was no longer strategic. So it might be empty.

He couldn't chance it.

Regardless, he needed a place to take cover, regroup, and work out a plan for making contact with the base, and this was his best option.

Ryker took his time going in, sweeping the entire first floor and clearing it before he carefully made his way up the single set of stairs. These were sturdy, metal struts, and though there was no worry over squeaking floorboards, he still stepped carefully, placing each foot deliberately, keeping noise to a minimum.

Infiltrating a structure like this was a dumb move without backup. He'd be a sitting duck if anyone came down while he was creeping up. But his job—the job he'd been trained to do—often meant working without a net. Dumb moves were the gig. And besides, this entire *mission* was a dumb move, with one guy marching through heavily occupied enemy territory, carrying the only hope for everyone in that base... just crazy.

Not even the craziest thing I've done, in this business, Ryker mused. Crazy was also the gig.

He heard voices before he'd ever reached the top floor. Two men, speaking in *Pashto*, talking mostly about their general boredom, and daydreaming out loud about engaging the enemy, killing the *American dogs*. Ryker paused, listening, trying to get as much intel as possible.

What he gathered was that they'd been at this post for days now, and the Americans were still entrenched behind the perimeter of the FOB, still holding the *Kharif* back, despite the Americans' inferior position and lack of reinforcements. It made for a tedious and drawn-out fight, and for men tasked with keeping watch it was boring, pointless business.

Both men longed to be where the actual *fighting* was. They wanted their chance to kill the infidel. They wanted their reward and glory. They wanted their chance to meet God, to spend eternity in paradise.

Ryker stepped into the room without making a sound, and before either man had noticed him he answered their prayers, putting a bullet in each of their heads with two quick, single shots from the M16.

Give my regards to God, Ryker thought, moving past them to sweep the rest of the room, prepared to fire if he spotted anyone else.

The shots had been quick, efficient, but also very loud. He paused, waiting, watching, listening. There was no sign of surprise from anyone out of sight, no stirring from any of the bunks. Which meant there was likely no one else in the building. Still, he did the walk, took the time, cleared each corner of the room, the latrine, each bunk top, down, and under. Satisfied he was alone, he rolled the two dead men aside, opening a path to the window.

He stayed low and was careful about being visible through the window. It was always possible that there was an American or Katakstan sniper across the way, waiting for his shot. Just because these two idiots hadn't taken a bullet before Ryker got here didn't mean someone at the FOB wasn't waiting for them to poke a head up. The distance to the perimeter was pretty far—just over a mile from the base. But Ryker had known snipers who could take that shot, if the conditions were right. The record was around 3,800 yards —or just over two miles. Which put this place *well* within range.

He didn't want to risk it.

This had really been a rookie move, leaving the downstairs open and empty while both *Kharif* insurgents lounged upstairs like kids at a slumber party. Lucky thing for Ryker, at least. But it was sloppy, regardless.

It told him something about the enemy—they were well-armed, but not necessarily disciplined. They followed orders, but didn't necessarily think *beyond* those orders. That could be good news for Ryker.

He couldn't count on every *Kharif* to be so negligent, but every scrap of intel he could pick up about the enemy could prove to be lifesaving. He took mental note of everything he'd learned, from their conversation to their current state as corpses, filing it away.

Now that he had his own perch, and some elevation, Ryker carefully looked across the way, scanning the pan of desert between him and the FOB, trying to get a better lay of the land than what he'd been given prior to his jump.

He was less than two klicks from the FOB now, but might as well be on the other side of the world. There was no chance of crossing that gulf of sand, rock, and bullets and getting to the base without being seen—or worse—either by the Americans or by the *Kharif*. And he might be able to avoid the live fire of one side or the other, but certainly not both. Eventually he was going to become someone's new favorite target, followed quickly by being just another corpse in the sand.

His only chance would be to signal the FOB and let them know he was incoming.

Comms were still down over there. The *Kharif* had used some new tech, an EM pulse, to knock out the electronics. They might also have some kind of signal blocker.

So no radio, no cellular, no satellite. How could he communicate with them, across that void?

He moved back down the stairs, and when he was outside he stared at the truck, studying it, thinking.

Old school, he thought.

But sometimes, he knew, the old tricks were the best tricks.

He slung the M16 over his shoulder and got to work.

TWELVE

US-Katakstan Forward Operating Base, Katakstan Border

Clayborne nodded as he chewed, and when he swallowed he said, "Ms. Adams."

"I'm sorry to interrupt your snack," she said.

He shook his head. He was a throughly stereotypical military man, standing at an impressive six-foot-three, with squared shoulders and an even more squared crop of salt-and-pepper hair, in a military-regulation cut. He had a bristle-broom mustache that was iron grey and looked as if he waxed each hair individually. They were as stiff as porcupine quills.

Despite his age, Clayborne was just about the most robustly fit man Jill had ever seen. Rumor had it that he could out-lift any man on base, in the FOB's gym, and that while he might not outrun someone on a track, he would definitely outpace them all over a long run. And despite all of this strength and toughness, there was a glint of gentle wisdom in his eyes. And maybe even a touch of kindness—of the stern-father, brooking-no-nonsense variety.

Though he could be ferocious when he thought someone wasn't doing their job, he was more often pragmatic and calm. His emotional discipline was off the charts, and Jill admired him for it. Though he hadn't exactly warmed to her in return, at least not at first.

He had welcomed her, when she'd first arrived, as if he was glad to see her. And yet she knew that he'd been coerced and ordered into letting her onto his base. She didn't know the particulars, but some of his junior staff had confided in her. He had not been happy to have her here.

But he hadn't shown it. Not even once. He was gracious and civil at all times, so Jill did her best to show him respect and not step on his toes. She needed him.

"You have caught me in a moment of weakness," Clayborne said. "I love bologna and mustard a little too much."

She smiled and laughed lightly. "I've seen worse vices," she said. "I have a few myself. In fact, that's why I came in here, hoping to find... well, let's say a bottle of vice. Preferably one about twelve years or older."

Clayborne smiled and chuckled. "You won't have any luck in here, I'm afraid. My orders are no hooch in the galley. And I never touch the stuff, myself. But I happen to know a few of my people have a bottle stashed here or there. I'm sure they'd be willing to share."

"There may be less laying around than you think," Jill said. "Days like we've had lately tend to burn through liquor."

Clayborne nodded. "That's true."

Jill stepped further into the kitchen and stood opposite Clayborne, the steel table between them. "Mind if I have a bit of that myself?"she asked, gesturing toward the bologna. She hadn't realized how hungry she was until she'd seen his sandwich. It had been a long time since her last meal. She wasn't even sure when that had been.

Clayborne, without a word, slid his sandwich aside and began constructing hers.

"Oh, I can do that!" she started.

He held up a hand. "No ma'am. I consider this my duty. Mustard?"

She smiled and nodded. "Please."

In only a moment Clayborne had finished his work and slid the sandwich across to her. She picked it up and took a bite, and immediately felt ravenous. She paced herself, but it was all she could do to keep from inhaling the whole thing. "I didn't realize how hungry I was," she said around a mouthful of bologna and bread.

Clayborne smiled. "Combat can work up an appetite."

She shook her head. "I'm spending my days under a conference table. I'd hardly call that combat."

"If the enemy is aiming their weapons at you," Clayborne said, "it's combat. The fight is to survive. How you fight makes no difference."

She considered this and nodded. Then, after a moment's reflection, she said, "It's not going well, is it?"

Clayborne had finished his sandwich and was cleaning up, tying off the bread, closing the plastic around the bologna, wiping the table with a damp rag. He paused, staring down at his hands, and shook his head. "It's not going well."

"How much time do you think we have?" she asked, quietly.

He looked up at her. "Let me put it this way—you at least have time to finish your sandwich."

She considered this, sighed, and nodded. "I'll take what I can get." She took a bite then, chewing deliberately.

He smiled at that, and then laughed. "You know, I didn't like you much, when you first got here."

She arched her eyebrows, as if surprised, and swallowed. "Oh?"

"Nothing personal," he said. "But you represented trouble to me. The CIA has used this base as a pass-through for getting their people in and out of the hot soup for the past forty years. I've seen a *thousand* CIA operatives come and go since I took over, including your brother, on more than one occasion. In all that time, nobody from Washington ever showed up to look in on any of those agents. Not until you arrived."

"Are you going to tell me I'm bad luck?" Jill asked.

"Not bad luck," Clayborne said, shaking his head. "A bad sign. I knew when you got here that things were going to get rough. The order to pull back, to withdraw and get our people out of here— that's a boneheaded order. But I followed it. That's what I do. That's what my people do. Even if it means doing it while people shoot at us. But when you got here, and I got my orders to accommodate you and help you find Agent Adams, I knew something had gone wrong, and that no one was telling me what it was."

He was looking at her, steady and strong, and she caught on to what he was asking.

"I... I'm not sure I can help with that," she said. "I only know what they told me."

"Which was what, exactly?" Clayborne asked.

She sighed. "That Mark was here. That he was in trouble. Captured. And that I might be able to help."

"And how would you do that, if you don't mind me asking?"

She shook her head. "I don't know," she said. "I didn't know then, and I don't know now. I don't know what the CIA expected from me. It's not like I'm a solider or an agent. I'm just a bureaucrat."

"Oh, more than that," Clayborne said with a wave. "I looked into you, when we still had access to the internet. You've held a bunch of offices in Washington, and you've been in and out of Senator Trait's cabinet most of your life. You're the youngest member of Trait's team, but still expected to sweep the vote and gets his seat, when he steps down. You're a prodigy."

"Maybe once," she smiled lightly. "Being a prodigy is something you outgrow, eventually."

The General nodded at this. "I think they wanted you here for another reason," Clayborne said, a note of warning in his voice.

She felt her heart thump and go cold. "What... other reason?"

He was staring at her, and shook his head. He started to speak, but was interrupted by the entrance of a Private.

"General Clayborne, sir!"

"What is it?"

"We're getting a message at the Southern wall!"

Clayborne looked confused. "A message? Are comms back up?"

The Private shook his head. "No sir, comms are still down. It's Morse code, sir."

Morse code? Jill thought. Then she felt her pulse quicken. She looked at Clayborne. "Mark?"she asked.

He met her look, then turned back to the Private. "Lead the way, son And brief me on the way."

As he followed the younger man out of the kitchen he glanced her way. She stood, hesitant, waiting. He nodded, and Jill raced alongside him, both of them on the heels of the Private, all marching toward the Southern wall.

And hopefully, she prayed, toward her little brother.

THIRTEEN

The idea was simple enough. Execution hadn't been so tough, either.

First, he repositioned the truck so that getting into the building would be both challenging and noisy. He basically rammed one bumper into the doorway, crushing through the door jam until the passenger-side window was more or less aligned with the opening. It wouldn't be impossible for someone to get through and enter the building, but it wasn't going to be a silent intrusion, by any stretch.

That should help keep him from meeting the same fate as his two *Kharif* friends, currently rotting under a tarp on the first floor.

Once he had the door obstructed, he then used his knife to remove one of the truck's headlights, and then to take the battery out of the truck itself, along with two lengths of battery cable. He climbed through the truck—making all the noise he was counting on for early warning, if the enemy arrived—and hauled the battery, light, and cables up the steps. He set all of it near the window.

The room he was in had two stacks of bunks, four beds total. He shoved one of these across the floor until it blocked the doorway, then worked the top mattress down between the bunk frame and the gap in the door. An extra barricade, just in case. It wouldn't stop anyone from either pushing their way in or shooting him through the mattress, if they were so inclined. But it would at least obstruct their view and slow them down. He should know they were coming long before they got him, at least. He'd take any advantage he could get.

He'd already worked out an alternate exit. Or an escape route, if it turned out he needed one. He'd spent a few minutes looping and knotting a length of rope he'd found in the truck while retrieving the tarp, and had tied one end to the metal leg of one of the bunks, leaving the rest in a neat coil near a window. He used the barrel of the M16 to clear this of glass shards and make a clean exit.

If it came to it, he could drop the whole coil out of the window and be out and on the ground in seconds. Maybe even without a broken leg or sporting a few new body holes.

With the room secured and an escape route in place, Ryker turned his attention to the headlight and the battery. He used the knife to cut away some of the insulation on the battery cables, and twisted the exposed ends to the dangling wires from the headlight. He attached the black grounding cable directly to the battery, fastening it down using the terminal. He held the red wire in his hand, and then touched it to the positive lead of the battery.

The headlight suddenly filled the room with bright light, and he lifted the wire free, throwing everything back into shadow, blinking rapidly until his eyes adjusted to the darkness again.

Basic, but it would do.

Keeping low and out of sight of the window, he moved the headlight upward until it was leaning against the aluminum window frame, now devoid of glass. He aimed the light outward toward the FOB.

The dawn was coming, and everything was starting to get brighter. Once again, he needed that darkness to hang on for *just a few minutes more.* Otherwise this trick might not work, his makeshift signaling device might be washed out in the growing daylight.

Of course, anyone who saw the flashing light might take it as an invitation to target practice. This little exercise could be over real quick.

His choices were limited to this or nothing, though. And given the results that would come from doing nothing, this was the better plan.

Wasting no time he began tapping out his message.

Morse code was still a requirement in the military, and for good reason. It was transmittable in a variety of ways, and sometimes could be cleverly hidden from the enemy, even in plain sight. POWs sometimes tapped out messages to each other from their cells, using whatever they could find—a spoon against a bowl, a stone on a wall, the tap of a foot, the rap of a knuckle on a surface, there were many variations. In some instances, when terrorists put a captured US soldier on camera, in a show of their impressive might in capturing and beating unarmed people, a soldier sometimes used the opportunity to send a message home by tapping a finger on a knee or blinking or even clinching and unflinching their jaw. Unless the bad guys were both paying attention *and* knew Morse code, the entire message usually went unnoticed. And more than one enemy camp had been raided based on intel secretly sent by a prisoner of war.

In this case, Ryker would be using the headlight to send a signal to anyone watching from the FOB. So being noticed was kind of the goal.

Noticed by the *right side,* at least.

In a sense, this was also a "secret" communication, thanks to the nature of the conflict at the perimeter. Ryker was essentially doing what the blinking, finger tapping, spoon clinking POWs did—transmitting a signal from right under the enemy's noses. And just like the POWs, there was every chance that he could be noticed, at which point things would go very, very badly. But he was playing the odds, that the enemy's attention was more focused on the FOB, and not looking back at turf they'd already conquered.

The Marines would surely be looking out this way, and they had a decent chance of noticing a repeating pattern of light. Meanwhile the *Kharif* should be focused on looking the other direction. The signal should pass right by them, unnoticed.

That was a lot of shoulds, but it was what it was.

There was always the chance that one of the bad guys might look back. Someone at the front line turns at the wrong time, someone slips away to take a leak, someone shifts position to reload, and that would be it. Spotted. And if they were so inclined, they might opt to send a mortar in Ryker's direction. For company.

There was another risk as well.

If the Marines signaled *back*, then they would essentially give Ryker away.

He would hope they'd have brains enough not to do that, but there was always the chance that someone over there wasn't too bright.

Chances. That's all these were. Good ones and bad ones. It was the worst sort of plan, depending on chance in one direction or another.

Ryker would do what he'd always done, and make the best of either outcome.

He had his message prepared.

US operative <stop> have intel <stop> have sat comm <stop> need path <stop>

He repeated this three times over the next hour, starting each series with the code that Agent Anonymous had given him—a twelve-digit alpha-numeric sequence that was the last access code the base had been using prior to comms dropping out. It was the answer to another sequence that the FOB would have transmitted, if they'd been able, and it was the only way Ryker had to authenticate himself.

Sending his own message was risky, and each time it went out that risk compounded. He needed to make sure he gave the folks at the FOB plenty of chances to see his signal, but couldn't overdo it. Timing was crucial.

He was also gambling that even if one of the *Kharif* out there saw the signal they wouldn't be able to interpret it. Because he was basically broadcasting "Hey guys, very important enemy target over here. Come shoot me!"

He could only hope this worked. And that the good guys didn't assume the enemy was trying to trick them. And that the bad guys didn't see anything and decide to come take a look.

After the third sequence he paused for a few minutes and then sent his final message.

I come to you <stop> cover me <stop>

Once that was done he dropped the hot wire, letting it dangle off to the side. They would either have seen his messages by now or they wouldn't. The fact that he hadn't gotten a response proved nothing, because 'no response' was exactly what he needed from them. A Catch-22, of sorts.

Ryker moved the bunk and mattress away from the door. He checked the M16, along with his pistol. He patted the pockets with the spare magazines, reassuring himself that he had plenty of ammo. Whatever that meant at a time like this. And after a quick few breaths to get his heart rate under control, he moved down the steps with the same cautious sweep he'd used each time, up and down.

Once on the first floor he squeezed out through the truck's cab and paused for a moment, looking out over the stretch of desert between him and the FOB. The landscape was now much brighter, with the sun rising to the East.

Time for my morning run, Ryker thought, and started jogging across the sand toward the only destination possible.

FOURTEEN

"What does he mean, he's coming to *us*?" Clayborne growled. He was peering over the desert using a pair of sand-camo binoculars, and had shaken his head in disbelief more than once.

Jill was standing in the back of the room, skirting the line of where she was told to be. She barely had a view of the window, which everyone in the room assured her was for her own good.

"Snipers," Clayborne had informed her in a curt grunt. "That glass is bullet resistant, but not bullet proof. You're better off staying out of sight."

And she believed him.

He seemed to have no fear of a sniper's bullet, however, as he swept the landscape in full view of the window. "Got him," Clayborne said. He lowered the binoculars and shook his head. "Man's crazy," he said, almost under his breath.

"Sir," one of the Marines said, "you're an all-American decoy right now."

Clayborne nodded, and stood aside. He caught Jill's odd look.

"Easy target," he said. "Right out in the open."

Jill nodded. "So you saw him just now? Mark? Is he... is he *walking* to us?"

Clayborne held up a hand and turned to his men. "I want cover for this guy. And a distraction. Get some people out on the East wall and start shooting the opposite direction. Heavy fire. Make it look like we're trying to clear a path over there."

His people acknowledged the order and were out of the room in seconds. With comms still down, every order had to be relayed by foot. It was a tight funnel for command, and Jill had heard the officers curse about it more than once.

Slow orders meant dead soldiers, at a time like this.

Clayborne turned back to her. "That isn't Adams," he said.

Jill felt her heart sink. She'd been hopeful. And she wouldn't have put it past Mark to pull a crazy stunt like this. She shook her head and looked Clayborne in the eye. "Do you know who it is?"

Clayborne shook his head. "Never seen him before. But he moves like he knows the devil's on his tail. My guess is he's CIA, probably whoever was dropped in the desert last night."

"Dropped in the desert?" Jill asked.

Clayborne put a hand on one of her shoulders and led her out of the room. "Best you stay out of there," he said. "Away from windows. In fact, I think it's time you went back to quarters. Go see if you can find some of that strong, brown liquid you were after."

"General..." she started.

He held up a hand again. "Ms. Adams, I've let you have a lot more leeway than I usually give, considering what's happened to your brother. But that isn't him, and that means your presence here isn't required."

She got the message, and as Clayborne and the others herded her down the corridor she didn't resist.

She waited until they'd moved on down the hall before she did any resisting.

Glancing around, making sure none of Calyborne's people were nearby, she made a quick sprint back to the room.

Here we are again, she thought, mentally projecting her annoyance to Mark, wherever he was. *Sneaking into mall security to get you out of another jam.*

It was a tune so familiar she could hum it in her sleep.

Clayborne's binoculars were sitting on the table where he'd left them, and Jill picked them up, took a few quick breaths, and then raised them to her eyes. She tilted, ever-so-slightly and cautiously, around the frame of the window. She held her breath for another second, anticipating a bullet piercing the glass and making a Jackson Pollock out of her brains. When it didn't come, she peered through the binoculars.

There, out in the desert, a man was darting between bombed-out buildings, debris and wreckage. He was pausing at each point of cover, then racing to the next, running in a low crouch and occasionally firing a machine gun or whatever it was, covering himself as he ran for the next safe spot.

Not that there *were* any safe spots out there.

He was close to the enemy, and inching toward the FOB's perimeter. And though a lot of the bad guys had repositioned themselves on the Eastern perimeter, there were still plenty of armed *Kharif* lingering behind, more than willing to take their shots at the obvious infidel racing toward the base they were currently trying to bomb into oblivion.

Jill watched the man move and dart, impressed by his courage as much as his skill. She found herself worrying for him and rooting for him.

But mostly worrying. Because his position looked *impossible*.

And then, when he was stationary for a moment, she got a good look at his face.

Clayborne was right. That wasn't Mark.

It was her boyfriend.

No... her *ex-boyfriend*. But still...

"Jim..." she said softly, the worry rising along with her pulse and blood pressure. "What the hell are you *doing*?"

FIFTEEN

What the hell am I doing? Ryker thought.

He was crouched behind the burned-out husk of a Jeep that had taken a hit from something hot and unfriendly. Something Ryker absolutely did not want coming back this way.

Flames still danced from the wreckage of the vehicle, and Ryker huddled behind it, using the motion of the flames to mask his own movements as he rose to peer out toward the FOB. He was a few hundred feet from the perimeter at this point—close enough that he might be able to make a dash for it—just before dying in a hailstorm of bullets plowing into his back.

He needed a distraction.

And lucky for him, the US military was there to provide one.

As he crouched behind the burned-out Jeep, there suddenly came a storm front of weapons fire off to the East. Ryker flipped down the goggles on his helmet and used the HUD to zoom in as much as possible. The optics were digital-zoom only, and the image started to pixelate. But it was clear enough to give him the gist of what was happening, and that made him smile.

Off in the distance, along the Eastern perimeter, the Marines guarding the line had started an all-out assault on the enemy forces there. Thousands of rounds were fired, mortars were launched, Ryker even thought he saw someone throw a rock. Though it could have been a grenade.

He hoped they weren't down to rocks.

From his vantage point, it looked like the Marines were clearing a path, preparing to evac the whole base in that direction.

It was a strategically dumb, desperate move—they were outgunned on all sides, and any attempt to get vehicles moving through even so much as a pinhole over there would end with everyone dead. The enemy was sure to swarm, pressing this new and obvious advantage, sweeping the place clean before rushing the base to loot it for all it was worth.

It was a desperate move.

It was a *brilliant* move.

Ryker had never met the base commander—General Clayborne. Or "General Claymore," as some called him. But he knew some of the man's reputation.

Ryker had only gotten the quickest of briefings about the guy from Agent Anonymous, but Anonymous had nothing but admiration for the General. He was a tactical genius with a bulldog's aggression and the patience of a tomb. In fact, the man had been on so many tours in Afghanistan it was rumored that the locals had started spreading legends about him.

It was pretty clear that Clayborne and his people had gotten Ryker's signals. Including the request for cover.

This was cover.

Ryker turned, sweeping and scanning the line in front of him. The bad guys were indeed distracted by the cacophony of noise from the East. If he moved now he might just close the gap without opening any new one's in his own chest or back.

He huffed three times, gripped the M16 in both hands, and charged.

He stayed low, and used literally anything in his path as cover, hopping from small rocks to wispy desert shrubs to burned out vehicles and barely standing matchstick structures. He dropped and belly crawled for a time, using the slope of dunes to obscure him.

It was working! He was making it! He was nearly...

Wap-wap-wap!

Plumes of sand rose all around him as multiple rounds struck the desert, just inches from his head.

Ryker cursed and then rolled away from the shots, hoping the move would put him at a lower eye-line. There was nothing for cover here!

More rounds struck near him, driving in a line toward him —*wap-wap-wap*—before ending abruptly.

They were sighting him, getting his range. And soon they'd have it. He was toast, if he stayed here, laying prone on the sand. He might as well be standing.

Ryker rose to his feet. No sense playing for cover. There wasn't any.

As he stood he opened up with the M16, spraying fire in the general direction of the shooter. Or shooters. He wasn't even sure of the enemy's position, much less their number.

His random spray must have been enough to provide some cover, however, because after a hard sprint he made it all the way to the crumbled ruins of a stone wall before the enemy returned fire. Rounds pinged from the stone near Ryker's face, chiseling the remains of the wall and sending chips and shards his way.

The goggles protected his eyes, thank God, and he rounded the edge of the wall to send some bullets back to his new neighbors.

The magazine ran dry, and he rotated back behind the wall, ejecting and reloading. This was his last magazine. He'd spent the others on the run in.

That made this his last stand.

So close to the FOB, but it might as well be a thousand miles away.

The enemy took the opportunity to return fire, and Ryker found himself once again cringing into the tiny wedge of corner that was all that remained of whatever structure had once stood here.

This wasn't going to take long.

He was pinned, and they had more bullets than he did. And more men, he was sure. He hadn't seen any of them, but there could be an entire battalion over there, for all he knew.

This was easy math. He was living on seconds now.

Bullets zipped by all around him, and he started to count down. If he reached zero from fifty, he was going to just go for it—round the corner with the M16 lit up, spend the magazine on whatever target caught his attention, and count on his vest to protect him long enough to give him some scrap of a chance.

Maybe he'd get lucky and take the bad guys out before they got him.

Or he'd go down in an instant, and everyone would be out of their misery in time for breakfast.

He had gotten down to nine and his heart rate was already spiking, his adrenaline already sizzling through his veins... when something odd occurred to him.

He was still hearing gunfire—but there didn't seem to be any *bullets*.

He heard the *rat-tat-tat* of automatic weapons fire, but he was no longer bombarded by shards of stone and raining dust.

Ryker steeled himself and then slowly turned to take a peek around the scrap of wall he was using for cover. He looked out toward where the bad guys must have been hiding, the direction that all the bullets had been coming from.

And he laughed, loud and sharp.

Across the way, a US transport had rushed the men who'd been shooting at him, and now a small contingent of Marines had swarmed out and taken down everyone in a quick burst. They were signaling all-clear to each other, and Ryker shouted for them, trying to get their attention without drawing their fire.

"Sir!" one of the Marines barked. "We're the cover you requested!"

"*You sure as hell are!*" Ryker shouted back and then sprinted for them. He was in the truck and they were rolling back to base just as the enemy realized what had happened. The truck took a few dozen pings of enemy fire before speeding back through the gate, where the rest of the FOB's people took over the fight, giving them cover as the gap closed in the fence behind them.

Ryker patted himself down, checking, making sure everything he'd been born with had come with him, and that he wasn't smuggling any extra lead into the FOB.

By some miracle, he was good. Barely a scratch. Nothing that couldn't be taken care of with a hot shower and a couple of bottles of Tylenol.

He'd made it. He was inside. For what that was worth. The base *was* surrounded by well-armed terrorists, after all.

That's the easy bit done, then, Ryker thought. *Now for the hard part.*

SIXTEEN

Ryker hadn't been given either his hot shower or his Tylenol when Clayborne had him dragged into a small. windowless room and unceremoniously shoved into a chair. There were two very well-armed Marines standing by, and neither gave Ryker the impression that they'd hesitate to shoot the guy they'd just risk four lives to bring in.

He had expected there'd be a debriefing. He'd even anticipated it would be a bit hostile. This place was under a full-on assault, and tensions were high. Ryker was a stranger, coming in from the sand with not much more than some stale codes to identify himself. Suspicion was to be expected.

He calmed himself, caught his breath, willed his body to relax, running through the sequence he'd been trained to do in the Army —top of the head, furrow of the brow, eyes and jaw, neck and shoulders. He kept the exercise going until he reached the tips of his toes, at which point his body was more or less relaxed, if a bit banged up and bruised. As there was nothing else to do, he started the whole process again. And then again.

It was a long wait.

Finally, after at least two hours by Ryker's reckoning, Clayborne entered the room with an aide in tow. "Start talking," he said without pausing. He stood across the table from Ryker, his arms crossed and his expression as firm as granite.

Ryker started talking.

He explained his mission—really two missions, when it came down to it. He was here to retrieve Adams. But he was also here to help get everyone out of the FOB and back to US soil.

"And how do you plan to do that, exactly?" Clayborne growled. "We spent half our munitions just getting you in here."

Ryker nodded. "I know, and I'm grateful for that, General."

"Save the gratitude and tell me the plan," Clayborne ordered.

"When I came in, I had a pack and some gear. There's a sat phone in there. I know your comms are down, so I was sent in to bring that to you."

"So we can call home to say *adios*?" Clayborne asked.

"So you can coordinate with the drone strike that's coming in twenty-four hours," Ryker said. He paused. "Actually, what time is it?"

"Oh-seven-hundred," Clayborne said.

"Ok, in that case, it's more like twenty-*two* hours. It took me longer to get here than I would have liked."

Clayborne was studying him. "You're CIA?"

"Mostly. For the moment," Ryker said. The full truth was too hard to explain, and likely wouldn't do much to assuage Clayborne's suspicions.

"And you're here for Adams?"

Ryker nodded. He couldn't divulge that finding Mark was only part of the mission, and not even the priority. Agent Anonymous had made it clear that no one at the FOB, including Clayborne, was cleared for the full details.

"We don't have the resources to back you up on a suicide mission," Clayborne said sternly. "Especially if we have to get ready for an evac in twenty-two hours."

Ryker shook his head. "That's fine. I don't need much backup. What I need is transport."

Clayborne was studying him. "You barely got across the desert as it was. And you're saying you want to go back? Alone?"

"Not my favorite plan," Ryker admitted. "But it's the mission. Actually, if it wasn't for the fact that I had to bring you folks a phone, I would have gone straight for where our intel says they're holding Adams."

"Well," Clayborne said, "Wasn't that *magnanimous* of you. We sure appreciate the thought, uh...?"

"Jim," a female voice said from the door. "Jim Ryker."

All eyes turned to see who had spoken. Ryker's eyes widened when he saw her.

Jill.

It had been over a year. And he'd thought, for all of that time, he'd never see her again. Even knowing she was here—the leverage that Agent Anonymous had used to lure Ryker back to this God-forsaken place—Ryker hadn't truly believed he'd see her. She seemed like a mirage. A fantasy.

"Ms. Adams," Clayborne said sternly, "I told you to get back to your quarters."

"Yes, General," she nodded. "But I thought I might be more useful here. Jim and I have a... history."

Clayborne looked from Jill to Ryker and back again. "I see," he said. "In that case, join us."

Jill entered the room and stood beside Clayborne.

"Hi Jim," she said.

"Hi Jill," Ryker replied. "Looks like Mark's at it again."

Jill nodded. "Yeah," she said. "Looks like it."

SEVENTEEN

They had a lot of catching up to do, but this was definitely not the time. Ryker had only just finished explaining the details of the rescue operation when a series of thuds shook the room they were in.

"Mortars," Clayborne said. He turned and gave orders to his people, then leveled Ryker in his gaze. "We have the *Kharif* held back far enough that most of those shots are near-hits, instead of direct. But that's enough to shake the hell out of us." He shook his head, paused, then said, "I can get you a Jeep and some provisions. That's it."

"I appreciate it, General, thank you."

Clayborne then nodded to Jill. "I suggest the two of you talk while taking cover. Ryker, I assume you'll be using the drone strike for cover, rolling out in the next twenty four hours?"

"Yes sir, General, that's the plan," Ryker replied.

Clayborne nodded, and he and the Marines left the room, leaving Ryker and Jill to face each other in awkward silence.

They stared at each other over a soundtrack of explosions and gunfire coming from somewhere that sounded distant, but was still far too close for comfort.

"So, you're not in prison," Jill said, finally.

Ryker shook his head. "Not yet. But I think it's only a matter of time."

"They let you go, though," she said.

"A long time ago. I've been bouncing around the US, doing odd jobs, keeping my head low."

"Not so low they didn't find you, I guess," Jill replied.

Ryker inhaled and let the breath out slowly. "They told me you were here. I think they figured that would get me here, just in case I had no loyalty to Mark."

"Do you?" Jill asked. "Have loyalty?"

Ryker shook his head. "I've never been disloyal to anyone in my life, Jill. Not Mark. Not the CIA. Not you."

Jill scoffed, and then an explosion shook the room and dust rained down from the suspended ceiling. She let out a yelp, stumbled, and leaned against the conference table.

Ryker was up and around the table in an instant, and had his arms around her, covering her.

"We should... get under the table," she said, blinking at him.

Ryker laughed. "You're as safe out here as under there. That whole duck and cover thing is just something to make people feel like they're doing *something*."

"It was at least a little *comforting*," Jill said, her tone hard.

Ryker was still holding her, and they faced each other, looking into each other's eyes. It had been well over a year since they'd last seen each other. It hadn't been the most amicable parting.

There was a beat, and they both looked down to Ryker's hands on Jill's shoulders. Another beat, and then a muffled explosion broke the trance. Ryker let his hands drop and Jill stepped back and away, looking off to one corner of the room.

"You know I was innocent," Ryker said, quietly.

"How would I know?" Jill said, looking back at him again. "You disappeared without a word."

"I left a note," he said quietly.

Jill scowled, her eyes set hard. Then, as automatic weapons fire rattled off from outside the building, her expression softened. She laughed, shaking her head. "A note," she said. "Thanks."

"It was for the best," Ryker said. "After everything that happened with Mark..."

"Oh, I know. It was the only way. I get it," she said. "And I knew there was more to it all than what I was being told. Mark wasn't saying a word. And none of my contacts were, either. For all I knew the note was a fake, and they'd shot you and dumped you in the desert or something."

Ryker sighed, then turned to lean back against the table.

Jill did the same.

"I'm sorry," he said.

She shook her head.

"When they told me you were here..."

"Don't," Jill said.

Ryker nodded, keeping his mouth shut.

He glanced over to see Jill staring vacantly at the floor, near the doorway. After a moment she said, "Are you going to bring my brother home?"

Ryker was watching her, and nodded. "I'm going to try."

She looked at him then, her eyes full of fury. "Don't *try*, Jim. *Do it*. You owe him that. You owe *me* that."

Ryker watched her for an instant, then nodded once again. "You're right. I owe you that." He wouldn't comment on what he owed Mark. "I'll bring him back."

She nodded. She was breathing heavy. Ryker was about to stand and leave when suddenly she turned, wrapped her hands around the back of his head and neck, and pulled him down sharply. She kissed him, and the kiss lingered.

And then she stood and left the room without a word.

Another mortar shook the building again, and Ryker thought about the promise he'd just made in the light of his mission.

His job was to bring Mark home, that was true.

Unless he'd given the enemy the weapon. Then, Ryker had other orders

Don't make me break my promise, Mark, Ryker thought.

EIGHTEEN

Kharif Stronghold, Somewhere in Katakstan

Faraz ran through the reports again. His people had been pecking away at the base for days, and were barely closer to breaking the perimeter than they had been when they started. And now, according to the intelligence coming to him, someone had gotten to the base from the *outside*.

Someone had entered the base from the territory that was supposedly in the hands of the *Kharif*. They had simply *walked* through *Kharif* controlled territory, straight to the base, as if none of Faraz's men were even there.

Though, that wasn't entirely accurate.

Reports had been coming to Faraz all night—an enemy aircraft had flown over, out of range of their anti-aircraft weaponry. At least one man had been spotted, parachuting to the desert. His chute and pack had been recovered—the chute shredded by weapons fire. How the man had survived to the ground was something no one could explain. But even more baffling was how he had managed to make his way from that landing zone to the forward operation base, alive and seemingly *uninjured.*

This man had crossed *kilometers* of desert, all of which was controlled and occupied by Faraz's own people, and had not only evaded capture but had managed to leave a trail of bodies in his wake.

Several men had been found killed, and it was clear it was the work of the stranger. They knew next to nothing about him, but Faraz had an instinct.

He was American. That much seemed certain. And well-trained. CIA, perhaps. But more likely Special Forces. Or perhaps both, just as their current American guest had been.

The deaths of Faraz's men had been quick, efficient. The man had used their own weapons, which meant he'd disarmed them, not just surviving but *dominating.*

He had stolen one of the *Kharif's* own vehicles, using it to get to the burnt-out guard shack near the base perimeter, killing the men inside. From there, he had proceeded *on foot,* through territory that was not only *controlled* by the *Kharif,* but was currently a hot zone. This man had marched through a literal *battlefield* to cover the ground between the guard shack and the FOB, somehow dodging fire the whole way.

He was clearly dangerous. And possibly insane. Which, Faraz knew, would simply make him *more* dangerous. The *Kharif* employed many men who might be considered insane—they made for powerful and efficient warriors. Insanity overpowered fear, and men without fear can do incredible things.

Though, as Faraz considered it, he would never entrust any of those men with something so strategic as what this American had accomplished.

The *Kharif* had managed to isolate and surround the American base. This man had completed a drop into enemy-controlled territory, and had managed to traverse the desert and not only reach the base but somehow *communicate* with them, to gain both their trust and their assistance. He would have had to convince the Americans, somehow, that he was not a Trojan horse—that he was an ally, not an enemy.

How had he done it?

Again, Faraz didn't have men of that calibre. Those who were insane enough to attempt it were too insane to be trusted to do it. It was such a delicate task, it could only be entrusted to someone who was bright, perhaps even brilliant, who was also astoundingly capable and resourceful. Someone who was completely lucid.

So, no, this American was not insane after all. He was... something else.

"Why would the Americans send only one man?" Ghazal asked.

Ghazal, Faraz's trusted man. His friend. His brother. His second in command. They had been friends most of their lives. Ghazal had been one of the boys who had played ball with Faraz, to help him spy on the Americans.

Faraz shook his head. He wasn't prepared to share his thoughts on this intruder—his speculation on what the man's presence might mean. "I can only imagine he was sent because his training gave him the best chance of breaking through our lines. He's..." Faraz thought about it, and the answer suddenly seemed obvious. "He's a *messenger*."

"Messenger?" Ghazal said. "What good is news to these Americans? We have them surrounded, and their communications have been severed. We will take their base in a matter of days."

"That may no longer be the case," Faraz said, thinking. Ghazal's words, *Their communication have been severed.* That had to be it. "Have the men use the EM pulse again."

Ghazal suddenly looked reluctant, even ashamed. "The device..." he started. He shook his head. "It was damaged, after we used it. Our people believe that some of its components may have been intended for single use. They would need to be replaced, each time. But since the device worked, and the Americans no longer have their technological advantage, we... did not bother repairing it."

Faraz scowled at his friend, and Ghazal hung his head in shame.

"Get it fixed, and use it again," Faraz said quietly. "Quickly, before this foolishness costs us dearly."

Ghazal nodded and hurried away.

Faraz—bitterly disappointed in his second, but keeping it hidden for now—turned back to the table where there were photos of bodies, recovered from the desert. The *Kharif* men this American stranger had killed.

Faraz studied them closely, poring over every detail, applying all he knew, trying to glean as much as he could about this man and his methods, from the wake of death he left behind. It was all he knew of his enemy—that a single man had killed so many *Kharif,* with their own weapons. That despite being alone, moving through a war torn landscape under the control of Faraz and his people, this man had not only survived, he had succeeded at his mission.

It wasn't much intelligence to work with, but it was enough, for now. It told Faraz the story he needed, anyway.

This man was dangerous. And they needed to be on their guard. Because it was almost certain that they had not seen the last of him.

Faraz left the strategy room and went down to the deeper levels, to the cells, the vacant and dark rooms where the prisoners were held and tortured for everything the *Kharif* could get out of them.

He stepped into one of the cells, and inspected the American hanging by his hands, his toes just making contact with the floor. The lights were on full, and music blared from four sets of speakers, keeping the man blinded and alienated. Faraz signaled, and the music stopped. The sudden silence rang like a bell, and the echo of the cacophony that had so suddenly ended was still very much a psychic presence in the room. Faraz had experienced it for mere seconds. This man had endured it for days.

"Are you prepared to share a bit more with me, my friend?" Faraz asked. His voice was honey and poison. The offer was there. *Cooperate, and you will be rewarded.* But so was the threat. *That reward may be a swift death.*

The American groaned, fully aware of what would follow.

Faraz did not disappoint him. He nodded to his men. And soon the raucous noise of the music was replaced by the screams of the American.

NINETEEN

They were just six hours out from the airstrike, roughly fifteen hours from when Ryker had managed to get into the relative safety of the base, and it had been one of the longest days of Ryker's life.

The constant barrage of mortar and gunfire didn't bother him all that much. While it was true they were all on the edge of being overtaken—any luck for the enemy could tip the balance in their favor, at any second—those were the conditions Ryker had lived under most of his adult life. The enemy was *always* one lucky break away from overtaking him, or his men, or whatever it was they were assigned to protect.

And that was the thing that was nagging at him most, the entire time he was hunkered down in the FOB. Memories. Regrets. Echoes of bad decisions and rotten luck from his past—some of which were scarcely a year old.

This was all too close to his last run through Katakstan—the events that had led to him being accused, drummed out of the company, barely avoiding being locked away, and set on a path of... whatever the path was. Redemption? Hardly.

Penance and punishment. Those old, rotten friends of his.

Being here, in Katakstan, in this base, with Jill so close she couldn't be avoided, much less forgotten—that was a sign to Ryker. It was a truth, about his reality. He hadn't survived that run across the desert after all. He'd died out there, with some *Kharif's* bullet in his head. Or maybe he'd died the second he'd jumped out of that plane, flung to the Earth like a wad of litter tossed out of a car window. Or, maybe more likely, he'd died out there on Avery's ranch, the sun baking his brains until they couldn't function any longer, delivering him to this after life that echoed with too many memories of the past.

This was hell.

Or at least purgatory.

Hell was coming up, he suspected.

He tried to stay out of everyone's way, particularly General Clayborne and Jill Adams. *Especially* Jill Adams. But though the base was large by most standards, there was really nowhere to go to just completely avoid everyone. Bumps were inevitable.

It had been easier at first. He'd spent the first few hours unconscious, in a borrowed bed. He'd finally been given his shower, and his Tylenol, as well as a bologna sandwich and a dark room. The noise and violence of the attacks might have kept him awake if not for the fact that he'd been running on pure adrenaline for most of the past 48 hours. Rebounding from that left him spent and exhausted. His body's need for sleep outweighed any fear of the roof coming down on him.

But even as exhausted as he was, he was wide awake after only around three hours of sleep. Circadian rhythms can be a bitch, and his were out of wack thanks to the rush of international travel and doing a death march across the desert. He awoke in darkness, and the noise of combat wouldn't let him go back to sleep. And so he found himself up and about, helping with whatever he could—or whatever he was *allowed* to help with—and wondering if there was any more of that bologna.

And, of course, he had to tiptoe to avoid Jill.

They'd bumped into each other several times, and each time was awkward. The kiss still lingered in Ryker's brain, along with a cacophony of confused thoughts about what it meant. He and Jill had spilt up more than a year earlier, and under some very rough circumstances involving her brother, and Ryker's potential fate. He'd made his choices, at the time. He hadn't been sure what outcome to expect, as he'd spent punishing hours in the chair, facing hard questions he didn't have answers to. He had taken full responsibility for everything, because that was his way. That was what good men did, he'd been taught. Even when he knew, with no doubts, that Mark Adams had more than his fair share of responsibility for it all. Ryker had been the one in charge, and so all of Mark's mistakes were Ryker's mistakes. That was just how it was going to be.

Severing ties with Jill seemed like the right thing to do, back then. It removed the conflict of interest Jill would have, for a start. And keeping his mouth shut about Mark's part in things also protected Jill. Her career, her trajectory toward the Senate, might have been derailed, if the truth came out. And to protect her, Ryker would take every bullet, sit in every cell. Whatever it took.

All of the bumping into each other and being unable to avoid each other, of course, only served to exacerbate the awkwardness, as well as the way Ryker felt, after that kiss.

And then there was the truth that Ryker had to admit to himself.

Forget rescuing Mark Adams. Forget keeping a weapon of mass destruction out of the hands of the *Kharif*. Forget whatever fate Agent Anonymous had in mind for Ryker, if he somehow managed to survive all of this. There was really only one reason Ryker was here.

Jill was the mission. Her survival was the only objective he actually cared about.

Which was why it was so torturous and confusing that he was forced to avoid her, to pretend that the kiss hadn't happened, to pretend that he didn't have an absolute compulsion to sweep her up and drive them both out of here, enemy or no enemy. They'd both die under fire, of course. Heroic fantasies were stupid. So, the only real way to keep her safe was to play the game just the way he was playing it, to complete the objectives he'd been given, and see it all through to the end.

The airstrike and evac were the only chance Ryker had of getting Jill to safety. Until then, he'd let life torture him however it wanted.

"Jim Ryker."

Ryker turned to see Clayborne, flanked by two Marines, standing in the doorway of the hangar where Ryker was helping prep vehicles for the evacuation. He left his tools and walked to Clayborne, and then allowed himself to be guided out of the hangar and into a small office.

The Marines left Ryker and Clayborne alone, the door closed.

"I was able to get in touch with Command, back home," Clayborne said. "Long enough to get details sorted. I... want to thank you for bringing the sat phone. And bringing some hope here."

Ryker nodded. "Yes, sir. That's my mission."

"Part of it, anyway," Clayborne said, eyeing him.

Ryker again nodded.

"I got a debrief on the situation," Clayborne said. "As much as they're willing to give me, anyway. I know about the designs, for the weapon. I had some idea of that before, but they've brought me into the fold. Mostly by way of telling me to give you any support you need."

"Thank you, sir," Ryker said.

"The trouble is, son, I don't *have* any support for you. I can't spare a soul to go with you. Munitions are running low enough that I'm considering throwing rocks at these people. That Jeep I offered you... the best I can do is one that's taken a lot of heat, patched up with duct tape and God's grace, and not much more. I don't know how long it will last you."

Ryker considered this. "I knew things were dire."

Clayborne laughed. "Dire," he said. "Yeah, I'd say so. This airstrike can't come soon enough. The folks back home have been in contact with allies in the region. We're getting air support, and there will be ground movement as well. Some helicopters are enroute to help with some of the evac, but it's mostly going to be trucks and Jeeps. There's no real plan to actually *beat* the enemy here, it's mostly about getting us out of here. They're planning to sweep the enemy in a big circle, all around the FOB. Then they'll concentrate fire on the Eastern and Southern lines. Same way you came in. We're supposed to go out the back and meet with US and Katakstan ground forces and choppers to the North. It's a solid plan—the *Kharif* aren't as thick on that side, and some well-placed ordnance should loosen their bowels a little. I also have orders to take out this base from the inside, and that's going to be a big enough bang to give us some breathing room. But it isn't exactly going to be a Sunday stroll, getting out of here."

Ryker considered this. "What can I do to help?" he asked.

Clayborne shook his head. "I was going to ask you the same thing," he said.

Ryker thought for a moment. And what he came up with didn't

exactly fill him with excitement. But then the memory of that kiss came back—the thought of Jill dying here was too much. He needed her out. He needed her safe. And he'd do whatever it took.

"I think I have an idea," Ryker said.

Clayborne peered at him.

"What if I leave a little early?" Ryker asked. "I'll take that Jeep. And if you can spare at least something that can make a big enough bang, I can get the bad guys shooting at me for a bit. Get them distracted, and maybe even clumped together so the airstrike is more effective."

Clayborne regarded him. "That's a suicide run, son."

Ryker nodded. "I'll do my best to prove you wrong, but I can't deny the risk. If it gives you all a shot of getting the hell out of here, it's worth it. But I have a request... I want Jill Adams on the first chopper out of here."

"Already done," Clayborne said. "I have a list of priority evacuees, and she's right at the top."

Ryker shook his head. "The problem is, she won't go willingly. She'll want to stay on the ground, and here in Katakstan, until Mark is safe. And that's kind of an issue..." he hesitated.

"Keeping Mark Adams safe may not be the mission," Clayborne replied.

Ryker was silent for a moment, then said, "I promised her I'd bring him back alive."

Clayborne grunted. "Foolish promise, son. Especially given what I now know."

"We don't really know *anything* for certain," Ryker said. "It's pretty likely they tortured him, and got everything they needed from him."

"Do you believe that?" Clayborne asked.

"I do until I know otherwise," Ryker said. "He might even be dead. But my mission isn't really about bringing him home. That's just secondary. It's about getting the plans, and making sure the *Kharif* don't have them. And I'm going to succeed in that mission."

"One man," Clayborne said. "And not even John Wayne or Chuck Norris."

"I've done this before," Ryker said.

"No doubt about that," Clayborne replied. "But now you're volunteering to be a diversion. Putting a target on your back isn't exactly the best way to sneak past the enemy. I'm pretty sure that wasn't part of the plan."

"All plans spin apart," Ryker shrugged. "My training is to *be* the plan. And don't worry—I'm not the only diversion happening. When this starts to go down, we'll time it so that I'm out there just before the airstrike. I'll go out of the North gate, and start drawing fire, herding the enemy. Clump them up so that when the strike comes I can make a run for it, just like all of you."

"Suicide," Claiborne said.

"Maybe," Ryker said. "Just make sure Jill Adams is on that chopper and out of Katakstan by morning. Even if you have to knock her unconscious."

TWENTY

Suicide.

The word just kept coming back, and Ryker couldn't think of any good reason why it shouldn't. Because this *was* suicide.

Clayborne hadn't been kidding about the condition of the Jeep. It was pockmarked with bullet holes, had no windshield, and the hood had been removed or maybe torn off, revealing the patched and jury-rigged engine. That was a problem—there'd be nothing to keep it from taking a hit that could disable it right out of the gate. But there might be a way to fix that.

Ryker had scrounged and scavenged to find any parts he could use to maybe sweeten his odds. There were no spare Jeep hoods or windshields laying about, but there were armored doors from some of the trucks and Jeeps that had been too damaged to revive and put back into service. Ryker and some of the mechanics seized these and welded them into place over the engine and the gap where the windshield would be, as well as over the door openings. Essentially, they shrouded the Jeep in steel, making a Frankenstein version of an armored vehicle.

It would be heavy, and there was no way to know how well the engine would handle the strain. It should be fast enough for what he was needing, but that was only if it survived long enough to ramp up to speed. Acceleration was going to be at a glacier's pace.

There were other modifications as well. Ryker and the mechanics cut a trap door into the roof of the Jeep, right above the spot where the passenger seat would go. They yanked the seats, mounting rails and supports to the bare metal floor. This would be a mobile launch pad.

It was ugly, but it was going to work. It *had* to work.

Time was up.

They'd lost sat phone communication about an hour ago. Ryker suspected that the *Kharif* had used whatever tech they'd gotten their hands on to brick the phone, just as they had everything else on the base. Including his fancy HUD night vision goggles. That was a crying shame, for sure.

He had no idea why it had taken them so long to use the EM weapon again. It had given the *Kharif* a huge advantage, and surely whoever was in charge would know that Ryker was bringing some form of communication in with him. So it made no sense that they delayed.

Maybe he'd ask them about it. He was going to be face to face with them pretty soon. If he survived anyway.

Thankfully, comms had lasted long enough for the plan to be cemented. The drone strike was coming, on schedule, and everyone still in the FOB would evacuate on cue. They knew the hour, and they knew what to do.

And Ryker knew what *he* had to do, and when.

Right now, he thought. It was time.

The Jeep revved and vibrated under him, and Ryker checked the clock. He nodded to the Marines manning the doors leading out of the garage, and when they slid open he gunned it, racing toward the North gate, which another team quickly cleared for him.

The enemy had been engaged in another round of fire on the base, and so it wasn't much of a shift for them to suddenly focus their attention and their fire on the lone American hauling ass across the desert in a Jeep that looked like it was built from LEGO scraps. As rounds ricocheted from the makeshift armor surrounding him, it sounded like he was driving through a lead hailstorm. Pings against the metal came in clips so rapid, the sound morphed into white noise.

Ryker downshifted, spun the Jeep's nose toward the East, and started what he hoped would be a Pied Piper march, leading the enemy straight for the primary strike zone, keeping them concentrated in one spot.

He had no idea if this plan was working, beyond the fact that the pings of bullets on metal didn't let up. He shifted again, racing through the maelstrom, speeding head-on into enemy fire, as insane as that was, hoping and praying his boldness kept them off balance, and that his makeshift armor kept their bullets on the outside.

He had a vague plan for when he reached the Eastern front. Vague plans were kind of all he had bandwidth for, at the moment. Most of his mental energy was being spent on praying that the drone strike came at the precise moment it was scheduled, and that he survived long enough to benefit from it. He needed that famous military precision right now, if this had any chance of working.

Ryker gunned the engine, raced along the wall of the FOB, took some hits but somehow was neither disabled nor killed.

He reached over to the floorboard beside him, to his right, where the biggest upgrade to the Jeep had been installed. It was janky, but it should work.

The passenger seat had been ripped out of the Jeep, first thing. In its place was an 120mm mortar launcher on its base plate, the bipod affixed to the firewall of the Jeep. It was loaded with a single mortar—a precious bit of ordnance that Clayborne had been reluctant to part with. It was called THOR, and like the Norse god for whom it was named, it brought the thunder, hitting like a 120mm mystical hammer, with a shockwave of flack and debris and concussive force that should give the enemy a face-full. But only if he could persuade them to gather round.

Ryker and the mechanics had rigged the launcher so that Ryker could engage it with the pull of a lever, from 'safely' next to the device. Hopefully it wouldn't blast his eardrums out of his head, but no one had the time for R&D. It was a purely mechanical setup, and it was going to take a hell of a yank to get the thing going, but it would work. It would also make him vulnerable to all of those bullets that were flying around.

A risk. But no more so than this entire, insane, unlikely plan had been from the start. And if it gave the evacuees even just a few seconds more time, it was worth Ryker's life in payment.

He huffed a few times, counted to five, and yanked the lever like he was pulling the emergency brake.

A piece of the roof of the Jeep flew away like an ejected canopy, and the barrel of the launcher sprang upward, aiming out of the new hole in the roof. Riker again huffed, counted, and then slapped the firing mechanism—a mechanical plunger wired and mounted to the dash.

The noise was positively *deafening,* and the Jeep was filled with acrid smoke that burned Ryker's eyes and lungs as the mortar was propelled upward.

Ryker gunned it blindly, coughing and wiping at his eyes with his sleeve. He had no idea what was in front of him, but he needed to be out of here as fast as possible before that thing finished its arc and came back to Earth to play.

He heard the explosion—*felt* it—moments later, and there was the sound of metal pinging on the Jeep's makeshift armored hull. Even this far away, fragments had been propelled with deadly force. If he'd been outside, he'd have been shredded like cabbage. Ryker coleslaw. Which meant that hopefully the enemy would be, too.

He kept moving, full speed, the smoke clearing as wind whipped in through the new hole in the roof and the top-most portion of the passenger door. He was vulnerable now, and he would need to stay aware of that. Though what caution he could possibly take, he had no clue. For now, he just had to drive.

That was it. That was the big move. Launching the THOR was meant to be the first hit, to not only cluster the enemy in the strike zone, but to disrupt them, disorient them, and keep their attention right where Ryker wanted it. And if his timing was right...

Another set of explosions shook the Jeep, threatening to knock it over sideways. Ryker cursed, gripped the steering wheel, shifted, and kept going.

The strike was in progress, and he was currently at ground zero.

But not for long. He hoped.

More explosions, more shaking, and suddenly, without warning, the Jeep was hit by a shockwave powerful enough that Ryker couldn't correct. The wheel spun in his hand, and some combination of gravity and inertia took over Ryker's life.

The Jeep rolled, toppling like a leaf in a strong wind, and Ryker's head slammed against the jutting metal of the makeshift armor surrounding him. As the vehicle went into an uncontrolled barrel roll across the desert floor, Ryker was tossed and scrambled inside. Another smack of his head against metal, and everything went black, save for the waves of pulsing light in his peripheral vision.

Ryker felt his consciousness slipping, felt himself sinking.

And the last thought he had was of Jill—beautiful, capable, but stubborn as hell—and as his awareness slipped his last thoughts were focused on hoping, *praying* that she got on that damned helicopter.

Then Ryker's life went blank, and blackness overtook him.

TWENTY-ONE

Jill was *not* going to get on the damned helicopter.

"Ma'am…" the Marine escort started, again. He'd been insisting, ever since then ground transport slammed to a halt and she was ordered out. This was the last of the helicopters to leave—the others had filled and lifted off immediately, and she was told numerous times that she'd been meant to be on the very first. Now, here she was, the last holdout. She looked at the rest of the evacuees, who were mostly military by this point, all hunkered, armed, ready to defend against the enemy if another wave of attack started. They weren't exactly safe here.

Jill refused to budge, and she knew that the Marine was getting ready to manhandle her into the craft, if he had to.

"Ms. Adams."

She turned to see Clayborne, looking remarkably calm considering he'd just led his people through hell, evacuating the

FOB. "Every minute that bird is on the ground instead of in the air, it's at risk of taking a hit. I need you on it. Now."

"General, my brother is still…"

He turned to the Marine. "Tie her to the seat, if you have to," he said.

"General Clayborne!" Jill shouted, but the general was already turning, leaving.

"Ma'am," the Marine said again, offering her one more chance to cooperate, touching her elbow.

She shook her head, but let herself be guided into the helicopter, feeling her choices had just been narrowed to nothing

The Marine guided her up and then buckled her in, cinched the belt tight, and gave her a smile and nod before smacking the side of the chopper, signaling the pilot to lift off.

Jill scowled at the man, but it was no use. He had already turned and jogged back to the line of trucks, where Clayborne was issuing orders to his men and to the reinforcement troops alike. She'd gotten only scant information about the plan from here, but it seemed as if the extraction was successful. All of the civilians who had been trapped in the FOB were now on their way to safety. She was the last holdout. The rest were military or specialists who would stay on the front to fight, slowly backing their way to more fortified lines, giving the civilians the gap they needed to get the hell out of there.

The *Kharif* had won this fight. She saw in Clayborne's eyes just how much that stung the man. But they had used the past 24 hours wisely, destroying anything that might give their enemy some advantage. All intel was burned or scrambled. Any weapons or ammunition they had would go with them. The only vehicles left were hunks of scrap, not even useful for parts.

And for good measure, Clayborne had charges set on every load-bearing wall of every structure still standing at the FOB. The whole place had been blown once the last soul was clear, dropping the base into a pile of rubble. If there was anything still of use to the enemy in there, they'd have to spend a month digging it out, at least.

Everyone was out. Everyone was on their way to safety.

Everyone but Jim Ryker.

She felt a stab of something hot and painful when she thought about Jim, and about how she'd treated him. That kiss had been...

Well, mostly *goodbye*, right? Or was it something else?

She hadn't even known she was going to do it, much less *why* she did it. But it made the rest of their time together awkward, she felt. She spent the next 24 hours wondering how big of a mistake it had been, but also avoiding Jim as much as possible.

Now she wondered if *that* had been the mistake. She knew the odds of either of them getting out of here alive were slim. One or the other, but more likely both of them, was bound to die here, if this evacuation hadn't gone well. There'd been that risk hanging over them from the start.

So why had she been so set on avoiding him, in what was probably their last moments together?

Because of Mark, she thought. Mark, who was chronically in trouble. Mark, who was the whole reason Jill found herself here, in this hellscape, in the first place. Mark, who she had slowly, inevitably come to realize was the real reason Jim Ryker had been drummed out of the CIA, cast as the villain, punished.

It was the toughest thing she'd ever had to admit to herself, in all of her life—the thing that probably should have been obvious from the start. Mark was basically a bad guy.

She was avoiding Jim because she was ashamed of the role her brother had played in Jim's downfall.

She was ashamed of her own role in it. She was the one, after all, who had pulled strings from all across the beltway, doing anything and everything she could to clear Mark of charges she wasn't even allowed to read.

The helicopter shuddered as it rose, angling away from the lines being held by Clayborne and his people. Jill felt her stomach flip as the chopper moved up and over the desert landscape at a an acrobatic turn and gut-dropping speed, banking as it rose away from the Katakstan sands.

When it finally leveled out, she heard sounds—like gravel hitting the bottom of a vehicle on a freshly paved road. She looked around, and the helicopter's only other occupant—a Middle-Eastern woman who had worked as a translation specialist at the FOB—handed her a set of headphones. Jill pulled them on, adjusting the microphone.

"They are firing on us," the woman said, a worried look on her face.

Jill nodded, sparing a quick glance out of the side of the helicopter. There was no door—she had a wide open view that was at first all blue sky. But as the helicopter leveled off she could see the first glimpse of the horizon, a line of hay-colored sand that stretched and rippled in all directions. It was like looking down on an immense scoop of vanilla ice cream, she thought. The gentle ridges and swoops of dimpled sand looked peaceful, rather than hostile. Like gliding over a sepia-toned cloud. It looked like a fantasy world. And yet it was the deadliest place on Earth, at the moment.

"Do we know what happened to Jim Ryker?" Jill asked.

A male voice came to her, presumably either the pilot or co-pilot. "Reports say his Jeep took a hit. We don't have eyes on him now. He's presumed KIA."

KIA. Killed in action.

Jill felt her guts clench at this news, and that feeling rose until it welled from her eyes, stinging her in streams that drifted over her cheeks.

Why had she stayed away from him, in these last hours? Why had she avoided him? Why had she allowed that last kiss to be... well, to be the *last kiss?*

She shook her head, and wiped at her eyes with her sleeve.

Not Jim Ryker, she decided. *That's not how his story ends. He's too... he's too* big *for that kind of ending.*

She couldn't say for sure why she thought this. She simply *knew* Jim. She knew how capable he was. She knew that no matter what the odds were, he always found some way to beat them. It was just who Jim Ryker was.

He'd been a guardian angel for Mark, when the two of them served together. When she'd met him, for the first time, Ryker had more or less become a surrogate big brother to Mark. And, though Mark would deny it if anyone asked, she knew that Ryker had been Mark's hero. Not just for the rescues, for getting Mark out of the trouble he always managed to get into. Mark seemed to have no ability to even *notice* that sort of thing. He'd been ignoring that trait from Jill, all their lives.

Mark had looked up to Ryker because Ryker was something Mark *wanted* to be—noble, honest, capable. Self-sufficient, but not self-serving.

Jill had seen all of that in Ryker, too. And more. He was a good man. Maybe a little too good.

When things had gone bad, right here in Katakstan, Jill knew that whatever it was had involved Mark. She knew only sketchy details, but having known Mark all his life, she could imagine the rest. And just as she always had, Jill had pulled whatever strings she could to keep Mark from facing the consequences of the trouble he'd found. But she'd never intended for Jim to take the blame.

Although she'd only known Jim for a couple of years—though they had dated and slept together, spent every moment they could together whenever he was in the States—she felt she knew him well enough to understand that he was taking the hit for something he probably had little to nothing to do with.

She had tried to use whatever political influence and pull she had to find out more, and ultimately to try to advocate for Jim, just as she always had for Mark. But it wasn't enough. Whatever had gone down here, on these sands, Ryker was being pinned for it. Someone had to be, it seemed. And Jill thought Ryker might have taken it on himself, rather than let Mark or anyone else under Jim's command become the scapegoat.

But she couldn't help wondering—*was* Mark responsible?

If she ever saw him again, she was going to make him tell her everything. Classified or not, he owed it to her. For this. For coming here, to this hell. For weeks of hunkering under a conference table, fearing the roof would come down any moment. For nearly getting killed.

For losing Jim Ryker.

There was a jolt, and then another. Suddenly the roaring white noise of the chopper's engines sounded different, strained, arhythmic. A screeching noise started, rising in pitch as the chopper jolted from side to side. A vibration had started, small at first but rapidly growing to a seismic tremble.

"Brace yourselves!" the pilot shouted over the din. Even with the headphones, Jill found it was hard to hear him.

The woman, the translator, screamed, and Jill looked to see she was holding her side, blood pouring through her fingers.

Jill tried to reach for her, to help, but the seatbelt yanked her and soon after a sudden jarring of the chopper threw her against the seat.

Her first impulse was to unbuckle, to rush to help the woman— why couldn't she remember her name? Why had she been so absorbed in Mark's drama that she hadn't bothered learning this woman's name?

Another jolt from the helicopter, and now Jill felt her guts reverse course, tumbling within her. She felt the vomit rise before she could do anything about it.

And then, suddenly, the blood and the vomit and the noise no longer mattered. They were hit so hard that the world became a torrent of uninterpretable chaos.

The chopper went down hard and fast, slamming into the sands of the desert before rolling across the dunes like an errant football. Jill found herself scrambled inside of it, slammed left and right, up and down, forward and back, until direction lost all meaning. Only the seat harness kept her from being hashed to bits in the helicopter's interior.

All of this happened in a sort of chaotic, cacophonic jumble of slow motion, then fast motion. Jill's awareness was keen throughout, noting with some detachment that she was being slammed in all directions, but somehow outside of it all—a third-person view of the violence happening to her.

And then, suddenly, everything stopped. Everything crystallized into a brittle stillness.

There was no more engine noise—just a faint clicking and tinking of hot metal. There was no sound of screaming or cursing. The headphones relayed nothing but a faint ocean of static.

Jill yanked off the headphones and worked at the seatbelt and harness. She managed to pry the buckles open, and fell slightly. The chopper was resting at an angle, but it wasn't severe. They were nearly upright.

The seatbelt finally snapped free, and Jill lurched forward. She used the seat to steady herself, and took deep, heaving breaths, as if she had just emerged from a tsunami and needed all the oxygen her lungs could hold. She felt a strange sort of lightheadedness creeping over her, and blinked away darkness from the edges of her vision.

Check on her, Jill's mind prompted. *See if she's ok.*

She crawled to the woman, and saw that there was a large, jagged hole in the metal wall beside her seat. Dust whirled in a beam of sunlight, penetrating through that hole. And following it, in a line, she could see that it was angled directly toward the woman, toward her side. A red, gory gash, where the miracles ended.

The woman was completely drenched in blood, soaked through her clothing, dripping down from her seat and into a sliding river on the floor of the helicopter.

She was dead.

Jill, who had only seen death a few clinical and sterile times in her life, could easily see it now. The woman's eyes were open, her jaw hung slack, her arms and legs were splayed at obscene angles, after the chaos of the crash. There was nothing to move them now, no motive force within the woman, nothing to use those arms and legs and hands for sensation or for interaction or for existing at all. Everything that was this woman was no longer within her, and what remained seemed *obscene*.

It was a shock, to see this woman dead. It was offensive, somehow. Jill had just—*just*—spoken with her. She had cringed under a conference table with her. She had said polite things in passing, as they encountered each other in the hallways of the FOB. And she *could not remember the woman's damned name, and now she was dead!*

Jill felt the vomit rising again, but her empty stomach had nothing to offer. She retched, gagged, and leaned away from the woman, to avoid whatever disrespectful thing she might add to this scene. She pushed away, and felt her legs going weak, felt herself wanting to collapse into a heap on the floor of the helicopter.

Jill shook herself. That was panic. That was shock. She had to get past that. She needed to get her shit together and *act*, not fall apart here. She needed to inform the pilot and co-pilot, needed to get out of this helicopter, needed to prepare for whatever came next.

Jill turned her attention to the cockpit... and froze.

The cockpit wasn't there.

Where there had only moments ago been a space beyond the steel wall of the area where Jill and the woman had been strapped in, where a glass canopy had domed over the two men who were piloting all of them to safety, now there was nothing but open air, framed by twisted metal.

She crawled forward, and saw that whatever had hit them had torn the helicopter in half, and only the section Jill was in had survived.

Only *Jill* had survived.

She felt the pain then. Like the sensation when novocaine wears off, after a trip to the dentist. Like the feeling of numbness subsiding after taking a bad fall, skinning your palms and your knees on a sidewalk, limping home to show your mommy. She felt awareness rise, and looked down to see it.

Her left leg had a gash across it—deep, red, but not bleeding. Seared, she realized.

A bullet had grazed her. Though that didn't quite describe what she was seeing. "Grazing" always seemed to imply some light touch, like a cut, or a rope burn. Painful, but minor. Something you could shrug off and ignore, like the heroes in a thriller novel would do.

This was deep.

And it *hurt*.

She shook her head. The tears were back, though now they came from the *excruciating* pain in her leg, as well as from the dawning realization of just how much trouble she was in.

She couldn't dwell on that now. She had to get out of here! She had to gather any supplies she could. Maybe find a radio. She had to figure out which way to go—to cross this desert and find her way to safety.

She scrambled. First things first, she needed to get out of this thing, to make sure she was safe. She could gather supplies after. She needed... she needed *out*.

The helicopter was more or less level, but they had crashed into a dune. Her side of the craft was blocked by sand, which sifted into the space and kept her from exiting. Going through the cockpit was out of the question—it was like a valley of twisted, razor-sharp knives waiting to grind her into hamburger.

The only way out was to climb over the body of the translator, to slip through the opening on her side of the craft, out onto the sand beyond.

Jill took several quick, deep breaths, and then forced herself to move. The pain was horrific, but that wasn't the thing that most slowed her down. She slipped on the woman's blood, at one point, and fell into her lap.

Jill pushed herself up, sobbing. And then managed to get a hand on the rim of the door. She pulled again, and managed to get to her feet, steadying herself with her hands.

And in a moment she was out.

Sand was sticking to her in every place where she'd been covered in blood, including in her wound. She wiped her hands on her jeans, trying to at least clear them. She'd worry about her injury later.

She stood, then, on the sifting sand, bracing herself against the helicopter.

Or what was left of the helicopter.

She looked out over the undulating dunes of the Katakstan desert. It was morning. The sun had only risen a short time ago— they had used the darkness as cover, as they'd evacuated. It lingered still, in weak patches of shadow, slowing melting in the rising sun. She could already feel the heat coming. She could feel it in her bones, like a weight gathering, like an increase in gravity prepared to crush her where she stood.

And the heat wasn't the only thing coming her way.

She saw them on the horizon—far off in that ripple of vanilla ice cream landscape. They were merely flea-sized dots at first, but she knew that soon enough they'd be too big to ignore. Too big to avoid.

And she knew, without quite knowing *how* she knew, that they weren't friendlies.

They were *Kharif.* There was something about the pattern of them, the barely organized swarm of them, that told her who they were.

Jill managed to stand, straightening herself as much as she could. She felt the pain in her leg and ignored it. She squared herself to face those dots as they grew in size, coming ever closer. She couldn't have run if she'd tried, and where would she run to anyway? This desert—this expanse of sand that seemed to stretch for thousands of miles in all directions—this was their territory. Their home. She didn't stand a hope in all this hell of getting away from them.

This was it, then.

Mark had finally gotten into trouble that Jill couldn't get either of them out of.

If she couldn't run from it, if she couldn't pull a string to untangle it, then at the very least, she was going to face it head on.

TWENTY-TWO

Ryker woke slowly, at first not fully sure of where he was or what was happening. All he had to work with was memories of noise—echoes of something big and loud played over and over in his foggy mind, on a loop that finished with a very real ringing in his ears and an even more real pounding in his skull. His eyes opened, eventually, to the interior of the mangled Jeep.

A beam of light slanted in from a bullet hole above him, striking him directly in his right eye. Had it been an actual bullet, this would all be over. The real thing must have missed him by centimeters at some point during the mad dash out of the FOB.

As it was, the shaft of sunlight was a knife, pushing its way slowly though his eye, slicing through his brain, until it would inevitably burn like a laser through the back of his head. He blinked, then stiffly, painfully, shifted position.

By God it was *hot* in here.

The sun had been heating up the metal of the Jeep for what must have been hours, and Ryker found himself slowly cooking inside. Sweat covered his body, and his clothes clung to him as he finally rose from the awkward and uncomfortable position in which he'd found himself. He had to grip the side of the seat to get into anything close to an upright position. His legs felt like lead, but at least he did *feel* them. Pain was a good sign, at least as far as letting him know he was, indeed, alive.

Message received, Ryker thought, trying to transmit it as a white flag to his body. *Feel free to stop broadcasting, I surrender.* But his body didn't bother dialing back, and instead simply stressed just *how banged up* he was over and again.

Bit by bit, ache by ache, Ryker managed to right himself, resting his butt on the oddly angled chunk of door that he and the mechanics had welded in place, just a few hours ago. That door, along with the others, had done the job and saved his life. So far.

The rest was going to be up to him.

He rose, standing first on the door beneath him, then on the edge of the seat. The Jeep was definitely on its side, and he managed to get enough leverage to push upward against what would be the passenger door, which had yet another chunk of metal welded to it to provide armor. Right now it was just providing dead weight, making it a hell of an effort to push the damned thing up and open.

It creaked as it finally rose, protesting its new state of being, and Ryker had to scramble to get up and through the freshly opened portal above. He struggled to keep the heavy, steel door swung wide enough to allow him some egress, without it dropping down like a guillotine to sever his fingers or maybe even one of his limbs. Or possibly to crush his skull, which might have been a mercy at this particular moment.

Finally, he emerged into the bright, blinding light of full daylight in the Katakstan desert. It was slightly cooler out here, by comparison, but that wouldn't last long. The sun was already brutally assaulting him from all directions, the heat starting to gather and cling like wet dryer lint, wrapping him in itself, stifling and strangling him.

There was a reason why most Katakstan operations took place at night, in this region. Cover, yes. On a moonless night in particular, the darkness here was a complete, inky abyss that even an entire platoon could submerge into for camouflage.

But in addition, the desert cooled down significantly without the constant press of the sun on its sands. And while it was perfectly possible to operate and survive, even thrive, in all of this direct and radiant heat, most of the locals tended to find the rhythm of doing their work in the mornings and evenings, with rest in the afternoons. Staying out of the heat of the day was a cultural necessity in a land that lacked such conveniences as air conditioning or even just clean water.

Speaking of which...

He took a quick inventory. He had water, enough to last him perhaps the day. A bit longer, if he conserved. He had rations as well. By necessity, both of these were in small quantities. He had known that if he survived, he would have to move quickly. He couldn't be weighed down by excess food and water. Even if such things might be necessary to stay alive. And they would be.

He would have to find other sources for what he needed, as he went.

Looking around at the horizon surrounding him, he saw plenty of signs of the enemy. There were vehicles—trucks, Jeeps like his own, various other hulking, smoking ruins dotting the sands—all, in fact, were tumbled or scattered or resting in burning ruin. His own Jeep had faired pretty well, by comparison.

The mortar didn't do this, he realized as he surveyed the carnage. *Not all of it, anyway.*

No, this had to be the result of the drone strike. And by the look of the landscape, Ryker had driven straight into the path of it—right into the heart of the maelstrom of bombs and weapons fire that had been laid down to keep the enemy suppressed while the FOB was evacuated. Ryker was supposed to be on the far side of it by the time that dropped, but clearly his timing had been off. Only luck had protected him, keeping him from taking a direct hit from a bomb or from a whole lot of bullets. He wondered idly how many of the Jeep's bullet holes were American made.

Jill, he thought suddenly, her name popping up from the random soup of thoughts boiling in his brain. She was supposed to be on the first helicopter out. And Ryker's plan had been to find an observation point beyond the strike zone, and turn back to try to visually verify how the extraction had gone. Obviously, he hadn't succeeded in that part of his plan.

He had no way of knowing whether she'd made it or not. He had no communications equipment, now that he'd handed off the sat phone. And besides, the enemy had used whatever EM device they had to brick everything anyway. He *might* be able to reach the strike force, to get an update, if he had so much as a radio to work with.

There was nothing in the Jeep. But maybe one of those burning hulks of enemy transport scattered across the desert floor had something he could scavenge.

He shook himself, trying to get some blood and adrenaline going for the slog ahead, then ducked back into the Jeep to retrieve what gear he could. He had stocked up with some supplies—a canteen filled with water, a backpack with some food and other gear. There was a coil of rope, and another of black Paracord. He had his fixed-blade knife and pistol. He'd even brought along the M16 he'd picked up during the run for the FOB, complete with exactly one half-spent magazine.

Ammunition had been in short supply, with most of it going to the extraction force. There was very little left for Ryker. He'd have to remedy that, if he had any hope of surviving long enough to complete his mission.

Luckily the enemy was using M16s as their weapon of choice, and he should be able to snag some ammunition from the fallen. First rule in these sort of covert ops was "adapt to use what the enemy uses." Even the most advanced and high-tech carbine rifle was useless if you didn't have bullets for the thing.

Scanning over his pitiful inventory, he shook his head. It wasn't much. But he'd made this kind of journey before, with a lot less. That didn't make it ideal, of course. And the sooner he could shore up some of his weaknesses and deficiencies, the better.

He pulled on the pack, tightened the shoulder straps and cinched the sternum strap, and then made sure his pistol was hidden but accessible. It was a last resort weapon, and the pack helped keep it out of sight, out of mind.

He began marching with the M16 at ease but ready to draw upward, as needed.

The desert sun was brutal. He'd have to find shade and ride out the hottest part of the day, conserving as much energy and water as possible, if he had any hope of getting to his next map point. But first he needed to assess the situation here, and snag any resources he could find.

He approached one of the smoldering hunks of metal, the remains of an armored transport truck about six-hundred yards from where his Jeep had rolled. Ryker raised the M16, sighting down the barrel as he crouched and sprinted, keeping cover as he could, alert for any signs of movement.

The cab of the truck—or what could reasonably be assumed to be the *remains* of the cab—had taken the biggest hit from whatever had dropped on it. The rear of the truck was a canopy-covered bed, and Riker drew his knife, plunged it into the canvas, and slashed downward, all while keeping to the side, M16 ready to swing around and light the thing up.

There wasn't a sound from the truck, no outcry or bullets fired.

He quickly peeked inside and backed away again, closing his eyes to picture what he'd just glimpsed. There were no signs of anyone in there. Now, cautiously, he tore at the hole he'd cut and opened things up a bit more.

Inside was a jumble of pipes and tools and other debris. No crates, no sign of weapons or even bodies. All of the truck's occupants must have been in the cab, when it... ceased being a cab.

Ryker reached in and picked up a stray piece of conduit, examining it through the hole in the canvas.

It wasn't anything he recognized, either in whole or as part of something else. Just some spare part for something or other. Junk, and worthless, just like the truck itself.

Except...

The canopy was basically one big tent. And with some venting, he could get some airflow going. It wouldn't exactly be an air conditioned suite at the Hilton, but it would block the sun and allow him to rest in the shade, cooled as much as possible by the desert breeze. It would certainly be much cooler than the interior of the Jeep had been—essentially a big, steel Easy Bake Oven, in the heat of the desert sun.

Ryker could call this base camp and ride out the heat of the day here, resting up so he could move at night.

It was a good plan. But he needed more resources, and more intel, if he was going to pull this off.

He reached into a pocket on the leg of his pants and took out a folded map and a pen. He had sketched the map by hand while killing time at the FOB, using a large wall map of the region as his guide, and had marked the locations of every enemy stronghold that Clayborne and his people knew about, as well as noting the coordinates that Agent Anonymous had given him—the potential location where Mark Adams was being held.

Hand drawn maps. Old school, but effective. The EM pulse the enemy used couldn't knock it out, at any rate.

Using the pen, Ryker made an X on his approximate location, using the smoldering ruins of the FOB as a primary landmark. He wrote *camp* next to it. Wishful thinking, maybe, but if he could find some supplies and get back here quickly, he felt he had a chance to make it to at least nightfall. In the cool of evening he might be able to find a few more resources, as he made progress toward his objective.

He tucked the map and pen back in his pocket, then started to march toward the next closest bit of wreckage.

This was a smaller hunk of burning metal. A small pickup truck, from the look of it. And unlike his new campsite, this spot came with bodies.

Three men were scattered on the desert floor. The first he encountered was what Ryker and his people would call *very dead*. Half the man's body was missing, including a large chunk of his head. Ryker could smell the guy's burned flesh, sweet and sickening. He shook off the nausea, and concentrated on the task of searching the remains. All he came up with was a pack of smokes and a lighter, and a photo. Presumably this was the guy's family. A woman, a little boy, and a much older man. Maybe the guy's wife, kid, and father?

Ryker studied it for time, trying to memorize the features. It wouldn't serve any purpose, really. He just... wanted to offer some kind of sympathy to these people. In all the years he'd done this work, Ryker had tried to keep perspective by forcing himself to lean toward empathy, even for the enemy. It wasn't easy, sometimes. But he'd yet to regret the effort.

This man would have killed Ryker, Jill, *anyone* who was in that FOB. It was probable that the man saw Americans as vile, inhuman, unworthy of breath or life. His entire culture wired him this way. And for many of these men, they fought less for ideals and religious zeal, and more because they felt their culture—their way of life—was being threatened. They had very little frame of reference to consider the other side.

How was that any different than the reasons American soldiers fought and died in places like this?

Again, seeing the other side of this kind of conflict wasn't something that came naturally to anyone, much less a people who had limited access and insight into the world of their enemies. They simply couldn't see the world the way Westerners could. So it was going to be up to people like Ryker to see it for them.

This guy was the enemy, but he was still a man.

He still had a life, and a family. And all of that was gone now. For reasons that he probably didn't even fully understand. Ryker was one of those guys, himself—someone who fought here, but couldn't really say why. He'd lost track of *why* years ago.

Ryker knelt and turned the man's dead hand palm up, freeing it from the sand. He opened the fingers and pressed the photo into them, angling it so that the eyes of his family were upon what was left of the man's face. It was the most Ryker could offer, by way of last rites or eulogy. He knelt there for a moment, knees sinking into the sand, head bowed slightly, silent.

After a few seconds he nodded and stood, raised the M16, and moved toward the next body, tossing the cigarettes into the sand but shoving the lighter into his pocket.

The next body, it turned out, wasn't a body at all. The guy was still alive, though from the look of him that wouldn't last for long.

He was missing an arm and a leg, and blood was seeping from him into the desert. He had managed to push himself into a seated position, leaning back against a wheel rim that had been blown off the truck, tatters of ruined tire still clinging to it. The rim was wedged into a small, sandy bank, and the spot was giving the man at least a bit of shade to die in.

"*American...*" the man rasped in *Pashto*. He moved his hand, waved it as if trying to threaten Ryker.

Ryker was cautious, moving forward with the M16 raised. He didn't see a gun, but that didn't mean there wasn't one. Or the man might have some kind of IED strapped to him, ready to blow them both into the next life.

Ryker doubted this, too. This guy, and the others, had been driving that pickup. They'd been chasing either Ryker or the FOB evacuees. It wasn't likely they were suicide bombers. Just foot soldiers, trying to gun down Americans.

"*Dog...*" the man said, and Ryker could tell that if he'd had it in him, he'd have spit in Ryker's face.

"*You'll die soon,*" Ryker said, bluntly. No sense pulling that punch, it was obvious. He didn't even lean into the Pashto accent. "*Make up for the evil of your life. Make your peace with God. Tell me how to find your headquarters. Tell me how to find Faraz.*"

The man laughed, then coughed, blood erupting from his mouth and nose.

It was only then that Ryker saw the man had suffered more than the loss of his limbs. His side was soaked in blood, of course. But Ryker could now see the tatters of the man's clothing, the gaping hole in his flesh. His lungs had been damaged, along with many of his internal organs.

He wasn't just *dying*.

"*I will end your suffering, if you wish,*" Ryker said. An offer. A mercy. Would the man accept it?

"*Suffering...*" he replied, shaking his head. "*It is my honor, to suffer for the glory of God.*"

He coughed again, and shuddered.

It wouldn't be long now.

Ryker slung the M16 over his shoulder and knelt. This was not a job for bullets. He needed to conserve ammunition, in case he didn't find more. He also didn't want the sound of gunfire drawing attention his way. This needed to be silent.

But mostly, mercy should be offered by hand, at close range. This wasn't a dog, to be put down quickly and callously, with a bullet to the head. This was a man—and even though he was the enemy, he deserved whatever respect Ryker could offer.

Ryker took the knife from his belt, holding it at his side. He reached with his other hand and removed the folded map from his pocket, opening it up and showing it to the man. With the point of the knife, Ryker indicated their location. "*We are here*," he said. "*The American base was here. Tell me, where is Faraz?*" One last chance, that's what this was.

The man shook his head, his eyes were bulging, his face looked pale. "*Die, American dog*," he said, weakly.

Ryker nodded at this. "*May God have mercy on you, then*," he said. With a quick and decisive strike he plunged the knife into the man's throat, pushing at an upward angle. The blade pierced the flesh with no trouble, and met resistance only as it encountered the spine at the base of the skull.

There was a brief gurgle from the man, and what little blood remained in him now trickled out of the wound, without even enough pressure to pulse and reach Ryker's hand.

Ryker pulled the knife, and let the man sag to the ground. He then searched him, finding a magazine for the M16. A bit of good karma, Ryker thought. Though every time he'd had to kill someone, he felt that some stain had spread on his soul. That was the job, though. Stained soul or not, killing was the job. At least this killing was done out of some sense of...

Well, was it truly mercy? Yes, in part. Ryker wanted to end the man's suffering. But he had to admit that there was also a bit of pragmatic *utility* in it. Killing the man meant Ryker was leaving no one to tell the enemy where he was, or what his objective would be.

In light of that, was this really a mercy killing? Or was Ryker simply covering his own ass? Did that taint the act? Was that what he felt, staining his soul?

Ryker had long ago stopped killing from a place of hate. Now, it was mercy or necessity. But perhaps far too much of the latter and too little of the former.

The rest of what the man carried was useless to Ryker. Like the previous man, there was a photo of family. Ryker repeated the rites he'd given the other, and positioned the photo in this man's remaining hand, ensuring the eyes of the family were on the dead man's face.

He stood, took a few deep breaths, and made his way to the third occupant of the truck. Another dead body this time. And in this man's hands was another M16. Ryker pilfered the magazine and rounds. And in his searching he found a treasure at last—another map.

This one was commercially printed, and had notations written in *Pashto*, but it very much resembled the one Ryker had drawn. Ryker tucked it away in the same pocket. When he was back at camp, he'd review it, compare it with his own map, combine the two.

All-in-all, this had been a decent foray into the wildness. Intel and ammunition were good finds. He would have appreciated some food, and perhaps more water. But as the sun beat down on him, it was time for him to call it a day and move back to camp. He would get into the shade, sip some water, compare and contrast his maps, and then get some sleep.

He'd need the rest, if he planned to trek the desert at nightfall.

TWENTY-THREE

Faraz wiped his hands with a dish towel, dropping it on the counter as he stepped out of the small kitchen and into the dusty courtyard. The trucks were returning. And they had brought him a guest.

The conflict at the American base had gone poorly, in Faraz's estimate. His people saw it as victory—they celebrated with chants and prayers, firing their weapons in the air, praising and thanking God. They smiled and danced, had their palms outward and tilted their head back in the ecstasy of communion with God.

But Faraz did not join them. Because despite the destruction of the FOB, despite routing the Americans out of the base and sending them to the border, this victory had been a failure.

The objective had been to capture the base, to add it to their resources as they had with so many other American weapons, vehicles, and structures within their borders. Faraz had intended to capture the personnel and use them for gathering intelligence and as hostages for bartering, or to make examples of them. He had planned this operation to such perfection that they had isolated the Americans for weeks, removing any possibility of communication with the outside world, and slowly taking ground and overwhelming outstations until the base itself was the only thing left standing.

The plan had fallen apart after a flock of American drones carpeted the desert with their bombs and weapons fire. And the walls of the base—the target Faraz had most wanted to acquire—fell like Jericho, becoming so much rubble among the sands of the desert. If there was anything useful left in that debris, it would take months to recover, and at great risk and expense. This made it effectively worthless, and all of their effort over the past several weeks was now a complete waste of time and resources.

It was not a victory.

It was an insult.

Faraz couldn't help but think that the arrival of the lone American man had somehow tipped the balance in this operation. It seemed impossible, but from everything Faraz was learning, from the men returning to report what they'd found, the moment of the man's arrival at the base had signaled the collapse of all of the *Kharif's* efforts there—the collapse of all of Faraz's planning.

The evacuation had been too well organized, too in sync with the arrival of the drone strike. This indicated that the Americans had somehow regained communication and coordinated with their reinforcements and allies. Something Faraz had thought would be impossible, since the *Kharif* had used an electromagnetic pulse and numerous strategically targeted mortar strikes to destroy their communication equipment. So it must surely have been the American operative who had brought them a way to reach the outside world.

And, because Faraz's own people had not done their jobs

properly, had not been diligent in their work, they had been in no position to block communication the second time.

Faraz couldn't tolerate that sort of failure. And though it saddened him, he knew that the one to pay the price would have to be his dear, childhood friend.

He had already had Ghazal tied and beaten. And even now, his old, dear friend hung by his wrists, dangling just high enough from the ground that his toes could just barely cut little circles in the sand as he spun.

It was just the beginning of his punishment.

The desert sun would teach his friend to be more attentive, Faraze determined. A day suffering in one of the hot boxes, baked in the full and collected heat of the desert sun, would burn all weakness from Ghazal. And the bitter cold of the night would harden Ghazal's soul against allowing that weakness to return.

After this day, should Ghazal survive, he would be nurtured back to health, and brought back into service. At a lower rank, of course. He could never again be entrusted with vital work, but he would be given the opportunity to prove himself useful to God and the *Kharif* once more. He would become a better solider. And a mourned and lost brother to Faraz, who would never speak to him again in this life.

The exile of the soul was the worst punishment Faraz could levy on a once trusted brother.

But now, Faraz was eager to greet his new guest.

She was the only American recovered alive, after the events at the base. The rest had either eluded capture or were killed on the sands. Though there were *Kharif* currently sweeping the area, actively looking for anyone who could be brought to the compound, or for any resources the *Kharif* could press into service, this woman was, at the moment, the only prize seized from the pathetic failure of their raid upon the FOB.

They had lost the battle for the base, but they were winning this war, Faraz reminded himself. The Americans may have escaped, but they had also been routed out, sent away. They had scurried over the Katakstan border, and the *Kharif* would ensure they never returned.

The *Kharif* were *winning* this war, on the battlefields of Katakstan.

More importantly, they were winning the war in the eyes of the *people*. The American dogs were being pushed farther and farther back, eventually out of Katakstan territory altogether, and all the way to their own shores. And the *Kharif* were the rising power here, the liberators. The *heroes*.

Like father, Faraz thought. As he always thought. His father's eyes were always there before him, always looking, watching, judging. Even after his uncle had been killed, even once Faraz found himself the sole remaining male of his bloodline, his father was always *there*. Always *watching*.

The American woman, his new prize, was pulled from the truck, roughly handled, but Faraz had given orders that she was to be kept safe. She wore a burlap grain sack as a hood over her head, and her hands were bound with rough grass rope, knotted tightly at her wrists. Uncomfortable, perhaps even painful, but nothing overtly harmful. The idea was to give her a taste, to create an expectation, as if this was just the start of so much more pain to come. He would let her fear and worry do the real work of breaking her. It made everything else go so much more smoothly, when their captives tortured themselves.

Faraz ordered that she be taken to a room especially prepared for her, and he watched as the men half dragged her to it.

He entered behind the men who had her in their grip, and watched as she was forced into a chair, the bonds of her hands loosened so that they could be retied behind her. Her feet were tied as well, and all of these bonds were pulled painfully tight, the reminder reinforced and amplified.

Faraz nodded, and all but his chosen left the room.

There were no electric or kerosene lights on in this space, at the moment, but diffused sunlight came in through windows covered in newspaper. It gave the space a soft, warm glow, in Faraz's mind. A surreal quality. The light cast gradient shadows over the walls and floors, from the posts and beams that supported the structure.

In the dimness, with masks removed and eyes blinking to adjust, one would see mostly shadows. Nothing comforting and familiar, no obvious hope of escape.

Faraz could hear the woman crying.

Fear. Which was appropriate.

He knelt beside her, and reached to pull the hood from her head.

She blinked as the room became visible to her, and she looked around wildly. Faraz could see her taking everything in, assessing her situation, as so many before her had done.

She had an air about her. He'd seen it before. She was afraid, yes. But also... brave. Or determined. Or perhaps simply stubborn and indignant, refusing to accept that this could happen to *her*. Such attitudes could be similar to bravery—their effect could be essentially the same.

Faraz would break her of any arrogance, if necessary. He had broken many of the *Kharif's* guests, in rooms such as this. Bravery or bravado, both would perish.

He had experienced women of her type before. *American* women could be like this. Trouble, in some respects. But also... admirable. In a shameful way, obviously. Faraz's father had warned him about American women, when he'd discussed Faraz attending University.

Their very existence and demeanor was an affront to God, Father had said. They were whores, shameful and lustful. Their independence had tainted their souls, fooled them into thinking they were the *equals* of men.

They were to be held in contempt, to be shamed, to be stomped out like a scorpion in one's rooms.

Father was right, of course. American women, indeed all western women, carried within them a toxin that, if allowed to settle into a man's heart, would lead to his destruction. But Faraz's time in the West had taught him to appreciate western women for what they truly were: *Untamed, wild, unbroken.*

Still very *tamable*, however. Still very *breakable*.

"Hello," Faraz said, smiling from his knelt position. His English was tinted with a British accent, which he knew made him sound exotic but also pleasant to Americans. It helped to soften them, he had discovered. The softer he spoke, the smoother his delivery, the more he could lure them into a sense of false comfort and trust. They became so much more manageable, when their lifetime of cultural bias was engaged.

The woman said nothing.

"I assume you realize that your situation is dire," Faraz said. "And that any attempt you make to escape will be met only with brutality."

He enjoyed speaking to his captors this way. The bluntness, the pragmatic directness, was something Americans found unsettling. Their whole culture was often circumspect, coming at the topic of conversation the way a rabbit might approach still waters. Cautious, ready to retreat at any sign of trouble.

Americans talked this way of death, with euphemisms that softened the topic, made it more delicate, more palatable. "Passing on," or "gone to eternal rest." It was as if Americans were afraid to talk directly of death, on the chance it might notice them and appear before them, taking them into its embrace then and there.

Faraz had determined, long ago, that a willingness to speak

bluntly about death or pain could give him a distinct psychological advantage, when dealing with Westerners. Particularly Americans.

"Yes," the woman acknowledged, and her own voice was quiet, small.

Good, Faraz thought. *No false bravado. No faux boldness. She is willing to be afraid.*

And so, she was brave after all.

Faraz stood and nodded to one of his men, who rushed out of the space on a predetermined errand.

He looked back to the woman. "I believe your name is Jill Adams," he said.

She didn't reply, but he could see that she had not anticipated him knowing who she was.

"I have been following your career," Faraz said, casually, kindly, as if engaging her in dinner conversation. "Many believe you will be a Senator soon. Very impressive, for one so young."

Faraz's man returned with a silver tray, carrying a pot of tea and two cups. He placed this on a small table near the woman's left knee, then stood back in his original position.

Faraz nodded again, and one of his men knelt to remove the bonds on Jill Adams' hands, while another brought a chair for Faraz. The first man then turned and poured two cups of tea, handing the first to Faraz, and the second to Jill.

She took the cup, her hands shaking slightly, and held it as if she had no idea what it was.

"You must be parched, after your journey," Faraz said. "My men have told me how they found you. Quite remarkable, that you survived that crash, especially under those conditions. Surely, God has plans for you."

He held his cup up, gesturing, and then took a sip.

She also sipped, and Faraz was pleased to see she had manners.

She has trained as a politician and a dignitary, he thought. *She has high ambition.*

He noted, as well, that she didn't speak. Faraz had engaged with many Americans in situations similar to this, and most would speak at this point. Usually in an effort to regain some sort of control over their situation, even if it was a hopeless sort of delusion. They might make some whimsical little joke, using humor to comfort themselves and to hopefully establish some sort of alliance with Faraz, perhaps seeing his overtures of kindness as a bridge they could use into his heart.

It never worked, of course. Faraz would laugh politely, nod appreciatively, and then casually let them know that they would die soon, and that he did truly regret it. But before it happened, they would have to suffer and give him whatever information he wanted.

That was the way most of these conversations went. But not with Jill Adams. She simply sipped her tea, and looked off to one dark corner of the room.

It was interesting to Faraz. But not altogether unexpected. He had, after all, met her brother. Had, in fact, had many conversations with Mark Adams, over the past few weeks. And though Mark was very much the typical American CIA operative—his attitude, his demeanor, his words all carefully controlled—when the subject of his sister came up he was far more guarded, and even a bit reverential.

Mark Adams loved his sister, of course. But Faraz knew, from their many conversations, that there was something else there. Mark respected Jill. He depended on her, as one might typically expect from a child toward his parent. He loved Jill as his savior, as his *home.*

Knowing she was here would worry Mark to no end. As it should, Faraz believed.

"You were in the forward operating base," Faraz said.

Jill looked to him finally, and nodded, still saying nothing.

"From the reports I've received, you've been there for some time. It must have been frightening."

Jill was watching his face, as he watched hers. He could see there was *something* brewing there. Some American defiance that wouldn't allow her to let all of this pass unremarked upon. Even if she was powerless, her liberated nature would demand she "speak truth power." It was the American way.

And yet she sat in silence.

He nodded, sipped his tea, and observed as she did the same.

Mirroring, he thought. And smiled in spite of himself.

She was using the mirror technique. Building empathy between the two of them by subtly replicating each move he made. She was letting him do all the talking, because her diplomatic training would have told her this was how he and his people would *want* things to go. His culture would demand that women be meek, subservient, bending to the will of the man.

He had learned all of this when he'd studied in Europe—the insights into human psychology, and into the psychology of his people, in particular, that were discussed in open-air classrooms filled with young people. As if the Katakstan people were simply some sort of curious animal that only Westerners could interpret, given enough study. One more way to degrade his culture, Faraz had come to believe. One more way to establish the sense of superiority that Westerners felt toward people from the East.

He sipped again, waited, and as she brought the tea to her own lips he said, "I have your brother here."

She paused, not yet taking a sip, the rim of the cup hovering close to her lips.

"Would you care to see him?

She was watching him now, and she lowered the cup.

"Yes," she said. And to her credit, her voice was steady. Strong. Controlled.

Faraz smiled, nodded, and took one last sip of tea before handing the cup to his man. He rose, and gestured for his people to cut the bonds around Jill Adams' feet. They pulled her roughly into a standing position, and she allowed them to guide her along behind Faraz as he walked.

Getting her to speak was the first victory.

More was to come.

TWENTY-FOUR

KATAKSTAN DESERT

The direct heat died down as the sun became mostly obscured by the distant dunes on the horizon. That just left the radiant heat of the desert, releasing all of that energy it had collected throughout the day to feed the great god of entropy. The slow heat death of the universe was at least providing some relief for Ryker, here and now.

Of course, the rapidly dropping temperatures could bring challenges of its own.

As much as the daytime was hot, the nighttime could be cold. It wasn't uncommon for the temperature in the Katakstan desert to drop to nearly -4°C, once the sun was down. It was one of the most maddening things about operations here. The freeze-or-fry nature of the place made preparation and survival a challenge. It was one of the things that made it so hard to fight these people, who were accustomed to the desert and had generations of tricks and knowledge to apply. It gave them an advantage—one that

Westerners could only match with technology and extreme discipline.

Ryker rummaged more layers of clothing from the dead, as he passed them, pulling on a second coat and rolling a third into a bundle he could carry in his pack. He wouldn't freeze. He wouldn't necessarily be comfortable, either, but given that he was about to march across enemy territory with patrols actively looking for him, comfort wasn't high on his list of expectations.

Aside from giving Ryker some protection from the elements, taking clothing from the enemy served the equally practical purpose of giving him a bit of camouflage. As he wandered the night, carrying the enemy's preferred weapon and wearing his enemy's uniform, sporting just over three days worth of bread growth, he might just stand a chance of passing by patrols without incident. As long as he kept his cool and didn't do anything to call attention to himself.

A long shot, really, but anything that improved his odds was good.

Plus, with US military out of the region, at least there was less of a chance of him being shot by one of his own.

The rapidly cooling desert air was a relief after spending most of the day hunkered and sweating in the transport. The vent holes Ryker had cut into the fabric of the cover had allowed some air to move, which combined with the shade to at least make things tolerable. But it was still like trying to sleep in a sauna for the afternoon. Being out here at night, it was almost as if someone had turned on the air conditioning. The first half hour of darkness, Ryker could feel the sweat of the day wicking away from him, cooling him even faster.

The cool air also had the effect of giving him a bit of pep. He had managed to nap for a few rough hours, although any sound from outside of the transport was cause for him to jolt awake, raising the

MI6, prepared to fight his way out of there. The closest he'd come to having to fight, however, was when some of the *Kharif* drove through in a beat up old Toyota pickup, cruising slowly among the minefield of debris, apparently looking for any signs of someone living.

Whether they were there as a rescue team or as a hunting party, Ryker couldn't say for sure. Maybe a bit of both. Though as he peered through one of the gashes he'd made in the transport's canopy, he never saw the search party stop even once. So either everyone out there was dead, or these people simply didn't care, and were just going through the motions. Maybe they were just scavenging, looking for something useful.

From what Ryker knew about the *Kharif*, they didn't exactly have a "no man left behind" policy.

He watched until the truck was out of sight, then settled in to resume his nap. It was a struggle to relax enough to fall asleep, but he managed it.

Before nightfall, after getting some rest and a bit of water, Ryker sat up and used one of the last, fading shafts of sunlight from one of the holes in the canopy to help him inspect his two maps.

The printed map he'd taken off of the *Kharif* proved to be only slightly more useful than Ryker's own hand-drawn map. The notes written in *Pashto* appeared to be mostly hastily agreed upon checkpoints, maybe meeting up to refuel or resupply. It was likely none of those sites were still active. But it did give Ryker a sense of the terrain, and some insight into the enemy's movements and habits. All of the checkpoints created a more or less straight path starting from a vague, distant point and leading to where he now stood.

He compared that map to his own. Agent Anonymous had given Ryker some coordinates of where the CIA *thought* Faraz would have taken Mark. But their intel was limited, and might be out of date. Best he had, though. His best lead, for now.

He ran his finger up to Faraz's suspected location on the hand drawn map, and then compared it to the printed map. The region where Anonymous had pointed him was near a couple of small villages. There were no waypoints marked on the printed map, in that area. But there was one about fifty klicks to the south of a town called Harat. More of a village, really, judging from the size of it.

If Ryker considered the meetup sites to be a trail of breadcrumbs, and if Anonymous had given him at least the right ballpark for finding Faraz, there was a good chance that Harat was where Faraz was holding Mark. Harat might be the *Kharif* home base.

It was a lead, at any rate. The best Ryker had, under the circumstances.

The problem was, Harat was about 90 klicks from his present location, and he was currently on foot.

Back in his military days, Ryker could run that sort distance in full ruck, in about ten hours. Less, if he was sufficiently motivated. But that was on generally solid ground, even with hills and rocks and other obstacles to navigate. And mostly, no one was shooting at him. Not real bullets, anyway. Dodging paintballs was a lot less of an obstacle than dodging lead.

Given the sandy terrain and the necessity to keep out of sight as much as possible, he estimated it might be more like fifteen to eighteen hours to get there. That would put him traveling in broad daylight for the last stretch. Out in the wide open, slowed by exhaustion—an easy target.

That was bad for him and bad for his mission. And it made finding a vehicle a priority.

As he marched through the growing desert darkness, he looked around at the vehicle graveyard surrounding him. There was little hope that anything here would still be functional, and it would cost him precious time to search or try to repair anything. Better to keep hoofing it until he spotted another search party or some other evidence of a working vehicle. Then all he'd have to do was somehow kill a bunch of well-armed, well-reseted *Kharif* and take their truck from them, without being injured or killed in the process.

Piece of cake.

He kept a steady pace, and kept his attention wide. All progress was good progress. And if his karma held out, maybe he'd just find a vehicle ready and waiting for him up ahead. Surely the universe owed him at least that much.

TWENTY-FIVE

About three hours after sunset Ryker ducked to the ground, crawling through the sand to stay as low and hidden as possible as headlights bounced across the desert, heading straight for him.

There was nowhere for him to go. Nowhere to hide.

This stretch of sand was barren and nearly flat in all directions, with not even one of the smoldering hunks of vehicles to hide behind. He wasn't sure if he'd been spotted or not. Regardless, if the truck ahead kept moving on its present course, in a few minutes Ryker would either be run down or gunned down. Neither option appealed to him, obviously, but he was damned if he knew what to do about it.

He had the M16 laying flat on its side, on the ground in front of him, his right forefinger resting on the trigger. His left hand was palm down on the sand, pushing flat against it like the rest of his body, as much as was possible. If it came to it, he could quickly pull the weapon upright and brace it with his left hand as he fired. He might even be able to take these guys out before they could get to him.

If not, he'd end up sending them a straight up homing signal to exactly where he was, so they could casually run over him like a speed bump. Or just open fire on him and turn him into so much bloody purée on the desert floor.

There was nothing to do but wait, and watch.

He watched, his chin pressed into the soft sand to the point where he couldn't open his mouth lest it went down this throat. He was *willing* himself deeper into that sand, hoping that maybe he could appear to just be some random lump of stone or debris on the landscape. The darkness should help with that, keeping him obscured.

Should.

To his relief, the vehicle stopped about 200 yards out. Still too close for comfort, but at least they weren't barreling down on him. That meant they hadn't seen him after all, which was nothing short of a miracle. Their headlights briefly illuminated everything around him, and himself, making him blink from the brightness, before they abruptly shut off.

No alarm. No shouting. No revving the engine in preparation for mashing him into the soil.

Ryker rose from the sand, slowly, brushing it off of his chin and lips with his sleeve. He kept low but got moving, running in quick sprints for a few feet at a time before dropping down and watching, waiting. In a series of crouching hops he closed the gap between himself and the vehicle. As he came closer, he recognized it as the Toyota he'd seen patrolling earlier.

Three men exited the truck, and were busy making camp for the night. One man dug a pit in the sand, dropped in some cords of firewood, and lit a fire. The others broke out an ice chest and some cooking implements—mostly a flat pan and a small kettle.

Dinner time, Ryker thought, and he felt his stomach rumble. His last hot meal had been days ago, and thousands of miles away, in a Texas safe house. The most nourishing thing he'd eaten in the past two days had been a bologna sandwich. Since then he'd been rationing energy bars, conserving for the trip on foot.

He'd expended a lot of calories, however. He could use that meal.

And that truck.

Having closed in on the makeshift camp, Ryker now belly crawled his way forward, stopping frequently to make sure he kept track of the location of all three men.

That part, at least, had gotten easier, as the men settled in for the night. They were chatting in *Pashto*, in quiet tones, and Ryker paused to listen long enough to get an idea of their plans, and to see if there was any useful intelligence there.

Mostly they were discussing who would take which shift, to scan and watch for signs of trouble. But they were also discussing the raid on the FOB, the "great victory" the *Kharif* had been handed over the Americans. It was all bluster and praising God and declaring victory over the American dogs.

And then, Ryker heard something that put the hairs on the back of his neck at full attention.

Speaking in *Pashto*, one of the men said, *"The woman from the helicopter has been delivered to Faraz."*

"Will he kill her?"

The first man responded, *"I believe he means to use her. I do not know all of the details, but I believe she is the sister of the American agent."*

This caught Ryker's attention for sure. All the details—there was really only one story that lined up. And it made him want to vomit.

They have Jill, Ryker thought.

He continued listening, hoping for more. Hoping that maybe he was wrong. But who else could it be? An American woman, retrieved from a helicopter crash, and who just happens to have a brother, an *American*, in the custody of the *Kharif*? It *had* to be Jill.

Ryker's heart pounded. How had this happened? Clayborne had promised to get Jill on the first helicopter out of there. So things must have gone really sideways, somehow.

The thought of Jill in the hands of the *Kharif*—and especially with Faraz and his people knowing exactly who they had—it chilled him to his core. His appetite, so strong and insistent a moment ago, immediately disappeared.

He pushed this all away.

He was no good to Jill if he let his emotions be in the driver's seat. He had to think clearly. Had to stay on mission. That mission now included rescuing Jill, that's all. Ryker had trained for this kind of shifting dynamic. Things went FUBAR, and people like Jim Ryker were the antidote to FUBAR. It was why Agent Anonymous brought him into this.

Well... that, and the fact that Ryker and Mark Adams had history.

Mark, Ryker thought. *Always Mark.*

Once again, Mark Adams was derailing Ryker's life, and putting him in the hot seat. Somehow, despite a year of distance between them, not even a text message of contact, Mark had managed to get Ryker tangled up in another of his messes. Last time it had cost Ryker his career, and had almost cost his freedom. This time, it could cost Jill her life.

Ryker was laying on the sand, and tilted his forehead to rest on his left forearm for a moment. He inhaled and exhaled slowly, centering himself. He needed to be calm for what came next. He needed to be present. He could channel his anger at Mark and his fear for Jill into a rage-fueled attack on these three men, and let the MI6 do the dirty work for him. But that might alert others, out in the darkness. It might call down hell on his own head.

Killing was easy. Killing strategically required a calm mind.

Once he'd run through a full centering routine, he raised himself up on this elbows, and sighted the MI6 on the camp, just to give him a way to focus his attention. He marked off distance, between him and truck, and from the truck to the men. The truck wasn't far, less than six meters. And about two meters beyond that was the campfire.

He rose, slowly, and took out his knife. He held it in his left hand, bracing the MI6 on the back of his forearm, his right index finger on the trigger, as he made a quick sprint to take cover on the other side of the Toyota. What he had planned was close-up work, but there was still the chance that he'd be spotted, and might have to fight from a distance. He had to stay ready for that.

Ryker made the last, quick sprint to the pickup and peered over the bed to see two of the men settling in for their meal. In his rush to take cover behind the truck, Ryker had lost the third man.

Dammit, he thought, turning and scanning, trying to spot him in the darkness. He'd give anything to have the night vision goggles back. Those, like all other electronic equipment, had been bricked by the device used by the *Kharif*.

The third man would be on patrol, watching for exactly the sort of thing Ryker was planning. And unlike Ryker, he would likely have no qualms over firing in the darkness. He had a significant advantage, at the moment.

But Ryker had an advantage of his own—one that blind luck had given him. In his sprint for cover behind the Toyota, he'd managed to slip by unnoticed. At least, there'd been no cry of alarm. So the man on patrol must have gone in the opposite direction. Ryker was now in a position where he could hide, and wait.

He lowered himself to the ground and crawled under the bed of the truck, positioning himself so that he would be able to watch the perimeter of the camp, but could also verify that the other two men were still at ease, with just a quick glance.

In this position, he waited. And watched.

TWENTY-SIX

It took the better part of two hours before the man on patrol finally drifted around to the far side of the Toyota. Ryker gave a quick glance toward the other two men. Both had settled in, laying on blankets next to the fire, and at least one of them was snoring. He felt confident they were both asleep.

As the third man moved past him, Ryker crawled out from beneath the truck. He quietly slung the M16 over his shoulder, and gripped the knife now in his right hand. He moved quickly, and caught up to the man in just a few seconds.

Ryker pounced on the man, gripping his forehead and pulling his head backward as he shoved the knife up and through the base of the skull. Severing the man's spinal cord instantly shut down even reflexive spasms. The man couldn't even cry out, as the connection between his brain and his body was lost.

The rifle he'd been carrying clattered to the sand, and Ryker lowered his victim to the ground beside it.

One down, and no shots fired. Ryker was sweating from the exertion, despite the icy temperatures. But he felt a deeper cold from the act he'd just committed than anything the environment could throw at him anyway.

He hated this. Hated killing. Hated that he was *good at it*, and hated even more that he was willing to do it, when the mission required it. Every kill, every time, left him feeling the chill of a stain on his soul. And he hated it.

Hating it didn't stop him from doing it, however. And Ryker hated *that* even more.

Turning the man over, Ryker could see he was really just a kid— maybe in his early 20s. Ryker shook his head, and wiped the blade of the knife on the boy's—the *man's*— clothing. He searched the body and among the odds and ends in the guy's pockets he found the keys to the Toyota. A stroke of luck.

Leaving the man in the sand, Ryker crept toward the camp fire. The two sleeping men had arranged themselves on either side of it, facing outward. Ryker moved as silently as possible, inching closer.

He held the knife ready, and knelt beside the first man he encountered. He was about to make a killing strike when the guy just opened his eyes.

He cried out, and reached for his weapon. Ryker was able to stomp on the man's hand and then fell downward onto him, using gravity to his advantage and driving his knee into the guy's sternum. He then drove the knife into the man's throat.

As he gurgled and died, his partner got off a shot.

The bullet grazed Ryker's side, as he dove into the sand. He hadn't yet even registered the pain when he reached out into the fire, taking one of the burning logs. Ryker rolled, getting to his knees in one motion, and swung the log up and into the man's hands, like he was trying to launch a baseball to the moon. The man cried out, and his grip on his weapon loosened, allowing it to fall away.

Ryker didn't waste the opening. He was on his feet and taking another swing at the man with the burning log. He made contact with the side of the man's head, sparks and embers flying in all directions.

The man screamed from sparks hitting his eyes and skin, and stumbled back, swatting at his face.

Ryker dropped the log, and picked up the dead man's weapon. He wasted no time firing a single shot, at nearly point blank range, into his enemy's forehead, practically taking off the top of the guy's head.

The body dropped to the desert sand, and Ryker huffed, standing in place, gripping the weapon so hard his hand began to ache. He dropped it to the ground and stumbled, angling toward the water cooler the men had unloaded from the truck. It was cracked and split in numerous places, the insulating foam bulging outward like a yellowing fungus. Ryker pulled the lid free and saw that it contained water—not quite clear and clean, but close enough.

He shrugged off his pack and took out the canteen. He filled this first. Then he took a wadded jacket from the pack and gingerly poured a bit of water on it, soaking it. He used it to wipe blood and gore from his face and neck, from his arms and hands. He hated to waste any water for something like this, but he couldn't abide being covered in the blood of his enemies. It was...

It was too much.

I left this life behind, he thought suddenly. *Bitterly.*

Not quite, it seemed.

He thought about Avery Clemmons and the old man's dusty, sun-baked ranch. He thought about the months he'd spent wandering the US, vagabonding across the country after being released by the CIA. He thought about being forced back into this life by Agent Anonymous, marching across the desert on a killing spree just to fulfill vague orders and unclear objectives.

He thought about everything that had led to his exile, to the sudden shift in the direction of his life, and his return to this hellish place, all because of Mark Adams.

He thought about Jill.

That last thought put the steel back in his bones. Jill, who was now in the hands of the *Kharif*. Jill, who was chronically anchored by her brother. The same man who had put Ryker in this position, here and now, in more ways than one.

Ryker shook his head, and wrung out the jacket, watching as the pink-tinted water sparkled in the flickering firelight as it sloshed to the desert floor. He thought about putting the jacket back in the pack, to hold on to it in case he might needed it again. But he couldn't. He felt a wave of revulsion over it. The thing represented something to Ryker, though he hadn't fully put it together what that was. Something vile, though. Something *unclean*.

He ultimately dropped it into the fire, where it hissed and sizzled and sent the smokey essence of his victims up to the heavens.

Go to God in peace, he thought. No sense harboring a grudge against dead enemies. Better to wish them some kind of absolution in the afterlife. After all, from their perspective it was *Ryker* who was the evil here. Ryker, and his Americanness. Ryker and his Western arrogance.

They were just doing their best to serve God and their own people. They saw themselves as the hero of this story.

And Ryker was the devil.

And hell, maybe he was. He had certainly been the devil to *these* poor bastards, and all the men he'd killed to get to this point. And he'd certainly be the devil to anyone else he encountered, until this damned mission was done.

He rose to his feet and began breaking camp, kicking sand into the campfire and scattering any evidence that someone had been here. He rolled up the blankets and gathered the pans. If anyone came through, he didn't want the remains of this camp calling their attention.

He put everything, including the cooler, with what water remained, in the bed of the Toyota. He searched the bodies of the three men, liberating them of everything from currency to bits of candy. He found yet more ammunition, which he gladly took. And the biggest prize of all, there were leftovers from the meal the men had prepared. He ate a bit of meat that he thought might be lamb, and some flat bread to help with the spice of it. He didn't eat all of it, instead wrapping the remainder up in a square of cloth and putting it in his pack. Just in case he needed the calories later.

His last task was to bury the dead.

This was less about ceremony, or even respect, than pure pragmatism. Bodies would definitely get attention, if someone came through. Ryker needed to keep attention down to its bare minmum.

He used the flat pan to dig a wide trench. Nothing fancy, but it was deep and wide enough to drag the three bodies into it, and cover them with just enough sand that they were invisible. Within a day or two the wind would likely excavate them. Or bury them deeper. The desert could be funny like that.

Finally this quick but grueling work was done, and he tossed the flat pan into the bed of the truck as he climbed behind the wheel of the Toyota and got it started. The fuel gauge read half a tank. There was a gas can in the truck bed. He didn't think he'd need the extra fuel to get to where he was going, so he opted to hold on to it. He still had the lighter he'd liberated from one of the dead men, earlier. Maybe he could put those two things to work somehow.

He was about to put the truck into gear and roll on, but paused, gripping the wheel with both hands. His knuckles began to whiten with the strain.

Ryker had his mission. Agent Anonymous had been explicit.

He'd also been the one to put Jill in this situation. She was *leverage*, right from the start. She had always been the reason Ryker was here.

So it was quite a coincidence that Jill's helicopter was shot down, and she was now in Faraz's hands. Wasn't it?

Did that mean Agent Anonymous had tipped Faraz off?

Ryker wouldn't put it past him. He didn't know the man, but he knew his type. He had worked with and *for* men like Anonymous for most of his career. They saw themselves as above the law, above conscience, above morals and ethics. They did whatever it took to get the job done, and to safeguard the United States. So yes, Ryker knew that if it came down to it, Agent Anonymous would certainly put Jill Adams in the hands of the *Kharif*, just to motivate Ryker enough to complete his mission. That was a fact.

But it didn't matter.

Ryker had been determined to go along with all of this either way, to try to get to Mark, to stop the *Kharif* from getting their hands on that weapon. He had agreed to the mission because Jill was in danger but even when he'd thought Jill was safe, he'd stuck to completing his objective. That's who Ryker was. It didn't matter what brought him here. He was here until the curtain dropped. He would get the job done.

Now he simply had more incentive. Getting Jill out of this country was one of his objectives now.

Ryker pulled the Toyota into gear and started rumbling across the darkened desert landscape, in the direction of Harat and, he hoped, wherever Jill Adams was being held. Which meant he was also headed directly into the home base of Faraz and the *Kharif*. The very gaping maw of the enemy who was most determined to kill him and all Americans, whatever it took.

It was time to drive right into the mouth of the beast.

TWENTY-SEVEN

Jill followed Faraz through the village, her arms gripped tightly by two of Faraz's men. She was focusing on the pain of those hands on her arms. The pain was letting her keep herself from freaking out. If she kept her mind on the pain, there was less chance of it wandering to worry about the state Mark must be in. Or what might have happened to Jim Ryker. Or what was going to happen to *her*.

There was the sound of screaming, up ahead. A man's voice, raspy and ragged. He'd obviously been suffering for some time.

Jill put her mind back on the hands that squeezed and bruised her. She kept her mind stuck on those twin points of pain. That, and each step she had to take, one foot in front of the other. She deliberately thought of each step. She counted them, kept them in mind. She might need that information later.

As part of her training, in diplomacy and foreign affairs, Jill had voluntarily taken courses on everything from cultural sensitivity to hostage negotiation. She had immersed herself in learning how terrorists thought and operated, worldwide. But especially in this region, where oil and other concerns kept the US both attentive and engaged, where war seemed a perpetual certitude, and where hostage-taking was common to the point of warranting a warning to anyone stepping off of an airplane in the region.

And the thought she was avoiding, the fact she was trying desperately to give no recognition to, the real reason she took all those classes, to know these people better: This region was where her brother was most likely to meet a grisly fate.

She had avoided thinking in those terms, for years now. But the more deeply embedded Mark became with these covert operations, the more certain Jill became that eventually she'd need some *uncomfortable* skills. The sort of skills that one hopes they never have to use. She had forced herself to face all the dark possibilities that Mark's life might bring down onto him like an avalanche, and had learned the things she thought might give him the best chance of survival.

What she hadn't quite considered, however, was that she might need those skills to get *herself* out of trouble.

They were moving closer to the screaming man, hidden somewhere in one of the buildings ahead. Jill refused to picture what would be revealed, when they finally got to him. She refused to let Mark's face come into her mind. She refused to imagine what was being done, to make that unnamed, faceless man ahead scream as he was.

The screaming got louder, and louder, until Jill realized they were directly in front of a door that led to the man in question.

And they moved past it.

She was confused. Even though she'd refused to picture Mark being tortured, deep down she'd *known* it was him. That screaming voice, rendered unrecognizable by torture, *had* to belong to Mark. So if Faraz wasn't taking her to see him directly, what was the plan here?

They'll bring him to me, she thought.

That had to be it. Though why they had to move her to a new location for this to happen, she couldn't quite fathom. Not yet.

She looked ahead, redirected her attention to studying Faraz. He moved with confidence, with no hesitation whatsoever. He had something in mind, and knew the way.

They stopped in front of a small building, a bit more substantial than most of the huts and structures she'd seen since arriving.

This village, Jill could see, was far from abandoned. People moved about in the business of their daily lives, here in the desert. They carried water, or other necessities, from structure to structure. They moved at a leisurely pace that said they were not only used to the presence of the *Kharif,* they *supported* them. This village might be small, might be lacking in certain amenities, but it was alive. Functioning. Maybe even *thriving*, by some standards. Unlike many of the small towns and villages that dotted the desert, this one certainly didn't seem to be lacking in food or clean water. It also appeared to be free of any sign of a US military presence, which was right on track as the current administration was pulling back here. Foolish or not, the current POTUS and his people were yanking troops across the Katakstan border, even if it meant leaving some—like Clayborne and Jill and the rest of the staff of the FOB —behind.

Not everyone in Katakstan was against the US military presence here. There were Western allies, for one, who now had to pick up the slack, in a hopeless and ever-growing conflict. But there were also many among the Katakstan people themselves. Some saw the *Kharif* for who and what they were—a violent group of extremists, determined to spill as much blood as possible. A threat to any progress here, to any hope of Katakstan joining the world stage as an equal to the Western powers, instead of as a pawn to be played by powerful people.

Those who supported a Western presence here saw it as intervention.

But many, especially in dusty pocket towns such as Harat, saw it only as *invasion*. And the people here might believe the *Kharif* were responsible for pushing the Americans out, and making this place safe.

It was the perfect hiding place for Faraz and his people, because it was a village *of* his people, Jill realized.

Faraz stood aside as his men brought Jill forward, their rough grips relaxing as she came to stand in front of a rough-hewn wood door. One of the few doorways with such a door, rather than a ratty curtain or a few hastily nailed planks.

"Be my guest," Faraz said, gesturing, indicating she should enter.

Jill nodded. She was playing the game, the best way she knew how. *Cooperation*. Keep the back talk tamped down. *Keep your eyes open and your mouth shut*, she heard one of her teachers telling her. *Do what you're told, until you see an opening. And know... know that you are probably going to die, either way. Use that knowledge to keep sharp, and to do whatever it takes, to maybe get lucky and prove yourself a liar.*

That last bit had sounded morbid, but Jill had come to understand the underlying directive hidden in it.

Know that you're going to die—so be willing to take any risk, any slim chance to live.

Or to put it a different way, *You have nothing to lose, so you might as well try any fool plan that comes along.*

So far, no plans—foolish or otherwise—had presented themselves. But she'd keep watching. Something was bound to come up.

For now, though, she would cooperate and do everything Faraz told her to do. And she'd keep her mouth shut while doing it.

She reached out a hand, trying not to let it shake. She placed her palm on the door, and she pushed.

It swung inward with a bit of creaking protest, but nothing obstructed it. And with the opening wide enough to pass through, she glanced back at Faraz.

He nodded, smiling, encouraging her to continue.

And Jill stepped inside.

And once inside, she stood, still as a stone, able only to blink in confusion.

"Hi Jill," Mark said.

TWENTY-EIGHT

He was seated at a table, in a corner of the room. There was a laptop open in front of him. And as she stood there, trying to make her mouth work, he reached and put his hand on a cane that was leaning against the wall near him. He used this to rise, wincing a bit. And Jill finally saw that his leg was bandaged.

"Mark..." she finally said. She turned just in time to see Faraz close the door behind her. And when she looked back she realized she was alone with her brother.

Her brother, who was *not* being tortured. Her brother, who despite a seeming injury to his leg appeared to be in good shape, even well cared for.

"There's... a lot to explain," Mark said. He gestured to a chair opposite from the one he'd been using. "Have a seat."

She shook her head. "Mark... my God. Did you... are you *working* with these people?"

He huffed, then shook his head. "Like I said, it's a lot to explain. Please, sit. Want something to drink? Are you hungry?"

"What the hell is happening, Mark?"

He studied her for a moment, then hobbled over to a counter mounted to one wall of the hut. There was a small refrigerator under the counter, and he sort of awkwardly stooped, opened it and removed two bottles. He rose, holding both by their necks, in one hand. Two bottles of beer. He smiled in triumph. "You have no idea how rare these are. And illegal, Faraz tells me. I mean, just the fridge is a luxury, in this place. The beer... you can be shot for drinking beer here, did you know that?"

She said nothing. She had nothing to say. She was struggling with confusion, and not a small amount of anger, she had to admit.

Mark hobbled back to the table, and placed both beers down. He reached for an opener, and smoothly cracked the caps one-handed. He dropped back into his seat, obviously relieved to be off his feet again, and he lifted his bottle as if in a toast.

Jill sat. She picked up her bottle. Rather than meet his toast, however, she tilted it back and drained nearly half of it. After her ordeal, the heat and the violence and the fear, the cold beer burned down her throat like a glorious stream of instant relief, and she could feel her body respond to it, relaxing some of the tension that had been building within her.

Unfortunately, the fear and tension was slowly being replaced by a darker mood.

She placed the bottle back on the table. "Mark, what the hell did you do?"

Mark was sipping his own beer, and smiled. He put it on the table, and shook his head. "I did what I was trained to do," he said. "I survived. And I cut a deal. A pretty good one, I think. I mean, I'm not free to leave or anything, but I'm in no danger of having a bullet put in my head. Not at the moment, anyway."

"But you..." Jill found she couldn't quite finish the sentence. She didn't *want* to finish it. But it had to be said and finally the bubbling anger within her forced the words out in cold, hard agates. "You're a *traitor*," she said, her voice dipping, going quiet on those final two fateful syllables.. She felt her stomach clench.

"Only technically," Mark said. "Our government does make some allowances for betrayal under duress."

She glanced around at the room they occupied—the single room of a freestanding building along a dirt street, in the village of Harat. It was far from luxurious, but she imagined that in a village such as this, with such limited resources, it represented great wealth and privilege. She looked back at Mark, who was by all signs healthy, aside from his bandaged leg.

"I know what you're thinking," he said, shaking his head. "I don't *look* like someone under duress. But you're only seeing the end result. I spent weeks being tortured for information. It wasn't until they realized they didn't have to break me that I gained an advantage."

"An... an *advantage?*" Jill said angrily.

He leaned forward slightly, locking eyes with her. "I did what I had to do, to survive," he said. "And to give myself a chance to get out of here. Of course, now that Faraz has *you*, I'm betting my chances are a lot more slim than they were twenty-four hours ago."

"Meaning what, exactly?" Jill asked.

"Meaning that now Faraz has a stick to go along with his carrot. If I try anything, he'll use you to punish me. So... that's a pretty solid way to keep me from trying anything."

Jill was shaking her head. She could hardly believe any of this. "Mark... I thought you might be *dead*. Or worse. I thought they were torturing you." She remembered the screams of the man. "Who was that? Who do they have? Who are they torturing?" *Torturing, while you sit here sipping beer,* she thought.

For once, a dark and haunted expression took over her brother's features.

"He's an American agent," Mark replied. "Someone who..." he hesitated, and Jill could see something in her brother's eyes.

"Mark..." she started.

He shook his head, waved a hand in the air. "I'm doing what I have to do."

She studied him. "What is that, exactly?"

For the first time, the facade cracked and Mark looked pained, even ashamed. She knew him, knew that face and that body language better than anyone else alive. She didn't need him to say a word in order to understand what he'd done, and how he felt about it.

Suddenly he was sixteen again, sitting in a mall security office, facing the real possibility of jail time.

Suddenly he was 18, and there was a girl—the first of many—who hadn't had her period in a while.

Suddenly he was 24, and there was a bookie who was more than a little insistent on being paid for a series of bad bets.

And there she was, again and again, over and over, helping him. Covering for him. *Fixing it* for him.

"I can't fix this one," Jill said, staring in disbelief at her hands on the table. This table, in a hut in some village tucked away in a country that thought women like her deserved to have their genitals mutilated, or worse.

Mark looked up, almost as if he was surprised she was there. He laughed, and shook his head. "Nothing to fix, Jill," he said. "Nothing that *can* be fixed."

"You're working for him," she said. "For Faraz."

"I'm... feeding him select information," Mark said. "Mostly

burned operatives, failed missions. He's after something, Jill. He has the hard drive."

"What hard drive?"

Mark looked briefly startled, and Jill realized that as cool as he'd been playing it when she'd stepped into the room, her brother was rattled. He got it together, quickly, pulled himself back to a place of calm nonchalance. His pose. His "got this together" face. She knew him too well to be fooled.

"I shouldn't have mentioned that. It's still classified."

"You think at this point it makes any difference?" Jill asked. "You're... you're a *traitor*, Mark. You're selling secrets to the enemy."

"I'm doing the *job*," he said, with some acid in his voice. "This is what I was trained to do. Work the enemy from the inside. Use whatever resources I have to stop them from doing what they plan to do."

"And what do they plan to do?" Jill asked.

He shook his head, then seemed to give up on the farce of keeping a secret. "That drive contains plans for a weapon. They've decoded some of it—they built a prototype device from what they could decipher. It's an EM weapon—electromagnetic. The one they built is small scale, highly targeted. But the plans they have on that hard drive could be used to build something *much* bigger. Big enough to... to just *brick* all technology as we know it. And its targeting is broader. No narrow beam. This is... it's worldwide."

"Shut down technology?" Jill asked, shaking her head. She remembered the FOB, the power going down, the communications equipment becoming non-functional. "Mark..."

"Don't you get it?" Mark snapped. He tapped his forehead. "Think about it. These people, they *thrive* here, in a world where war tech is about as advanced as hitting someone in the head with a rock. They're using M16s from the fucking *Soviet* era. That is, until recently, when our own people basically armed them by leaving tons of shit behind." He shook his head, as if *this* idea, not his betrayal, was the truly appalling thing.

"They know how to conduct warfare without the gear" he said. "They know how to survive on next to nothing. How to *thrive* with *nothing*. No food. No water. They *thrive*, Jill. And they know how dependent the West is on all of that technoloy. They know that most of the world—the parts they hate—they can't *exist* without all of this." He motioned to the laptop.

"This thing isn't even online, I can't even Google anything, but it's still the most advanced technology in this village. And without it, I couldn't do the work that Faraz is making me do. He brings me files, things lifted from the CIA assets I burn for him, and I decrypt them. I use my training, and my access, and I open as many files as I can. Faraz uses that information to go find what he's after—more case officers, engineers, caches of weapons and equipment. I'm pretty sure he knows I'm dragging my feet, not giving him quite everything. But as long as what he does get gives him an advantage out there, he lets it slide. Though... that's probably done. Now that you're here."

"Mark, I don't..."

He interrupted. "They have a plan, Jill. They want what's on that hard drive. All of it. With that, they can make the whole *planet* a third-world country. They can drop humanity back into the stone ages, and then march through the land, taking whatever they want. They have operatives everywhere, waiting. They're so much bigger than we think, Jill. There's so many more of them than we ever thought."

"But you're keeping them from getting to the data," Jill said. She was asking more for assurance, more to insure that Mark still had a line he wouldn't cross, a sense of *right* he would still cling to. Some thread of a way out of this. She would use every ounce of influence she had to pull that thread and drag him out of this, if it was possible. But she needed to know he was there.

Mark nodded. "I mean, it's not hard to keep the data limited. I have no idea how to fully crack the encryption on that drive. And so far, none of the assets I've located for Faraz have the key, either. I don't... I don't think any of them could have kept it secret, through what the *Kharif* do to them."

"Torture them," Jill said, her stomach twisting. She wanted to vomit.

"Torture and kill," Mark said. "I don't know how many, so far. They don't tell me anything. They just make sure it all happens close enough that I hear the screams." This last bit was said with a bit of haunted regret in his voice, to Jill's relief.

He's not that far gone, she thought. It was hope, at least.

Then she realized it. She heard—or rather, *didn't* hear—the reality.

There was no screaming. The man she'd passed, behind the walls of some filthy hut, was silent.

She looked at Mark, and he stared back. There was a brief motion, a tiny nod. An acknowledgement, that what she feared was right. That what she suspected was true.

Jill settled back, then downed the rest of the beer. Mark did the same.

She couldn't dwell on it. And so she forced her mind to focus instead of on what all of this meant for *her*, personally, and for her brother.

She was at a loss. Faraz had shown her to Mark, clearly as a means of leverage. She knew what that meant. Faraz *did* know that Mark was holding back. And now, Jill would be the stick, just as Mark had said. Faraz would threaten her, torture her, if Mark didn't step things up.

"You can't give him what he wants," Jill said. "No matter what they do to me."

Mark laughed. "Jill... you're still trying to rescue me. But it's too late. It was too late the minute you set foot in this country. You've been a pawn since the beginning. There's nothing to do now. There's no... there *is* no country now. No US, no Katakstan. There's just Faraz, and what he wants. And anyone who stands between him and what he wants..." He shook his head. There was no need to finish that sentence. Jill knew exactly where it was going. The silence still hanging in the air said it all.

Mark sank back into his chair, and Jill let her attention and gaze wander.

It had finally happened. All these years of looking out for Mark, of taking care of his messes, and finally one of those messes had gotten on Jill herself.

She'd been so concerned, so determined to find and rescue her brother, she'd let herself be manipulated. Right from the start. She was either the tool of the CIA or a tool of the *Kharif*, but nothing else. Nothing more.

Jim, she thought, suddenly.

Jim Ryker was out there. He was on his way here. He had orders to find Mark, to determine if Mark had turned, and to extract Mark from this place. Or, if it turned out Mark was a traitor, to end him. That had been the unspoken thing between them, back at the FOB. She'd known it, even if Jim wouldn't say it out loud. The truth that had remained a quiet reality that Jill hadn't dared to acknowledge.

She instinctively thought about how to convince Jim that Mark was innocent, that he should be spared. That old instinct, back again, even just seconds after finding out what Mark had actually done. Was *still* doing.

She didn't know if Jim would believe her. And it didn't matter.

The more important fact was that Jim was coming. He was out

there, somewhere, and he was coming *here*. She knew that. She knew he would find a way. That was just who he was.

She had to keep that knowledge secret. No matter what they did to her, she had to make sure they didn't know that Jim Ryker was on his way.

Which meant she couldn't tell Mark.

That realization, that she couldn't even trust her brother far enough to offer some kind of *hope*, that was the deepest cut in this. That was the blow that left her stunned, and unsure of who she even was now, in light of Mark's betrayal.

The door to the hut opened and Faraz stood there, looking at the two of them. He motioned, and Jill rose without a word, turning back to her brother. She wanted to say something. Wanted to tell him not to give them what they were after. She wanted to tell him to hold out, that help was coming.

Instead she turned her back on him and followed Faraz out into the darkening streets of the village. Nighttime had come. The only sources of light, as far as she could see in all directions, were flickering flames—lamps, candles, cook fires. Light that required no electricity, no wires.

Mark was right. These people knew what it meant to survive without technology. They would know how to take advantage of the Westerners who blinked and fretted at the loss of electric light, who panicked as their mobile phones and laptops and electric cars ceased to work. Not to mention the chaos and death that would come as life-sustaining electronics shut down—pacemakers and respirators, and all the tech that humanity had adapted to overcome human frailty, to extend life for those who would otherwise die. The emergency broadcasts that would be muted, leaving entire populations in chaos. The satellites that would go dim, preventing these mighty nations from communicating and coordinating. Jill imagined airliners falling from the sky, elevators trapped between floors, train line switches becoming non-functional. All the ways to die, when technology disappeared, were nearly infinite.

Shutting down the technology meant eliminating a large swath of the population without even firing a bullet.

Everything that would follow that EM pulse that would blanket the Earth—it would all be blood and suffering and death. And easy pickings for the *Kharif*.

Jill followed Faraz out into the darkened dirt street to a small hut, with planks of wood nailed together and fastened with rope hinges, to cover the door. And once she was ushered inside another of those planks was dropped across it, and that door was locked tight behind her. She could see through a small window, boarded with rough-hewn timber, that there was at least one guard posted outside the door. There was no other exit, no way out. No back doors or other windows. No way for her to escape. She was here for the duration.

But Jim Ryker was coming.

It was the only hope she had. And as she curled up on a dingy mattress, she prayed silently.

Come here, Jim. Drop onto this place like the wrath of God from above. And do your worst.

TWENTY-NINE

Agent Anonymous sat alone in a large conference room in CIA headquarters, waiting. This was the closest thing he had to an office these days. It would do.

His actual name—the name he currently used, at least—was Michael Malleus. Formerly *Director* Michael Malleus. The surname meant "hammer" in Latin, because in terms of his work with the Company, that's what he was.

The Company's hammer, treating every problem and every crisis like the nail that it was. That was his job with the CIA, for almost four decades. And now he was retired.

Or had been, until the moment the CIA reminded him that retirement wasn't a real thing in their world. Retirement was more like a vacation of indefinite and indeterminate length. So smoke 'em if ya got 'em, eat drink and be merry, and live like there's no tomorrow, because there probably wasn't.

Clichés were how high level CIA folk liked to play at being

clever and jovial at the same time, while letting you know they owned your ass, and shit was alway dire.

Malleus didn't mind. He'd used those clichés to goad other spooks and operatives to do what he told them to do, for years. Turnabout was fair play. He'd been expecting it. And he'd expected that at some point, the Company would need its hammer back. The world was full of nails.

Sitting in the conference room that was serving as his office, Malleus studied the tablet in front of him. A progress report. The FOB had successfully evacuated everyone on site, with a minimum of casualties, and only one capture. That one happened to be Jill Adams, budding superstar and potentially the next freshman Senator.

What a stroke of luck, Malleus smiled. He couldn't have planned it any better.

He'd had nothing at all to do with getting her captured, of course. It really was luck of the draw. Fate. Karma. But if he could have arranged things perfectly, this would have been the way.

Jill Adams was only in-country because Malleus wanted her there. It was the only real way to force Jim Ryker to do what needed to be done. Malleus knew that Ryker would do any job he committed to, even without incentive. It was just the man's noble character. But getting Ryker to *commit* meant putting on some pressure. Jill was that pressure. And that plan had worked—not only motivating Ryker to board a plane and parachute into a hot zone, but to march across enemy-controlled territory and facilitate getting everyone out of the FOB before that drone strike. Jill Adams had turned out to be one hell of a carrot.

Having her in the enemy's hands was a sweet bonus.

It would definitely get Jim Ryker moving, but that wasn't really necessary. Ryker had already started making his way to Harat—which, at this point, Malleus was now convinced was the *Kharif* base of operations. Ryker couldn't have known Jill was there, when he'd started moving. So he was just acting in character, finishing the job because that's what you do when you're an army of one who operates on a code of honor—*God bless America and all her patriotic farm boys.*

Malleus had watched satellite and drone video of both Jill Adams being taken and Jim Ryker doing some truly brutal stuff in the desert, both on their way to the *Kharif* home base. It was like watching the stars align.

The major perk to come from Jill Adams being taken was that Malleus now knew for absolute certain that Faraz and his people were in Harat. There had been numerous prospects for where they were hiding, but once they'd snagged Jill from the helicopter crash site the CIA had been able to track them all the way to the little village deep in the guts of Katakstan. And now that he knew that Harat was the place, it became a target.

In a pinch, if it came to it, Malleus could give an order to raze the whole village to the ground. Harat was so far out in the absolute middle of nowhere, no one would even realize it was gone before the desert sands swept over it and buried it for future archaeologists to dig up. He already had the drones circling the area.

There was really very little to keep Malleus from giving that exact order. It would likely end all their current troubles with the *Kharif,* though that would probably be just a temporary relief. The *Kharif* were not so centralized that a solitary drone strike would rid the world of them all for good. Another faction would simply rise to power, and the game would start all over again. But taking out one of the hydra's heads, taking out Faraz... that would be a serious blow, at least. They'd recover, but it wouldn't be immediate. And it might give them the opening to deal even more damage to the *Kharif.* It could be the first of a series of swift cuts that led, ultimately, to the *Kharif* bleeding out.

The trouble was, it was still uncertain whether Faraz was *actually* in that village, and whether or not he had the hard drive there. It was also unclear if Mark Adams was there, as well. And Malleus very much wanted to hit *all* of those nails.

Adams was selling secrets, Malleus knew. It had become obvious, once operatives started disappearing all over Katakstan, and the forward operating base was surgically dismantled from a distance. And using an EM weapon—even a crappy, weak one with limited range and capabilities—that was certainly no coincidence.

The fact was, as painful and shocking as it would be for the public, burning a few assets and sharing a few strategic secrets might not be as treasonous as it sounded. It might actually be how Adams was working to keep Faraz from getting his hands on the full schematics and designs contained on that hard drive. An acceptable tactic, in a certain light. But it was still safer to put Adams down like a rabid dog rather than let him keep at this game until he ran out of rabbit trails and ended up giving Faraz the whole hare.

It would be even more useful to the Company, as well, to make Adams the face of the FUBAR for this mission, and display his corpse as a show of victory. *We have overcome the snake in our own garden.* Western audiences would eat that up. It would dominate the news cycle for weeks.

So, there were multiple targets in play, in Harat. Faraz, the hard drive, and Mark Adams. Malleus could have a drone strike sent that would send that whole village to hell in minutes.

But he needed *confirmation*.

Resources in the region were limited, with the FOB down. At best, Malleus would have two, maybe three more drone strikes to deploy before US resources were tapped out. After that it would take months to restock and replenish. With the *Kharif* displacing the current Katakstan government, and Westerners getting the boot at all corners, it might take even longer. It might not happen at all.

So any strike would require confirmation.

Jim Ryker would be that confirmation.

He had orders to signal or make contact, to show something to the drones circling practically from orbit. His job was to infiltrate, verify, and make *a very big bang*. Malleus was pretty damned confident that Ryker could do it, too. And at that point, Malleus would give the command and the hammer would come down.

Malleus smiled at that—the pun hadn't been intended, but it might as well have been. This was the job he'd done for the CIA for all those years. He'd lost count of how many villain-of-the-week terrorists he'd put down, over the span of his career. And with every one down, a new one always popped up. The job was never done. Which was fine. Malleus liked this work. Always had.

Of course, there was every chance that Ryker could pull off his assigned mission—the *cover story* mission that Malleus had given him, to help Ryker justify doing the job, to his overblown sense of honor and ethics.

It was possible that Ryker could *actually* retrieve both the hard drive and Mark Adams, and could take down Faraz and deliver a serious blow to the *Kharif*. He could maybe even get the girl out of there alive. Malleus wouldn't put it past him. He had studied Ryker's file and his history. If anyone could be referred to as "a one-man army," it was definitely the man calling himself Jim Ryker.

So, for now, the play was to wait. To watch. To see what Ryker did, and *how* he did. The drones were ready, either way.

"Officer Malleus?"

He looked up to see a younger man, practically an intern, standing in the doorway of the conference room.

"Sir, you wanted to know the instant something changed with the asset."

The asset. The only name that anyone here knew for Ryker, for the moment. Malleus was keeping things close to his vest with that one. It was insulation, for the people above, since Ryker had been heavily implicated in "the bad shit" that went down in Katakstan, a little over a year ago. Bad shit that Malleus happened to know should have been squarely on the shoulders of Mark Adams, not Jim Ryker. But that wasn't the way things happened with the Company. It wasn't always the one who deserved the blame most who got it. Sometimes it was the one who gave everyone else the biggest political advantage. And Mark Adams had a sister on the rise in DC.

"What do we have?" Malleus asked.

"The asset has acquired a vehicle. Three *Kharif* dead. Based on the course he's set, he should arrive at Harat within the hour, if he can avoid a convoy just to his west."

Malleus perked up. "Convoy? What are they carrying?"

"Intelligence says they're moving recovered weapons and equipment from the site around FOB. Salvage, mostly. They're moving toward Harat, pretty slowly. But there's a slight chance they may intercept the asset before he gets there."

Malleus thought about this. Could it be that easy? Could he be that *lucky?*

He opened the laptop, and typed in the key sequence that only he and two other humans on Earth knew.

"Sir?"

Malleus looked up. "That'll be all," he said.

The young man nodded and left. And as he closed the door, Malleus returned his attention to the laptop. He typed in the command, and hit the Enter key like he could physically smash the convoy under his finger.

He practically was.

"Hello nail," he said, grinning. "Looks like I get to drop the hammer after all."

THIRTY

KATAKSTAN DESERT, NIGHT

Ryker rumbled along in the Toyota with nothing but the running lights to illuminate the desert ahead of him. Unsafe, for absolute certain. But he was trying to stay invisible, to avoid being seen by the string of trucks and other heavy machinery off to his west.

He'd spotted them about ten minutes ago, and saw that inevitably he was going to cross their path. They were slow, but still moving at a speed greater than he could pull off in the little Toyota —which was doing a fine enough job moving along in the deep sand of the Katakstan Desert, but not so great that he could match the speed of a bunch of trucks with huge, turf-grabbing tires. He was just barely ahead of them on his route to Harat, but that lead wasn't going to last long.

He was weighing his options, and calculating how screwed he was.

He couldn't see much more of the convoy than their headlights, but by his count there were at least ten large vehicles and half a dozen small ones. It was a pretty safe bet that each had a fair number of well-armed *Kharif* onboard.

So his conundrum was two-fold: If they spotted him, they might investigate closer, discover the American in *Kharif* clothing, and then turn him into a fine mist of blood and ground meat spread across the desert sands; or alternatively, they could roll on past him and arrive at Harat, fortifying it with even more men and weapons, and his delay to let them pass could put him arriving in broad daylight. Again... a fine mist of blood and ground meat seemed a likely outcome.

Ryker had resolved himself to the idea that he was marching headlong into a town full of armed and eager *Kharif* soldiers anyway. That was always going to be his night. But this convoy pulling into town just ahead of his arrival was going to stir the ant pile.

Even if it was still night when he got there, rather than coming upon a sleepy, mostly unsuspecting village that he might stand some chance of sneaking into unnoticed, he was going to arrive at essentially a lively military base full of amped up, wide-awake men with guns in hand and the aroma of victory pouring off of them, exciting everyone they encountered. They would get the *Kharif* in town all riled up, in other words, and they'd be adding to their numbers besides. That was going to nix any chance Ryker had of getting in without being seen, and severely reduce the chances of getting out without being shot.

He toyed with pulling over and waiting, anyway. He could maybe let them get there, let the festivities play out, and go in once the excitement died down.

But that was a terrible plan. For a start, Ryker suspected that this convoy was rolling into Harat from the FOB, loaded down with the spoils of battle. Taking down the American base was a *big* victory. Celebrations of that magnitude could go on for *days*, and there was simply nowhere for Ryker to hide out safely, long enough to wait it out.

He suspected a sandwich-sized wrap of mutton and a cooler one-quarter full of dirty water wasn't going to get him through several days of hiding. He would need to find provisions. That meant taking risks that could get him caught, putting himself and the mission in jeopardy.

Putting *Jill* in jeopardy.

All the options were bad. But waiting was the worst.

So he would have to push on. He'd have to just try to beat the convoy to town, to get in and get hidden before they got there. If he was going to hide out, his chances might be better if he was already behind enemy lines.

Which was dumb, of course. The truth was, he was screwed here, there, and everywhere. His best chance at this would come only if that convoy was halted, or redirected, or, God willing...

There was a sudden series of screeches in the air, followed immediately by a punch to his senses, as the Katakstan night was lit by dozens of fiery explosions. The landscape went from pitch black to hell on Earth in a blink, and even all these miles away and inside the cab of the Toyota his ears were assaulted by the noise of it all.

Ryker slammed on the brakes, put the Toyota in park, and stepped out to watch. From this distance, he could see the trucks scattering. Some had been hit by whatever had flown over—Ryker suspected it was another drone strike, just like the one that had opened a path for everyone to escape back at the FOB.

The remaining trucks, about three of them, were scurrying in different directions.

Another series of screeches filled the night, followed by more bombs, more noise, more explosions.

No doubt, now. This was definitely a drone strike. Ryker cheered and hooted, and pumped a fist as he looked up into the night sky. He couldn't see the drones. But just knowing they were there was giving him a hell of a rush. Ever since Agent Anonymous had snagged Ryker from Avery's farm, it had felt like Ryker was on his own. Knowing he had an ally looking down on him—whoever the hell it might be—was comforting.

He wasn't fooled, of course. That strike wasn't entirely about saving his ass. It was a strategic hit, taking out a convoy that could put some lead back in the pencil of the *Kharif*. Taking it out was just something that had to be done. Ryker just happened to benefit from it.

But he'd take any angels he could get, even if they couldn't care less about him.

He leapt back into the Toyota, slammed it into gear, and raced forward, popping the headlights back on as he went. There was no need to hide now. Not for the moment, anyway.

The convoy—what was left of it—was still far enough from Harat that it was unlikely anyone heard or saw that attack, but there was no way to know if anyone from the convoy had gotten word back by radio. There might be reinforcements coming any minute.

Or not, he realized.

After all, the damage was done. And, as Ryker thought about it, Faraz might not want to tip his hand and reveal his location, especially now that he knew there were drones in the area. It would be better to cut his losses and leave the convoy to smolder, unavenged, than to send help and risk confirming his location to those eyes in the sky.

That has to sting, Ryker thought. He didn't know Faraz personally, but he had the sense that the man thought of himself as a master tactician. And indeed, a lot of what he'd pulled off with the onslaught on the FOB showed that he really was pretty brilliant. He knew when to throw a punch, and when to pull back and put his guard up.

Right now, it was safer to keep the lights out and the city gates closed, and accept the black eye without even complaining about it.

Ryker bounced along now, smiling. It was going to be safe travels over the remaining klicks between him and Harat. Faraz would probably even pull back all of his patrols, get everyone into the town, and go dark.

For sure, they'd be armed and waiting, on the lookout for another drone strike. But they'd be looking for the US military. They'd be watching for an envoy of armed vehicles barreling down on them, or drones bearing down from above. They'd be waiting for an army.

But they were getting Jim Ryker instead.

THIRTY-ONE

Jill heard the commotion from the streets of Harat, and got up to peek out through the sliver between the rough boards covering her window. It was pitch black in the hut, and not much brighter outside, but she could see the guard still there at his post. She couldn't quite see any activity on the streets, but she heard the shouting.

She wished she'd pushed herself to learn the language here. She only knew a few basic phrases and words. She did recognize the *Pashto* word for "explosion," and "dead." It wasn't much, but it painted a bleak picture.

She dropped back onto the dingy mattress, sitting with her back pressed against the wall and her knees pulled up before her. She pressed her face into her knees and rocked gently.

She was in trouble. Mark was in trouble. And there was clearly trouble brewing outside.

She looked up, suddenly.

Could it be Jim?

That filled her with some hope, and it shook her out of the fear that had her sitting here feeling helpless and sorry for herself.

If Jim was on his way, then there was a chance they could get out of this. She could use that kind of hope right now. And maybe, *maybe*, she could find some way to use this energy to actually *help*.

But what could she do?

She got up and started moving around the room. It wasn't much. There was just the one door and the one window. The walls seemed to be stucco over bricks. She remembered from some of her cultural classes that most homes in the region were indeed made from mud brick, patted and shaped by hand and baked to hardness in the brutal sun.

Tough and durable.

But also brittle.

She glanced back at the door, then started her search again. This time she was looking for a spot, the perfect place to do her work. She was also looking for anything she could use as a tool.

In a corner of the room was a small, square cabinet. It was flat on top, and mounted to the wall in the corner. She pulled aside a small curtain of fabric on its front to reveal a barren and empty space inside. She knelt and squinted in the darkness. The back of the cabinet was open to the bare wall. Some of the stucco had flaked away to reveal the mud bricks beneath.

Ok, good start, she thought. *I can Shawshank my way out through here.*

She could work on the wall inside the cabinet without the results being immediately visible. Just cover the opening with the curtain. It was no Rita Hayworth poster, but it would keep her work hidden. If she didn't do anything to call attention to it, chances were good that no one would bother even looking in there.

Now she needed a tool. A spoon, a stick, a shoe heel... *anything.*

There was nothing in the cabinet itself, and the floors and walls were all bare. Aside from the dirty mattress, there was no furniture in the place. It was a barren cell.

She wondered idly what she'd have to do to get the luxury accommodations her brother had managed to pull off. But she shook this thought away. She couldn't bear to think about her brother right now.

She and Mark—there was a problem there. It ran deep. But this wasn't the time to dig into it.

She stood and wandered back to the window again. The boards had been nailed over it from the outside, but she could reach a hand out and touch them. There was no glass to block her.

She pulled her hand away sharply as she felt a stab of pain her finger.

In the anemic slant of light coming in from the slit between the boards, she could see a black splinter lodged in the skin of her middle finger. She worked this out, and sucked on her finger, thinking.

She leaned closer to the boards. Outside, the guard was distracted by the noise in the streets. He had stepped out a couple of feet. No chance for her to make a break for it, even if she could somehow bust through the door. But his attention was on something else, at least.

She inspected the boards over the window, and saw that they were rough hewn, with plenty of jagged splits. She reached out again, and this time found a large, splintered wedge. She was able to push her fingertips under it, and a gap opened up. She looked at the guard again, and held her breath. Then she started pulling at the shard of wood.

It creaked and groaned, but the guard didn't seem to notice. The rising noise in the streets was masking the sound of the splintering wood.

She pulled a bit more, and there was a loud crack, which did get the guard's attention.

He turned, and she froze. He tilted his head slightly, then turned his gaze upward, inspecting the roof line. After a moment, he turned back around.

Jill waited a beat, then pulled again. The sound this time was muted enough that the noise from the street was overwhelming it. Or more to the point, as Jill worked, she noticed that the noise outside was getting *louder*.

People came jogging down the street, shouting in *Pashto*, wielding guns above their heads like spears. The guard waved and shouted and conversed with some of them as they jogged by.

Jill didn't waste the opportunity. She gave the splinter of wood a yank, and it cracked as it broke backward, then came free in her hand. She once again held her breath, watching and waiting, but the guard made no sign that he'd heard her.

She quickly shoved the rough wedge of wood into her back pocket and retreated to the mattress, just in case. She waited, listening to the raucous noise from outside. It passed after a moment, fading somewhat as it continued on down the street.

Jill stayed in her spot for several minutes, silent and unmoving, until it was clear that the guard hadn't heard anything, and wasn't coming inside.

She moved then to the little counter. She pulled aside the curtain, and started digging away at the mud bricks inside. She was pleased to see how easily they crumbled away in tiny rivers of dust, each scrape of the wedge creating a thin divot in the brick.

This wasn't going to be quick, she realized. The bricks might be dry and brittle, but they were dense and tough by design. Progress would be slow.

But there would be progress.

She would have to be careful. The dust from the bricks wasn't a problem, with the floors of the hut being dirt themselves. But at any hint that someone was coming into the hut, she would have to close the curtain and try to get back to the mattress, without seeming suspicious.

She glanced at the mattress, on the far wall. It wasn't more than a meter away, but it was still too far. The room was tiny and she could cover the gap in just a couple of quick steps, but there was still too great a distance for her to risk it.

She stood, closed the curtain, and went to the mattress. She grasped its edge and pulled, and it slid along easy enough. Soon she had it on the wall next to the small counter.

Would they notice? Would they realize she'd moved it? And if so, would that make them wonder enough to go investigating?

Maybe. It was a risk. But this way she could have the curtain closed and be curled up on the mattress in seconds, before the door was unlocked and opened. She could take that gamble. It was as close to a sure bet as she was likely to get, anyway.

With that settled she again opened the curtain and got to work. Sliver by sliver she went about the business of scraping an opening in the wall, to wherever it might lead. Even the destination was kind of a dice roll. But that didn't matter.

If Jim was on his way, if it was him causing the ruckus outside, she at least intended to *do* something. She intended to up the odds, and help in her own rescue, in any way she could.

THIRTY-TWO

Faraz stepped out into the street in a near rage, but calmed himself. He turned to the men who served as his hands, and said to them in a quiet but stern voice, "Get this under control."

The blood of the *Kharif* was running hot tonight. They were riled up over the drone strike that had robbed them of the scavenged supplies and weapons carried by the convoy. They saw it as an affront, a slap to the face after the victory God had given them over the Americans, and the destruction of their base.

Fools, Faraz thought. As if they were *entitled* to those spoils. But didn't they see that if God had wanted them to have the base, to have the weapons, to have the people who had been hiding in that place, all would have been delivered to them?

Instead, all was *taken*. All was *kept* from them, and the only one who could do that... it was not the US military. It was the hand of God.

What they needed now was to go silent. To wait.

Faraz blamed himself for the current riot in the streets. He should have ensured that the message from the convoy was kept quiet. There had been only a small number of men in the room with him, when the radio had come alive with the sounds of *Kharif* frantically shouting, in some cases screaming, accompanied by the booms and static that came from bombs dropping on top of them. Drones, they had said. US drones, just like those that had swept through the *Kharif* surrounding the US base.

The drones gave the Americans an air advantage that was difficult to overcome. But Faraz was close to a solution. All he had to do was *push*.

It was time.

He barked orders to his men, told them to get the town quieted within the hour. Told them to use force, if necessary, but all of Harat would be *silent* and *dark* within the hour, or it would be in flames. If not from the American drones, then by Faraz's own hand.

They'd gotten lucky, in a way—perhaps blessed was a better way to frame it. If that convoy had made it to Harat, it might have served as confirmation of where the *Kharif* were hiding. And that drone strike might have been here, in these streets, instead of out in the distance. God had blessed them, sacrificing a few of the *Kharif* to preserve the many. Losing the spoils of their battle was a cheap price for that sort of miracle.

If all of this unusual activity and commotion in the streets kept up, however, it could *still* be confirmation that the *Kharif* were here in Harat. The Americans could be watching, looking for anything unusual. And a riot of armed men in the streets of a sleepy village deep in the heart of Katakstan, waving torches and firing weapons in the air in the middle of the night for no obvious reason, that could be signal enough.

Faraz left the men to settle things, and marched through the chaotic streets on his own. He needed to see the American, Mark Adams. It was time. It was well past time, in fact.

He nodded to the guard posted at the American's door and pushed his way inside. There was no lock. The American wasn't likely to leave, or even attempt to do so. The guard would shoot him in the attempt, at any rate. But Faraz knew that Mark Adams wouldn't try anything.

He had come to know this man better than perhaps Mark Adams himself even realized.

He knew, for example, that Adams was holding back. He was giving Faraz good leads, revealing the whereabouts of many American spies and resources within the Katakstan borders. So far, every one of those leads had panned out with a prize.

But Faraz wasn't fooled. He knew he was getting low-hanging fruit. These were CIA and US government assets who were mostly burned already, or resources that were abandoned or no longer critical to the Americans. Faraz could see the hints of greater intelligence to be won, bigger prizes to be captured.

He had let Adams continue to play the game. Because though it was a play for time, the longer it went on the more mired and entangled Mark Adams became.

It was a bit like *Kali Eskrima*.

Faraz had been fascinated to learn about the martial arts styles of various cultures, during his time studying in the West. He would lay no claim to having mastered any given hand-to-hand skill, though he was proficient in several forms. But knife fighting was one that particularly interested him, because nearly every culture on Earth had some form of it. The weapon itself was ubiquitous, and even easy enough to improvise from scrap materials or even sharp stones or shards of glass, in a pinch.

Kali Eskrima was the fighting style of the Philippines. It was a close-up fighting style, using a variety of readily available, even improvised weapons. But the deadliest and most cunning methods were the Filipino knife fighting techniques.

What fascinated Faraz about the Filipino style was the strategy of making quick feints, and taking tiny nicks with the blade. A flick of the wrist and a quick, tiny cut was more or less the objective. And because of this, the fights could be drawn out, stretching for several minutes rather than being quick and brutally ended. The energy was paced, rather than frenetic. The fighter could conserve energy by simply evading and moving while making even the smallest strike on his enemy.

A tiny cut, a minuscule amount of blood. On its own, practically nothing, equivalent to perhaps a paper cut, a nick while shaving. But as combat continued, and one received more and more of these tiny cuts, the amount of blood lost would soon add up and overpower them.

"Death by a thousand cuts" was the phrase. And the fighter, who started off strong and vigorous, would find himself growing more and more weary with the loss of blood, until he became weakened to the point where he was easily overcome and defeated.

A war of attrition. And by the time the fighter realized what was happening, it was already too late.

This was how Faraz thought of the American operative and his work. The assets that Mark Adams was exposing were mostly insignificant. They were tiny pieces on the board, losses that the Americans were prepared to part with. And Adams could not be blamed for turning them over, out of duress. It was likely his people would see that he was doing his best to buy time, to keep the *Kharif* from cracking the encryption on the hard drive and retrieving the full designs for one of the most potent weapons on the planet.

But with every nick and cut, Adams was bleeding just that much more. Everyone else he burned, every asset he turned over, it was stacking up. And at some point, if it had not happened already, Mark Adams would find that he was too weak, too powerless, too entangled—that his fate was sealed.

At that point he would go from *pretending* to work for the *Kharif* to simply being one of them.

Faraz stood in the doorway of the hut, looking in at the unabashed luxury of the place. It was true that this would barely be considered livable by most Western standards. But here, deep within the borders of Katakstan, a place such as this was a mark of high wealth and privilege. Just the fact that it had electricity made it enviable to the rest of the village.

This had once been the home of the mayor of this village—a man who had opposed the *Kharif,* when Faraz and his people had first arrived. And thus, he had been removed. His blood had long ago soaked into the sands of the desert. His flesh fed the animals and insects, returning his life force to the world so that it could be put to better use.

It made Faraz sick to think of the American living so well while the people of this village continued to light their homes with sheep dung or candles made of rancid animal fat, and carry water here from miles away, in containers made from goat bladders. The people here lived hard lives, while this American "slummed it" at their expense.

But this had been part of the plan. A small cut, as it were. Putting Adams up in this place may have felt like a reward to him, but for Faraz it was nearly the flick of a blade, a tiny cut that the American hadn't even noticed. A trickle of blood.

And every asset that Adams handed over, every resource he provided Faraz with, was another. And another. And another.

"I trust you had an enjoyable reunion with your sister," Faraz said. His voice was pleasant, but hard. He smiled, but there was malice in it.

Mark Adams had been sitting before the laptop, as he often was. He said nothing, but nodded.

"You have enjoyed a great deal of our hospitality," Faraz said. "But I think that ends tonight."

Adams again said nothing.

"You are unusually quiet, Mark," Faraz said, peering. "Perhaps you've already worked out that the game is over."

"I have," Adams said. "I won't be able to keep delaying. Not now, with you having Jill here."

Faraz was impressed by the man's honesty and willingness to accept his circumstances. He nodded. "I'm glad you see the reality of your situation. And what does that mean for you? What do you intend to do, now that things have changed?"

In answer, Mark turned the laptop around, and leaned back against he wall. He said nothing, but watched Faraz's face.

Faraz shook his head once, then bent to examine the contents of the laptop. His eyes widened as he looked up.

"Unlocked," Adams said. "All of it. Well... *almost* all of it. There's one file remaining. And I know the code to open it. I also know that a wrong code, *any* wrong code, will delete it and wipe the drive clean."

Faraz straightened and laughed. "Oh, well done. You're going to make a final play. A... what do Americans call it? A Hail Mary?"

"Something like that."

Faraz shook his head. "You should know, I'll never release your sister. Or you. If you delete the files I'll simply kill her in the slowest possible way, and I'll have you sitting there watching. You won't be able to help it, because I will have your eyelids and your tongue removed, along with your arms and legs. You will die only when I have them remove the feeding tubes and leave you in the desert to roast in the heat of the sun and sands, as you slowly dehydrate. If God has mercy on you, perhaps some creature of the desert will make a meal of you right away." Faraz said all of this as pleasantly as if he were discussing the weather.

"Very graphic," Adams said, nodding. "But unnecessary. I'm not an idiot. I couldn't leave here if I wanted to. I've given you too much. My people would see me as a traitor by now. No way around it. Whether I like it or not, I'm one of you now. But to be honest with you, Faraz... I'm fine with it. I think I could thrive here. If you give me a chance."

Faraz laughed. "Well, that's an interesting proposition. But of course, I could never trust you. How could I? As you say, you're a traitor."

Adams shrugged. "Trust has to be earned. I'm prepared to do that."

"How, exactly?"

Adams leaned forward and turned the laptop around. He tapped at the keyboard, and with a decisive punch of the Enter key he turned the screen once more so that Faraz could see.

"Unlocked. All of it. You have your designs."

Faraz gave another quick shake of his head, not quite believing. Not sure what game the American was playing. But as he inspected the data, he could see that everything was there. He was no engineer, but he understood the schematics and plans well enough to see that they were complete.

He looked up at Adams, who was again watching him.

"You've given away your hand," Faraz said.

Adams nodded. "That's right."

"Do you think I'll be so grateful that I'll just let you live? That I'll be so impressed by this sudden 'loyalty' that I'll make you one of my inner circle?"

"I figure there's even odds you'll kill me and Jill, now that you don't need me anymore. But my hope is that you'll see this for what it is."

"Surrender?"

"A first step."

"To what?" Faraz asked. He had to admit, he had become intrigued.

"The weapon, this EM device, it can level the playing field worldwide. You can selectively target and knock out technology for any enemy you face. But just because you have the world's biggest hammer doesn't mean you can just go striking any old nail. You need a strategy. And I know, you're smart. You've studied the West, and you know our strengths and weaknesses. But I have something you don't have."

"And what's that?"

"Something to prove," Adams replied. "Well, I mean, *that* and knowledge of some of the most sensitive targets for most of the world powers out there. I also know people. Some of them are a little *fluid* when it comes to ethics and loyalties. If you can make sure they get paid enough, though, they'll make sure you get everything you need. A lot of them are not all that fond of the US or its allies."

"You would help the *Kharif* take down your own homeland," Faraz said, skeptical but intrigued.

"I would help the *Kharif* burn the US to the ground if it meant that my sister and I were safe and... taken care of."

"I see," Faraz said. After a moment he nodded. "Very interesting."

"Interesting enough that I keep my eyelids and tongue?" Adams asked.

Faraz smiled tolerantly. "For now." He reached out and closed the laptop, picking it up from the table. "You seem comfortable enough with what this will do to your status among your countrymen. Have you considered what it will mean to your sister?"

"She's... not going to like it."

Faraz chuckled. "American, you are certainly not boring." He held up the laptop. "My people will inspect this. If it is as you say, then perhaps I'll consider your proposal."

He turned, leaving the room of electric light, stepping back out into the darkness of an ancient world. A world that he and his people understood, and could thrive in. A world that he might just be able to introduce to those of the West, sooner than he had anticipated.

The American was playing another game, Faraz knew. But he also knew that this game was about his continued survival. His, and his sister's.

He could never be trusted, on his own. But the message was clear.

You can trust me as long as you keep my sister safe.

Faraz shook his head. No. That wasn't it. The message wasn't about trust. There would *never* be trust.

But there could be control.

The American was giving Faraz a leash. He was telling Faraz how he could continue to control and use Mark Adams, to get the most out of him.

Well played, American, Faraz thought. *I'll take you up on it. I'll put you to work.*

The chaos of the night was already dying down as Faraz walked back to his temporary quarters. He would hand the laptop to his people, have them duplicate its contents and get to work. They already had the prototype weapon. That should serve as a starting point. Their progress should be rapid. And then... soon.

Soon, they would have the power to cast the world into darkness, where they would rise as God's vengeful light.

THIRTY-THREE

Ryker ditched the Toyota on the other side of a rise of hills that bordered Harat. He'd gone back to running without headlights for several miles before that, and had found a good spot to hide the truck, in a gap in the hills. It wouldn't keep anyone from spotting it if they happened to pass by in the daylight, but it was off the beaten path at least.

Now, having picked his way into the darkened hills, moving carefully to avoid stumbling and falling to a painful death on the crags of stone below, he sat on a protrusion of rock on a hillside overlooking Harat.

It was a fairly standard Katakstan village—small, short on modern amenities, unpaved roads and mud-brick huts. There were flicking lanterns and torches lighting both streets and homes. And like most small villages and towns in Katakstan, the streets were empty once night fell.

Mostly empty, in the case of Harat.

Ryker had arrived in time to see the riots being dispersed. Some of the rowdier folk had to be taught some manners by *Kharif* wielding the stocks of rifles like war hammers. Even from this distance, Ryker could see that a few of these nudges got out of hand. Bodies had fallen and remained in place as the crowds slowly broke apart and drifted back to their homes or wherever they were supposed to be.

He gave it about an hour, watching through a pair of binoculars and studying the patterns of movement as the activity in the streets winnowed down to just a handful of armed guards, marching through the mostly-darkness of Harat with rifles ready. They were slow but meticulous. Ryker was counting guards and mapping routes, and above all he was making note of what was and was not important to the *Kharif*.

The guards tended to keep to certain streets. And they more or less avoided the residential areas. Except for a few small buildings on the Eastern edge of town.

In fact, most of one whole block was very obviously occupied by the *Kharif*, with armed men coming and going at irregular intervals.

Which meant that it must be their HQ here in the village.

Ryker focused his attention on that area, counting off guards and looking for weak spots. It took a bit to figure out where the main base was located, in a series of small, low-slung buildings at the center of the block. That had to be where Faraz and his core team were quartered.

But what was with the two buildings down the block?

One of them clearly had electricity. A steady, warm light could be seen shining through the curtain-covered windows, rather than the flickering of candle light. It was almost obscene in its luxury and wastefulness, compared to the rest of the village.

Someone of great import was in there, Ryker reckoned. Though he doubted that it would be Faraz, or any of the *Kharif*. They would want to appear humble, to avoid seeming to think of themselves as above the villagers who were caring for them and keeping them hidden.

So, not the *Kharif*.

Instead, it would be the most likely place to find his old friend Mark Adams.

And it was a sign. If Mark was living it up in this place, he was paying for it in the shekels of betrayal. Agent Anonymous had been right after all.

That made Ryker sick to his stomach, knowing what it was he'd have to do next. Because despite everything, despite what Mark had done over a year ago, despite how Ryker had taken the blame and suffered because of it... well... Mark *was* Ryker's friend. He was one of Ryker's team. And, above all else, he was Jill's brother.

Jill.

Ryker swept the binoculars back over the street and peered at the second guarded hut. This one wasn't quite as luxurious. In fact, it was as dark as a tomb. That had to be where they were keeping Jill. They would want her away from her brother, so that both would have to wonder and worry about the other. They wouldn't want to torture her, fortunately. Not yet. They would keep her locked up and miserable, to try to break her spirit and make her cooperative without having to waste any energy on her. First the scary stuff, *then* they might try enticing her the way they had Mark. Give her some food, some amenities. A clean bed, some candles for the darkness. And when she was allowed to see her brother, it would only be so that he'd know she was safe, so he'd stay in line.

Then, every now and then, they'd beat her mercilessly and let Mark look at her bloodied and bruised face. As a reminder. As a slight yanking of Mark's leash.

The thought of them hurting Jill was even more gut twisting than the thought of what he was going to have to do to Mark.

He settled back against the rock and dug the wrap of mutton out of his bag. He ate, forcing himself to chew slowly and thoroughly. He drank from his canteen, to wash it down. And he fished in his pocket and retrieved a piece of hard candy—he'd been saving it for the past couple of days. He pulled the wrapper off of it, and popped it into his mouth. The flavor wasn't one he was familiar with, but it was sweet and tart at the same time. He sucked it as he smoothed and flattened the plastic wrapper, tucking that into his shirt pocket.

He sat there for a few minutes, letting the food settle and getting himself centered and calm.

His trek across the desert—twice now—had been all about instinct and training. It had come down to pushing himself and playing the odds. Luck had definitely given him a couple of wins.

But what came next was going to take more than instinct or luck. He had to be clear-headed. He had to have a plan.

He took out his hand drawn map and the pen. In the pale moonlight he could just make out the lines he'd scribbled, representing the region. He turned the map over, rested it on his knee, and drew a rough rectangle to represent Harat. He sketched in the grid of streets and buildings. He then made notations for all of the guards he'd observed, with dashed lines representing their routes. He noted where he believed Faraz was, as well as Mark and Jill.

He considered what he was seeing and what he knew. His objectives were pretty clear.

First, he had to get to Mark. He had to find out what his old friend had shared. How much he'd given the *Kharif*. And he had to deal with him, as appropriate.

Then he had to retrieve the hard drive, or otherwise destroy anything the *Kharif* had managed to unlock. That meant hunting down the prototype EM weapon they'd used on the FOB, and making that a special kind of non-functional. With fire, probably.

He had to kill Faraz, of course. That was a given. It might even have been number one on the list, but it ensured the bad guys didn't get their hands on those plans was the ultimate priority.

And then there was the fourth objective—he had to find and rescue Jill. She was going to be tough to handle, when he told her that her brother wasn't coming. She might resist. He might have to tell her the truth. Things could get messy.

Which was exactly why he should definitely take that objective *last*. She was currently under guard, tucked away and essentially safe. He'd leave her there, and try to take out the first three objectives as quietly as possible, then circle back for her on his way out of Harat. That was the best plan.

The last of the candy dissolved on his tongue, and he washed back another bit of water. He stood and folded and stored the map, along with the pen. He checked his M16, and felt the multiple magazines in various pockets. He patted the .45 tucked into his waistband—backup, if he needed it. And finally he checked his knife, which would be the preferred method for killing, once he was down there.

He was as ready as any one man could be, when that man was about to stalk right into an enemy-controlled town all alone, with no backup and no real plans for escape.

That was the bit he kept trying to keep out of his mind.

It was the reason he would rescue Jill last, when it came down to it.

He knew—had known all along—that he wasn't really *meant* to escape this place. He was meant to fail at his objectives. All except the one where he sent a signal that could be seen by drone or satellite, to confirm that Faraz and the *Kharif* were holed up here.

That was the real mission. The one that Ryker suspected was the only one Agent Anonymous really cared about.

It was the drone strike out in the desert that had sealed it. Agent

Anonymous had sent Ryker here mostly as confirmation, to give them the green light they needed to light this place up. They wanted to be sure that Faraz was here, that the weapon was here, that the hard drive and Mark were both here.

The plan, Ryker knew, was to turn Harat into a smoldering pit in the desert, and take the *Kharif* out with one strike. And if Ryker and the Adams siblings were taken out with the bad guys, that was just "acceptable losses."

That was the plan.

But Ryker was the *backup* plan.

And he intended to make things go another way.

THIRTY-FOUR

STREETS OF HARAT

Getting into Harat wasn't as challenging as Ryker had worried it would be. It wasn't a piece of cake, either, but he managed to do it without alerting anyone to his presence. Or killing anyone.

So far.

Coming in by foot, along the ridge line of the hills surrounding the town, had allowed him to stay stealthy. He had been on alert for any signs of *Kharif* on patrol in these hills, and he was not disappointed. Twice he had to lay low and wait as a patrol passed, and once they were gone he sprinted to make up the time.

He was on the clock now. Dawn was only about five hours away, and he didn't like his odds once the sun came up and people started moving into their day. Right now he had the advantage of darkness and mostly empty streets, and he needed to push that advantage as much as possible. He'd have no hope of blending in, as a white-skinned stranger among the villagers. So if he couldn't get this done by daylight, things would get nasty.

As he came down out of the hills he found that there were several opportunities to get into the town proper, without being seen. He ducked down an alley between two of the mud brick huts along the outer edge of town, and stayed to the shadows as he moved.

Up ahead, not far from his current location, was the street with the two guarded huts. One of which, Ryker was certain, held Mark Adams. The other, he suspected, held Jill.

It was taking everything in him to avoid going straight to her. But he had his objectives.

The priority was Mark. Not out of any sense of loyalty to the guy. As far as Ryker was concerned, by this point in their relationship Mark could rot. He'd taken enough bad turns that Ryker felt his character was pretty clear. He couldn't be trusted. He would his betray his country, betray anyone and anything out of a sense of self preservation.

That might even include Jill, Ryker thought. Though he doubted it. Jill was Mark's safety net. His mother figure, really, given that their mother was long gone. If Mark had any loyalty in him, surely it would be for Jill.

Ryker just wasn't willing to count on it.

So Mark was the priority, but only because he was the richest source of intel. Ryker could press him for information about the *Kharif,* and about Faraz. But more importantly, Mark would know the status of the hard drive and its data, and how close the *Kharif* were to having their hands on the full designs for the EM weapon.

The best bet for finding Mark, in Ryker's mind, was the hut with electricity. There were two guards in front of it—or there were, when Ryker was doing surveillance. And if Ryker moved along the street he was currently on, he could come around behind the building. He'd have to avoid one of the patrols, but at this point they should be nearly a block over. He had a window.

He kept himself pressed against the buildings as he moved, sticking to the shadows. That wasn't difficult, considering that there were no streetlights or even lamps lit in this part of town. Shadows were there in abundance.

As he approached his map point, he slowed, scanned the streets around him, looked for any signs of guards he might have missed. He was holding the M16, ready to fire, but trying to avoid it as much as possible. Even a single shot would be enough to put the whole village on alert, and he'd have *Kharif* swarming the streets.

He pulled his knife, holding it in his left hand against the hand guard of the M16. He moved then, slowly, quietly, until he could peer around the edge of the building.

Light still shone from inside, shining through a set of curtains and casting a warm, waving pattern onto the dirt street. Ryker could see a guard leaning with his back against the wall, on the other side of the door from where Ryker was standing.

One guard.

Where was the second?

Ryker looked both ways down the street, but saw no one. There was no sign of the second guard anywhere.

This was bad.

He could easily take out the guard who was still standing there. The guy wasn't paying attention, and might even be sleeping standing up. In a sense, it was kind of a blessing. Dealing with two armed men without anyone firing a shot was always going to be a challenge.

Ironically, having to deal with just the one guard was much more of a problem. If the second guard was nearby, if he heard a scuffle, he might start shooting, never giving Ryker the chance to close the gap between them and take him out. The noise would definitely alert everyone in town. But worse, there was a better than good chance that Ryker would be dead anyway.

Still, Ryker's training was to deal with what was right here, right now. He couldn't see the second guard, so he couldn't plan for him. He also couldn't just stay still and do nothing. He had a window here, and he needed to act.

He slung the M16 over his shoulder, tightening the strap so that it wouldn't bounce as he moved. He kept his grip on the knife in his left hand. He could use his right hand—his dominant hand—to fight, grip, even position his enemy so that his left hand could strike.

Silently, sticking to the shadows, he slid around the edge of the building. The guard didn't move, hadn't noticed him. Ryker was close enough that he could smell the guy. And with a quick step and turn he reached the guard, shoved his right hand into the guy's mouth, and stabbed him in the throat.

He held him there for a long moment, the man's eyes wide and catching what little light came from the street. His hands spasmed outward, grasping, trying to shove Ryker away.

Ryker had him firmly under control, he wasn't moving, and eventually he wasn't even fighting. Finally he died, standing there, his hands going limp and dropping to his sides.

Ryker let him slide down to the ground, and then he turned, looking for any sign of the second guard. No one. Not yet.

Ryker dragged the first guard around the corner and dumped him in the shadows of the ally. No last rites ritual, this time. He couldn't afford the sentimentality. Instead, Ryker had to make a decision.

He had access to the hut where he suspected Mark Adams was being held. He could get in there with no trouble. But the second guard...

He wasn't sure what he'd find inside, and whether Mark would even be cooperative. And with that second guard floating around, it would be too big of a risk to slip inside. Coming out would make him vulnerable to attack.

So there was nothing for it. He had to find that guard.

Leaving the first guard in a heap, Ryker once again started sliding along the walls of the nearby buildings, keeping an eye on the street. He crept along until he was a full block away, then turned and started back in the opposite direction.

He passed the hut once again, and kept going until, finally, he spotted the guard. The guy was chatting with another *Kharif*, the one patrolling the street in this part of the village.

Ryker cursed silently. He had no doubt he could take out both men, but doing it without at least one of them firing a shot was going to be a challenge. Maybe even impossible.

He had no choice. He had to wait.

Long minutes stretched by, and Ryker went through the cycle of calming exercises, getting his nerves to chill. He gripped the knife so tight that his hand ached, and in the crouching, hiding position he was in his thighs were starting to burn.

He waited.

Eventually the two men stopped the chit-chat, and the guy on patrol went on his way, walking away in the opposite direction from the hut.

The second guard turned and started moving toward Ryker.

Ryker was in a good spot, hidden, with visibility all the way down the street in that direction. He waited until the second guard passed him, then slid out and followed, moving silently.

The second guard was almost to the hut when Ryker pounced on him, driving him to the ground with a knee in his back and Ryker's palm pressed against his mouth. The man's gun clattered off to the side, and the guard grasped for it with flexing fingers.

Those fingers suddenly went into a spasm, however, as Ryker

drove the knife in and up through the base of the skull, severing the spinal cord and ending the guy's life.

Once again Ryker dragged a corpse through the streets of Harat, dumping him next to his compatriot in the alley beside the hut.

He checked his watch. The guy on patrol wouldn't be back this way for another 30 minutes, adjusting for his little side chat. That should be plenty of time.

Ryker opened the door to the hut, let his eyes adjust to the light, and stepped inside.

Mark Adams was sitting up on a bed along one wall. He looked up, startled.

"Jim?"

"Mark."

Mark shook his head. "Jim... this is... this is terrible timing."

"Tell me about it," Ryker replied. "Get up."

"I'm still injured," Mark said. "Can't exactly run." He motioned to a cane leaning against the wall next to his bed.

"That's fine, Mark," Ryker said. "We'll take our time."

THIRTY-FIVE

Jill scratched frantically at the mud bricks under the counter, peeling away crumbles of dust in thin lines with each pass of the splinter.

She'd been at it for hours. Or so it seemed—for all she knew, she'd only been doing it for ten minutes. She had no way to tell what time it was, and she was in a very heightened state.

The noise and chaos from outside had died down a long time ago. When it did, she worried that the guard outside would hear the scraping and come investigate. So far, however, she hadn't heard a peep from him. And she kept going.

She'd made pretty good progress. The back wall beneath the counter had gone from a more or less flat surface to being concave. She wasn't sure how thick the walls actually were, but she envisioned being mere inches from breaking through. It was how she kept at it, despite her hands and arms aching from the effort.

As she worked, she thought about Mark. She *worried* about him.

Because this was bad, and she wasn't at all sure she had the pull and influence to get him out of this one.

Worse... she was starting to wonder if she should even try.

All of Mark's life, Jill had been there to keep him safe—from bullies, from school officials, from the police. But mostly from himself. She'd been his guardian angel practically since he was born, and the biggest threat she was always protecting him from was his own tendency toward self destruction.

Maybe she hadn't done him any favors.

When he'd gone into the military, and then into the CIA, she'd been so proud of him. So *hopeful.* He was growing up, *finally.*

But it became obvious in time that he was still the same Mark, still pulling the same crap, still getting into the same trouble. And she was still playing her part, backing him out of it all, covering up his mess, and pretending like there wasn't a problem.

She was complicit in this. *All* of this. Mark's betrayal, the hard drive getting into the hands of the *Kharif,* the destruction of the FOB. This was as much on her as it was on Mark.

And that other thing.

A year ago.

She could hardly believe it, when she'd started hearing the rumors, reading the reports. Most of those had been marked "classified," but she'd used that *wunderkind* influence of hers to gain access to them. She was tied to the two principle players, after all— her brother, and her lover.

They were pinning all of it on Jim. And Jim, being who he was, took it all on himself without trying to pass the blame on to anyone else. Jim legitimately saw himself as the one at fault, because he was the one in charge. Mark may have been the one who... who...

Who killed all those people, Jill forced herself to think and admit. After a year of denying the very idea, now she knew.

Her little brother, trouble magnet, had attracted bigger trouble than he could get out of. Even with the help of a guardian angel.

It was a village not too different from Harat, Jill thought. She imagined it so, anyway. According to the reports, there were fewer than three thousand people living in that village.

Jim was leading his team in an operation to search the area, to see if rumors of a *Kharif* occupation were true. And there had been some evidence of it, though according to Jim's debriefing he came to believe the *Kharif* had moved on months earlier.

Jim, as team leader, had given orders for a final sweep. The twelve-man team had split into two groups of five and one group of two—that last being Jim Ryker and the team's Captain, hanging back to run the operation from the temporary base they'd commandeered upon arrival. Mark was leading one of the other groups, into the village's interior.

The mission was infiltration and verification. And it was going well. Based on reports from inside the village, Jim and the Captain had determined the *Kharif* were no longer present, and they were waiting for the two groups to complete their sweep and return for extraction. That's when things went wrong.

Details were sketchy. Jill had read the reports, and had tried to imagine how it could have happened. But now... she was pretty sure she knew. The gaps in who was where, who did what, who made what mistake—she was certain now that she knew what role Mark had played. She had denied the whole idea, at the time, and played almost a doe-eyed innocent over it. But she knew. The story was right there for her to see, even though the names had been redacted. She had known, even then. She just hadn't been willing admit it. Not until now. Not until she'd seen, with her own eyes, what Mark was capable of.

The sketchy details suddenly became clear.

One of the infiltration teams—she now could admit it *had* to be Mark's team—had managed to keep a low profile going into the village, but when they entered one of the supposedly abandoned buildings they unexpectedly came across a group of people. What they were doing in the building, no one could say. But according to the after action report they were armed, and they were about to attack. The team commander gave the order to open fire.

The village was only lightly occupied, but upon hearing gunfire there was a sudden surge of men, women, and children bursting from every building. They rushed into the streets, inexplicably *toward* the sound of fighting. At first they encountered the second five-man team, catching them off guard. The villagers attacked, using mostly tools like shovels or rakes—what amounted to sticks and rocks, according to the report.

But it was enough. They'd caught the Americans by surprise, and that had given them enough of an advantage that they were able to kill all five men. They continued on to the abandoned building, and in a fury they rushed inside.

The first team's commander, seeing that they were being overrun, ordered a retreat.

And to cover the retreat, he threw a grenade into the crowd.

The resulting explosion brought the building down on top of all of them. Most of the men were crushed beneath a mass of brick and stone and wood. And only the team leader—only *Mark*—managed to get out alive.

When the dust settled, according to the reports, Jim and the Captain called in reinforcements, to help in excavating the scene. The villagers who survived were hostile, but helped in clearing debris and recovering the bodies.

And that was when the true horror of it all came home.

Among the bodies, there were dozens of young boys. Kids, who had been playing in the abandoned structure. Playing solider, it appeared, with "guns" carved from scrap wood, dabbed with pitch to paint them black.

Boys. Kids. *Children.*

Her brother had opened fire on a bunch of kids playing in an abandoned building. She couldn't deny that now. The evidence was too much to ignore.

And the result had been their deaths, along with dozens of locals and nearly all of Jim Ryker's team of US operatives.

Jill had cringed with every word of the reports. And, foolishly, she had refused to even *consider* that Mark was the one responsible. Even though...

Even though, deep down, even with everything struck through with black ink... she'd known. She'd always known.

But Jim had given her an out from having to admit or face the truth.

The mission had gone wrong in a horrific way, and someone had to be blamed. Jim Ryker decided that someone had to be him. Because that's who he was. *Of course* that's who he was.

She'd fought for Jim as hard as she had for Mark. She pulled strings, called in favors, even begged and pleaded with CIA officials. And it had worked. Or had mostly worked.

Mark got a slap on the wrist. An official reprimand on his record that presented that heavily redacted version of events that was squeaky clean compared to the reality. And Jim...

Well, she wasn't entirely sure *what* had happened to Jim, at the time. She'd managed to keep him from being indicted on any charges, but after the hearings he'd just disappeared. Mark had assured her that Jim was ok, that he wasn't in a cell either in the US or in Katakstan. But he didn't know exactly where Jim had gone after the hearings and interrogations. He'd just vanished.

And then, a couple of days ago, he'd shown up to save her and everyone at the FOB. And now...

Now she was *certain* he was on his way here to save her again.

Jill kept scraping at the wall, with suddenly a bit more vigor than she'd had for the past hour. She was feeling a range of emotions she couldn't quite explain, none of them good. And having something to focus on helped her to deal with it.

Why had she treated Jim as she had, back at the FOB? Why had she ignored him? Turned her back on him? She'd spent most of the past year wondering what had happened to him, where he'd gone, why he'd left without a word. And then, seeing him marching across the desert like some kind of movie hero, she'd felt nothing less than joy.

But that joy turned into something else when she'd finally gotten to talk to him, face to face. And it was only now, as she scraped her way to what she hoped was freedom, that she realized exactly what she'd felt.

Shame.

She'd gotten confused, thought that she was feeling some kind of resentment toward Jim, maybe for leaving her without a word of explanation. But now she knew, that wasn't it at all. She was feeling *shame*, and regret, and even self-loathing. Because in her mad dash to try to clear her brother, she had indeed tried to help Jim as well. But in the end she'd been perfectly willing to let Jim be the scapegoat, on the altar of her brother's freedom. If it meant Mark could go free, she would let Jim take the blame for something she knew he had nothing to do with. And she would pretend, all the while, that Mark was really innocent.

She'd been living with that for the past year, though she'd never admitted it to herself. And worse, though she'd thought about and wondered about Jim that whole time, she'd secretly been *relieved* when he'd taken the blame, and when he'd left. It had made it easier, all around. For Mark. For her. She *had* to back her brother. That was just what family did.

And now, having faced her brother in this God forsaken place, she realized that all this time, all these years, she'd been backing the wrong man.

Mark was a self preservationist. He was a narcissist. A sociopath. A traitor.

In a flash of anger, Jill tightened her grip on the shard of wood and stabbed at the wall, in the center of the concave carving she'd made. She hit hard, and was surprised as the tip of the shard penetrated through. Bits of brick crumbled and fell away, and as she pulled back she could see a bit of light visible. Not much—just the slight cast of an anemic moon in the sky above. But much more light than she could see in the rest of the room.

Just a wispy beam. But it might as well have been a floodlight, for the amount of joy it ignited in Jill's heart. She felt tears well up in her eyes and run down her cheeks.

She glanced back over her shoulder. She was half afraid that now that she was this close, the guard might have heard. He might be unlocking the door to enter, right now. But after a pause, listening, prepared to leap back onto the filthy little mattress, there was nothing.

Jill took a deep breath and let it out slowly. She turned her attention to the hole in the wall. Just big enough to put a hand through, at the moment. But as she scraped the shard of wood around its edge, the brick crumbled away in bigger chunks now, its integrity broken. In a moment the hole was twice as big, and a few minutes after that it was twice more.

Big enough to squeeze through.

THIRTY-SIX

"It's good to see you," Mark whispered as he hobbled along, using the cane to keep himself stable.

"I can't say the same," Ryker replied. "Somehow you keep dragging me into a world of crap and making me dig you out of it."

There was a pause in the conversation, even as Jim nudged Mark to keep moving. They were sticking to the shadows, just as Ryker had when he was coming in. Their destination was a few blocks away. The plan was to deal with Mark quietly, closer to where Faraz was hiding. The walk was all about gathering intel, though at the moment Ryker was finding it hard to open his mouth without telling Mark he intended to kill him.

Plus, talking out here on the streets of Harat was a dangerous prospect, and one he would have preferred to have avoided. Ideally they should have had this conversation in the room where Mark was being "held captive." But it was too dangerous to stay there. The *Kharif* on patrol would be swinging back by on his route soon, and he was sure to notice that the guards were not at their posts. It wouldn't be long after that for him to discover the two bodies hidden in the alley, and eventually the missing prisoner as well.

The window would be closing soon, and Ryker had to make sure he was close enough to Faraz to complete the next two objectives, before he put Mark down.

The wrinkle in this plan was Jill.

Once the *Kharif* knew Mark was missing, they would assume he had somehow overtaken the guards and killed them. The next logical place for him to go would be where Jill was being held, to try to rescue her. Which meant that the *Kharif* would go to her next. What they might do from there was hard to guess, but it put Jill in danger, regardless.

It was a tough call. But Ryker had to make sure that the hard drive was destroyed, along with any technology the *Kharif* had managed to get their hands on. And he had to make sure Faraz went down. Someone else would inevitably take his place, but his death would destabilize the *Kharif* for a time, at least, giving the CIA an opportunity.

Of course, the CIA was probably planning a drone strike on this village, once they knew for sure that the *Kharif* were here. Which might take care of Faraz and the tech at the same time, Ryker figured. It would also take care of Jill and Ryker—a fate Ryker was hoping to derail.

He would give the signal that Agent Anonymous had ordered him to give. He'd just be giving it while he and Jill were rushing out of this village, to somewhere safe.

"Jim, listen," Mark whispered. "I'm... I'm sorry, about how things went down last year. I wanted to tell you, I'm really grateful that you took the blame. You didn't have to do that. Not for me."

"It wasn't for you," Ryker said. "I took the blame because it really was my responsibility. That's what being a leader means, Mark. Your screwup is my responsibility."

They moved in silence for a few minutes more, and Mark said, "That's just noble bullshit, Jim."

"Not the kind of thing I'd expect you to understand," Ryker replied.

There was a sound from up ahead, and Ryker pulled Mark back against a wall, stretching his arm across Mark's chest.

Two *Kharif* footmen were walking past up ahead. They weren't part of the patrols that Ryker had accounted for. But beyond them, by less than half a block, was the building that Ryker suspected was the headquarters for Faraz and the *Kharif*. These two were guards, then. Making an impromptu patrol.

Ryker and Mark stood still for long minutes, and Ryker was practically holding his breath. If they were spotted, they'd have to engage in a firefight. That would draw *Kharif* out of the woodwork.

The first bullet Ryker fired would be into Mark's head. He'd be a liability in more ways than one, and Ryker couldn't afford to let him live.

The shame of it was that he hadn't yet gotten the intel he was after. He'd wasted time, trying to control his rage toward Mark instead of questioning him. Now it might be too late.

The two men up ahead finally turned and wandered in a different direction, and Ryker felt the tension go out of him. He lowered his arm, letting Mark step away from the wall.

Ryker turned on him. "I need to know if Faraz is here in Harat."

Mark nodded. "Yeah. He's here."

"And how much did you give him?" Ryker asked. "Did you unlock the hard drive?"

Mark hesitated. "Jim, you have to understand… they have Jill."

"I know," Ryker said. "How much did you give them?"

Mark sighed. "All of it. I unlocked all of it. I'm... I'm trying to keep her safe."

Ryker wanted to believe him, but given everything he knew about Mark Adams, he couldn't bring himself to forgive and forget. He could see that Mark was playing yet another game. He'd given Faraz the hard drive as a way to protect himself, and protecting Jill was just a bonus. He'd probably offered more intel, as a show of loyalty, to cement the deal with Faraz.

But Mark was also playing Ryker, right here in the shadows of Harat. He kept invoking Jill's name. He was playing all of this as a move to keep *her* safe. But the reality, Ryker knew, was that Mark was doing whatever it took to make sure *Mark* survived. He would want to protect his sister, if he could. Ryker believed that. But the cards in Mark's deck all bore his own face. He was playing a solo game, and everyone else was a wildcard.

Ryker was still gripping the knife. It would be easy, to just gut Mark right here, leave his body in the dirt. But he hesitated. Something was stopping him.

Jill. He was hesitating because of Jill.

He turned to look at the building up ahead. It was dark and quiet. He might be able to sneak in and get to Faraz without being seen. He might even be able to search the place for the hard drive without setting off any alarms. *Might. Maybe.*

There was a much better chance that he'd be dead within the hour.

Agent Anonymous had told him to send a signal. He'd said they'd be watching, and they'd send in help, for the extraction. Ryker didn't believe a damned word of it. He knew that any signal he sent would trigger a drone strike.

He looked at Mark, hobbled and limping on the cane.

If I'm not killing him, I can't leave him here, Ryker thought.

He pulled Mark's arm and started moving in the other direction.

"What are we doing?" Mark asked, bouncing to try to keep up.

"I'm getting you out of here. But first we have to find Jill."

"And then what?" Mark asked.

"Then... I have to send a signal."

THIRTY-SEVEN

KHARIF HEADQUARTERS

Faraz had turned in for the night. He needed rest. The past 72 hours had been challenging, and the long hours and lack of sleep were taking a toll. And so he had given orders to his men, and retired to a small room with a cot. Once again he thought of the American, with an actual bed and electricity.

That was fine. Who was the slave here, and who the master? Faraz purposefully chose a more spartan life, as a reminder—he lived as many of the Katakstan people lived. He slept as they slept, ate as they ate, dressed as they dressed. He was one of them, and always would be.

Let the Americans have their creature comforts. That was, after all, the key to their undoing. They lived lives of comfort, wealth, and luxury. They were *soft*. But the Katakstan people knew a harder life. And when the day came, when the weapon blanketed the world with a signal that made darkness fall over all of humanity, the *Kharif* would rise to destroy the West, once and for all.

It was a pleasant dream for Faraz. He had just drifted off when one of his men, Soban, pulled aside the curtain and spoke his name.

"What is it?" Faraz asked.

"The American... he has escaped."

Faraz sat up immediately. "How?"

"The two men guarding him were found dead," Soban reported. "Stabbed and left in the alley beside the American's quarters."

Faraz stood. "And the woman? His sister?"

"Her guard is still there, and reports that no one has opened her door all night, as you instructed. We have placed two more guards there."

Faraz nodded. "Keep watch. The American is sure to try to rescue her. Get more men on the streets. I want him found."

Soban nodded and left.

Faraz felt a strange sort of shakiness. He'd been deep in sleep when Soban had awoken him, and he was having trouble coming fully out of it. He pushed through the curtain and moved to the small kitchen, where there was already a kettle of hot water for tea. He made a cup, sipping it slowly, willing the caffeine into his bloodstream.

He would never tell anyone, but one of the things he most missed about his time in University was coffee. He had been introduced to it by his classmates, who were actively rebelling against the custom of tea in the UK. Many of them were fans of a more American style of morning beverage—coffee overloaded with cream and sugar and flavored syrups. All far too sweet and rich for Faraz's tastes.

But he had developed a fondness for the black, bitter beverage in and of itself. He particularly liked the bright flavors of lighter roasts, which he'd been told tended to have a much higher caffeine content. Something he could use, at the moment.

As he sipped his tea he thought about the American. It seemed odd, that this man who had only hours ago given Faraz and the *Kharif* the keys to the weapon would suddenly attack and murder his guards and escape. Why unlock the hard drive's encryption and share all of the secrets he had so carefully preserved all this time, if he planned to escape?

Soban had said the men were stabbed.

There were no knives or glass or anything in that room that Adams could have used to stab and kill two armed men. And besides, Adams was still injured, hobbling about on a cane. While it was possible he might have been able to attack the men regardless, it seemed unlikely he would be successful in killing both of them.

"Soban," Faraz said, looking up. "The two men... you said they were stabbed. How?"

"One was stabbed in the throat, and the other through the base of his skull," Soban reported. "The American must have taken that one by surprise first, and then attacked the second."

"Where were the bodies found?" Faraz asked.

"In the alley next to the building."

Faraz nodded and Soban went back to his duties.

The details of this story did not make sense. Mark Adams was a highly trained operative—there was no doubt that he could take out two armed men. But he was not in peak condition, and Faraz could think of no way he could have armed himself. He would have to have opened the door of the hut without either guard challenging him, killed the first and then the second in very rapid succession, and then somehow drag both bodies off to the side, despite being dependent on a cane to walk.

Faraz was standing in front of a small table that was almost completely covered by a map of the region. He saw the dashes of red ink, an X for every loss of personnel they'd suffered over the past few weeks. There was a trail of X's that meandered to the FOB, from the drop point of the American who had, somehow, taken out several *Kharif* as he marched straight into the American base. This man, who had brought communication back to the FOB, and aided them in coordinating an evacuation and a drone strike.

Faraz had assumed the man had escaped with the others, or perhaps was killed during the evacuation.

But what if he was *here*?

And another detail floated up from his memory.

"Soban, you said the guard in front of the woman's quarters—he reported no activity?"

"No, Faraz."

Faraz thought, then shook his head. "There is someone here. The American, who dropped in a few days ago. He is here." He looked up at the startled Soban. "Put everyone on alert. Search the streets. But we are looking for someone else, not just Mark Adams. The man is here. Find him and kill him."

Soban nodded and was out the door, issuing orders to the men within seconds.

Faraz sipped his tea, and glanced back at the map.

Whoever you are, he thought, *you are too late.*

He turned to his people. "Load the laptop and all of our research into a vehicle, along with the prototype. Let me know when it is ready."

"Yes, Faraz."

"Bring the keys directly to me," he replied.

THIRTY-EIGHT

"They're onto us," Mark whispered. "There are way more *Kharif* on the streets now."

Ryker had noticed this himself. This was the third time they'd ducked for cover, allowing a patrol of at least four armed men to pass. That activity on the streets was picking up, and it was particularly concentrated on the street they were navigating. The street that led to where Jill was being confined.

This wasn't going to work.

"We have to adjust the plan," Ryker said.

"There's a plan?"

Ryker looked at Mark, up and down. The man was in no shape to make a run for it. In fact, he was just slowing them down. He was a liability. Maybe he should put the guy down after all. It would certainly make things simpler. If the *Kharif* found Mark's body, it might distract them, get them to end the search. That could give Jim an opening to get Jill out of there, and then send the signal.

But Jill was the main reason Ryker wasn't killing Mark. It was for her that Ryker kept the traitorous son of a bitch alive. That, and even with his leg injured Mark was still a trained operative who could handle himself in a firefight. That might come in handy, and sooner than Ryker would have liked.

"Jill's being held up ahead," Ryker nodded in the general direction. "But that's exactly where the heat is thickest. We're never going to make it. So we need a new strategy."

Mark nodded, then took a deep breath and said, "Give me a gun."

Ryker nearly laughed out loud. "Give you…"

"Look, Jim… I know, ok? I'm… I'm basically the bad guy in this. I'm the traitor. Even if I get out of here, by some miracle, I'm screwed. Life in prison, if I'm lucky. Probably just a bullet in my head, to save the trial. But for now, I can still help. I can still… I can help you get Jill out of here." He was watching Ryker's face, and added. "Besides, I'm pretty sure this plan has crossed your mind already."

"Not the 'give you a gun' part," Ryker said.

"No, maybe not. Maybe you thought about shooting me and then running. Let the noise draw the *Kharif*, and let them assume one of their own people got me. That about it?"

"I hadn't quite thought it that far ahead, but now that you mention it…"

"It will be a lot more believable if I go down fighting," Mark interrupted.

Ryker shook his head. "Jill would never forgive me."

"She'd learn," Mark said. "Or she wouldn't. But this is the best chance for her to be alive to hate you, at least."

Ryker studied him, this man who had been a friend and an ally, a teammate, a traitor. "You're not this noble," Ryker replied.

"Never have been," Mark said. "But Jill... she's been there for me my whole life. She's always bailed me out. This time, maybe I can return the favor."

Ryker was about to respond to that when a shot cut through the night, pinging the wall behind them. Ryker cursed and dragged Mark down for cover, behind a wooden cart. He had unslung the M16 when it became clear that the *Kharif* were on the hunt, but had hoped he wouldn't have to use it. Now he rose, took aim, and squeezed off several rounds.

"*Surrender, American!*" their attacker shouted in *Pashto*. "*Put down your weapon!*"

This was followed by several more shots, which had Ryker ducking for cover once again.

There seemed to be only one of them, at least. But that wouldn't last long. Others were sure to hear the gunfire, and come running.

Ryker again rose to fire a few rounds, but stopped when he saw the street ahead of him. There was enough light to show that the man who had been shooting at them had dropped his weapon, and was grasping at his throat. He stumbled forward, and finally fell to the ground.

Cautiously, Ryker rose and stepped around the cart, moving forward quickly, the M16 ready to fire.

He knelt and checked the man, turning him over to reveal that there was rough wooden spike driven into the man's throat. Blood was still pulsing from the wound, but that stopped after a few seconds, as the man's heart ceased beating.

"Jim?"

He looked up at the sound of a woman's voice.

"Jill..." he said.

She ran forward, and he stood just in time for her to leap and embrace him.

They leaned away from each other, and Ryker asked, "How...?"

"I escaped," she said. "Dug my way out."

Ryker smiled, nodded. "Ok, maybe you can explain that a bit later."

He turned, and Jill followed his gaze to the cart, where Mark slowly rose.

"Hey," Mark said.

Ryker spared a glance at Jill, expecting to see relief. Instead, her expression hardened. She looked angry.

There was a sound from down the way, shouting, running.

"We have to move," Ryker said, dragging Jill after him. Mark joined them, hobbling along as fast as he could mange as they hurried back down the street.

"We can get out of the village down this way," Jim said. "Into the hills."

"I'll never be able to keep up," Mark said, huffing.

"Keep up," Ryker replied.

The sounds of shouting were all around them, and Ryker was not at all sure they could make it to the point he'd used to get into the village. And if they did, he wasn't sure whether they'd get through without being seen. But it was the best plan he had, at the moment.

The fact that Mark was lagging behind didn't bother him. Not now. Jill had clearly come to some epiphany about her brother, and maybe that would allow Ryker to have a bit more leeway. Maybe, if it came to it, Jill wouldn't be quite so willing to risk everything to keep her brother alive.

Still... blood was blood, and family ties ran deep. Jill had spent a lifetime looking after her little brother, and no matter what she was feeling now, it was unlikely she'd willingly let him go down.

Even now Ryker was noticing Jill hanging back, pausing, letting

Mark catch up. She didn't speak to him, didn't even look at him. But she was still caring for him, in at least this small way.

They reached the gap, and Ryker motioned for them to follow him as he squeezed through the narrow opening between two structures. This was where he'd found a way in.

It was tight, and Mark had some difficult with it, but eventually all three of them were standing outside of Harat.

"I have a vehicle parked not far from here," Ryker said. "Not exactly close, but I could probably get to it in under ten minutes. If I go alone."

He watched Jill's face.

"You want us to stay here," she said.

He nodded. "You can hide in the hills. Stay low. They aren't looking here. Not yet. And soon they'll have a whole other problem to deal with."

She turned and looked at her brother, who was huffing and sweating, his face showing that he was in a lot of pain. He leaned heavily on the cane. "About that gun," he said, feigning nonchalance.

Ryker checked the M16, popped the magazine and replaced it with a fresh one. He took the spares out of his pocket, and moved toward Mark and Jill.

Mark held out a hand, but Ryker turned and handed the M16 to Jill. "You know how to fire this?"

"I... not really."

"Mostly, it's point and shoot. Mark can fill you in on the details of reloading, clearing the breach, whatever you need. I suggest you go over it a few times, while you're hiding. Don't fire on anyone unless they've spotted you. I'll be back soon."

"Jim," Mark started. "It would be better..."

"You need to count yourself as very, *very* lucky that I don't just put a bullet in your head and take Jill with me," Ryker said.

That was that. The message was clear. Ryker was only leaving Jill behind because he knew that, despite everything, she would want to keep her brother safe. This was the compromise.

"Be safe out there," Jill told him.

"No such thing," Ryker replied. He drew the .45 from his waistband and sprinted away in the darkness.

THIRTY-NINE

KHARIF HEADQUARTERS, HARAT

Faraz gave the order for the men to keep searching, and then turned to Soban. "You will come with me," he said.

Soban nodded and climbed behind the wheel of the SUV. Faraz checked the metal case one last time. Inside was the laptop, in its own protective case, and the components of the EM prototype they'd been able to build from scant data and designs. This would be the foundation of a much greater weapon.

There were also hard drives and reams of paper and notebooks, collected research that the *Kharif* had acquired thanks largely to the intel they gained from Adams. He had turned out to be a valuable asset. Faraz was sad to see him go. But his usefulness had certainly come to an end.

He had, in fact, become a liability.

It seemed likely that the American who was leaving a trail of dead *Kharif* across the desert was here in Harat. He would be here to reclaim Mark Adams, though it seemed more likely he would kill the man who had turned traitor. And though a single American operative couldn't hope to overtake the hundreds of armed *Kharif* patrolling the streets of Harat, he could certainly call in a drone strike. Just, as Faraz suspected, he had done at the FOB, and then again with the convoy.

Faraz should have ordered that this man become a primary target. He should have been eliminated as soon as he appeared in Katakstan.

But that wasn't a fair judgement. By the time Faraz had even heard the news from the front, this man had already marched into the base. And in all honesty, Faraz had no actual confirmation that the American was here in Harat at all. This was all just a guess, and it was entirely possible he was wrong. But he had what the Americans called a "gut feeling." His intuition told him this man was here, and that he was a sign of even greater trouble on the horizon.

There was little chance that Mark Adams could have taken out both of his guards. He was unarmed, hobbled, and had also just given up what Faraz had wanted from him. His sister was a hostage, as well. Adams had neither the means nor the motive to escape.

No, all the pieces were pulling together to show Faraz a picture of something unexpected. The American who had been dropped into Katakstan a few days earlier was here. And if he could do all he had done thus far, then he could do a lot more.

The city of Ghezna was a littler over three hundred kilometers from Harat. It was a far more metropolitan area, with an international airport and modern amenities. And though the Americans had a small embassy within the city, their presence was very limited. *Kharif* had infiltrated the city's security presence, and Faraz would be guided to a facility where the metal case he carried would be most welcome.

This had always been the plan. Faraz was always going to bring everything he found to this base. The time table was being accelerated, that was all.

They were in the endgame now. Close the victory. Soon they would have the weapon that many of the *Kharif* referred to as *the fist of God.* And with that, they would crush and remove the biggest advantage the West had over the Katakstan people.

First their technology would fall. Then they would follow.

Faraz climbed into the passenger seat of the SUV, and in moments they were out of the village gates, rumbling along the rough road leading away from Harat. They were nearly a hundred kilometers from a proper paved road, so this was going to be a long and rough ride.

FORTY

Malleus watched the screen, studying every flicker, every movement. It was night in Harat. The infrared image gave him a clear enough view of the town, but the mass of heat signatures was a little short of the sort of detail he was looking for. Then, he saw the first signs.

Three signatures were cutting out of the village, and moving into the hills.

Ryker, and the Adams Siblings? Malleus felt certain that was exactly who it was. But he needed confirmation.

This feed was coming from a satellite. And though they had some very sophisticated birds in the air, the truly powerful eyes were really on the drones. With this top-down view, Malleus could see a sort of ghost outline of the buildings of Harat, the red and yellow blobs of *Kharif* running the streets, and otherwise a lot of blackness. Even with infrared and other night-breaking tech, no light meant no details. At least not the kind that Malleus wanted.

The drones were better for this, with their invisible spotlights of infrared LEDs. But he was holding all of those drones on reserve. The strike on the caravan had severely reduced the number of drones he had on hand, and he needed this batch to play out one more highly strategic hit. He was keeping them well back and on low-power mode, essentially circling Harat until he was given the signal. And he knew he'd get a signal.

From the three blobs breaking away from the village, Malleus watched as one of them moved deeper into the hills, leaving the other two behind. That would be Ryker, Malleus figured. He was retracing the route he'd used to get to Harat, after ditching the truck on the other side of the hills.

What was he up to? Probably planning an escape. But why leave the Adams' siblings in such a dangerous spot?

It didn't matter. Malleus knew that Ryker would eventually send that signal, and at that point Harat would become a ring of ash that could be seen from space.

Hundreds of innocent civilians would die.

That didn't sit well with Malleus. He was indeed a cold hearted bastard, but even he wasn't as cold a man as that. He was trained and willing to make the hard calls, to do the reprehensible things in order to serve and protect his country. Taking any innocent life, that wasn't what he signed on for. But it could, sometimes, be the job. The hammer didn't get to decide *which* nails he hit.

Besides, that town was absolutely overrun with *Kharif*. In fact, one of the highest-ranking among the *Kharif* was reported to be hiding out there. If that could be confirmed, this hit would send shockwaves of chaos through the whole organization. It would upset the apple cart enough that they might stand a chance of ending the *Kharif* threat once and for all.

Killing hundreds of innocent people to save billions elsewhere... that wasn't even a contest for Malleus. It was an immediate "go."

The single blob running through the hills was now descending to the desert floor. There was little doubt now that this was Ryker. He was headed directly for the pickup he'd left hidden in a ravine, before infiltrating Harat.

"What are you up to?" Malleus asked aloud.

The glowing red dot was suddenly invisible, as Ryker climbed into the truck. A moment later, the front of the truck began to glow a light yellow, fading toward red, as the engine was started and warmed up. Then it started moving.

It rounded the hills, and barreled straight for Harat, where hundreds of *Kharif* fighters were swarming the streets like ants.

Surely Ryker wasn't nuts enough to barrel into town and start fighting? He must have some other plan.

As Malleus watched, however, he spotted another movement, on nearly the opposite side of the village. Another vehicle, what looked like an SUV, went bouncing out of the village and speeding through the desert night.

Malleus couldn't explain how he knew, but he knew...

"Faraz," he whispered.

The man was escaping. And it was very likely he had the hard drive with him. And probably more.

Malleus looked at the red blob representing Ryker's truck. Whatever he was planning, it would be for nothing. Or almost nothing. If he was going to call in the drone strike, they would take out a bunch of *Kharif*, sure. But Faraz was getting away. And Malleus had no way to tell Ryker, or to do anything about it.

Except...

For the second time that day, Malleus punched in a series of codes that only a few people on Earth knew. This time he had to be a bit more crafty with his commands. He had to punch in a sequence of events, and get them just right. And this plan was one of his trickiest so far.

It was going to be close, for one thing. He needed to time this right, and it was a good damn thing that he already had drones circling.

Now, all but one of those drones started their course toward Harat. May God have mercy on their souls—and on his.

That last drone, however, was moving toward Ryker's truck. Malleus had a man to kill. And this was the only way.

FORTY-ONE

The Toyota was bouncing along at a dangerous pace, jarring Ryker to the bones. The headlights were illuminating a crazy, animated landscape, as the truck sped through the night on the rough terrain. He dialed back, slowed a bit. He couldn't afford to break an axel.

He was closing in on the village. The route around the hills was taking him longer by truck than it had taken for him to travel overland by foot. He was relieved to see signs of firelight as he rounded one of the rolling hills.

He slowed some more. Up in the hills, Jill and Mark were still hiding out. There were no signs of a firefight happening, so that was good. He had half a mind to stop, hide the truck, and go find them. They could be speeding away in no time. Ghezna was a couple hundred miles from here—they could get to the US embassy and be on a flight back to the States in just a few hours. Mark would have to answer for what he'd done. Jill could go back to her career, and hopefully the stain of her brother's betrayal and her own failure to keep the tech out of enemy hands wouldn't stick to her for too long.

And Ryker...

Well, there was no sense even pretending. Ryker's life belonged to the Company now. Whatever happened next, it was up to them.

Still, the idea of getting Jill and Mark and climbing into this truck and lighting out for Ghezna, that had its appeal.

But the problem was, the *Kharif* had the designs for the weapon. And that meant that no one, anywhere on Earth, was safe. And Ryker couldn't allow that.

Ryker's mission was to signal for a drone strike, to take out this threat. That was exactly what he had to do.

He pulled over, not to go and retrieve Jill and Mark, but to grab the gas can from the bed of the pickup.

He'd saved it for exactly this sort of thing.

In the bed of the truck was a rag someone had used for checking the oil, and Ryker took this and soaked it in gasoline. He stuffed the rag into the spout of the gas can, then fished the lighter from his pocket. He'd taken this off of a dead *Kharif* less than a day ago, and somehow that seemed significant. Or just poetic, maybe. All of this, the truck and the gas can and the lighter, it would be the harbinger that brought destruction and death to this place. All of it had come from the *Kharif*, and now he was going to give it all back, with interest.

Ryker moved the gas can to the passenger side floorboard of the pickup. It would have more fuel to burn inside the cab, and there was less chance of it bouncing and tipping, its own fuel putting out the flame.

He searched and found a tire iron under the seat, and using his knife he cut a slit in the seat itself, so that he could wedge the iron in place. The other end would press the gas pedal.

Ryker then used the knife to cut away the seatbelt, and tied the steering wheel so that it would be held straight.

When he started the engine, all he'd have to do is shift into drive and release the parking break. The truck would shoot off in a straight line, ramming into either the village gate or one of its walls. Either way, there would be a fireball to light up the Katakstan sky. And that should be signal enough.

Bring hell down on this place, Anonymous, my job is done.

"Jim!" he heard a voice say.

He turned, and felt his guts drop.

Jill, with Mark leaning on her for support, was guiding the two of them down the hillside. They must have been closer than he'd expected.

"What the hell are you..."

"Don't be mad," she said. "Some *Kharif* were starting to search the hills, and we saw your headlights go out as you stopped here. Mark suggested it would be better to regroup than to start a firefight, which might call attention to you down here."

Ryker looked from Jill to Mark. He was right. It also meant that he needed to get this plan going. If the *Kharif* found them before he could put the truck in gear, this whole plan might fall apart.

He circled the truck and opened the passenger door. He was about to light the fuse on his makeshift bomb when he heard a familiar sound echoing over the landscape.

It was the whine of a drone, coming in fast.

He looked up to see it moving toward them, from the direction he'd driven in.

"They're going to do the strike now?" Ryker asked. "I haven't..." He was going to say, *I haven't given the signal*, but he stopped.

What was happening here?

Agent Anonymous had been pretty clear about the sequence of events. Ryker was to send a signal, confirming that this was the place where all the lines met. The *Kharif* home base, Faraz, the hard drive. They wanted confirmation—some CYA for the CIA.

Is he about to take us out?

Ryker wouldn't put it past him. He was Company, through and through. And it was altogether possible that the Company had deemed Mark a traitor, which might lead them to believe that Jill was working with him against US interests. And basically, Ryker was already on their target list, or he wouldn't even be here right now.

Dusting them off the Earth while taking out a *Kharif* base of operations was vintage CIA, for sure. No need for a signal, Ryker, we'll take it from here.

But something was off.

The drone wasn't moving at top speed. Instead, it was moving at barely the speed needed to stay aloft. It was also running low, just feet above the ground. It was still several miles away, but Ryker could see and hear it clearly. Which mean the enemy could also see and hear it, too.

This was dumb. No stealth, no tact. It was like running a bullhorn, announcing that there was a strike incoming.

"That damned thing is going to bring the *Kharif* right down on us!" Mark shouted.

Ryker agreed. This was a dumb move. Unless you wanted to get your operatives killed for no good reason. Or...

Or you wanted to get their *attention*.

The running lights on the drone began blinking in series.

Blink, blink, on, blink. Blink, on. Blink, on, blink. Blink, on. On, on, blink, blink.

"That's Morse Code," Ryker said.

"F-a-r-a-z," Mark replied.

The drone veered off, skirting the edge of the village, moving toward the West.

Ryker thought for a moment. What did this mean? Faraz... was Faraz on the move? Moving West?

Moving in the direction of Ghezna.

There was a rise of noise to their South again. The sound of more drones, in the distance.

Ryker turned, looking at the walls of Harat, barely visible in the night. He looked at Mark and Jill.

Suddenly he reached into the truck and pulled the gas can out. He removed the rag and replaced the cap, dropping it into the truck's bed. "Get in," he told them.

"Jim, what's..." Jill began.

"No time, just get in!" Ryker shouted.

He raced to the other side of the truck and began cutting away the seat belt tied to the steering wheel. That was when the first shots rang out.

"Inside!" Mark shouted, shoving Jill into the cab of the truck.

More shots were fired, pinging from the hood and door of the pickup. Ryker heard Mark scream, but couldn't spare a moment to look up. He was hacking away at the seatbelt, trying to cut it loose as fast as he could.

"Mark!" Jill yelled.

"I'm... ok. Just, go. We need to go!" He was in the seat now, and Jill was sitting in the middle. Mark slammed the passenger door shut just as more shots pinged into it.

Ryker finally cut the seatbelt free and tossed the tire iron into the floorboard. He leapt into the truck, started the engine, and was speeding away before he'd even managed to shut the driver-side door.

More shots were fired, but they either missed or hit non-crucial parts of the truck.

Ryker slammed the door closed as they bumped along at high speed. "You're hit?" he shouted to Mark.

"Yeah," Mark panted.

"Where?" Ryker spared a glance at him. Jill had torn away part of his shirt and was pressing the wad of cloth to his chest."

"It's... fine," Mark said.

His eyes met Rykers.

And Ryker knew.

Suddenly there was a screech and roar from overhead, and as the Toyota veered onto the dirt road heading West, the entire village of Harat ceased to be.

Along with hundreds of *Kharif*.

Along with hundreds of innocent civilians.

Fire lit the night sky, and as each drone swerved and circled for another pass, Jim tilted the review mirror up and toward the ceiling of the pickup.

He didn't want to see that light. It was blinding.

It burned his very soul.

FORTY-TWO

WEST OF HARAT, THE ROAD TO GHEZNA

The Toyota was riding a bit smoother, at least, compared to his drive across the desert. This was an established road, even if it wasn't much of one. There was little to distinguish it from the desert terrain itself, in fact, beyond the graded and compacted soil and smoothed stones that had been placed to fill pot holes. It was still a hell of a jolting rumble, though, if you were moving too fast for it. And Ryker was moving way too fast for it.

"Where are we going?" Jill asked. She was still pressing the cloth to Mark's chest, and it was soaked with blood.

Mark looked pale, but was still conscious, for the moment.

"I think someone was trying to tell us that Faraz is on his way to Ghezna," Ryker replied. "And I'm betting he has the hard drive with him."

"More," Mark said hoarsely. "He... has a weapon. Prototype."

Ryker nodded. "The device they used to knock out all of the tech at the FOB."

"The thing that shut down communications?" Jill asked. "And knocked out the power?"

Ryker nodded. "Now imagine that on a global scale."

They were quiet then, thinking. Mark groaned, and Jill did the best she could.

It wasn't good, Ryker knew. Mark was losing a lot of blood. The fact that he was still alive, still conscious, meant that the bullet had missed any major organs or arteries, at least. But it was still a serious injury, and they were hours from any hospital.

Not to mention, somewhere up ahead of them was Faraz, the leader of the *Kharif*. He was sure to be armed, and certainly would not be alone. Ryker's goal, at the moment, was to catch up to him, and kill him. But that plan might be a little underdone.

For a start, it would put Jill in mortal danger.

True, she'd been in mortal danger for weeks now. And she was safer with Ryker, at the moment, than she would be anywhere else. So really, there wasn't much to be done to change her situation. The mission now was to kill Faraz and destroy that hard drive, and the prototype.

Mark might slow them down.

Unless he died quicker.

That was an option. All it would take was pulling over long enough to leave him in the desert. Or to put a knife or a bullet into his brain, if Ryker wanted to be a bit more humane about it.

But despite Ryker's willingness to do the job, to complete the mission at all costs, and despite the fact that Mark Adams had betrayed not only his country but Ryker himself... he was still, somehow, a friend. He was still someone who had risked his life for Ryker, and vice versa, on dozens of missions. And he was Jill's brother—Jill, who Ryker...

Loved?

Maybe. It had certainly felt like it was going that way, a year ago. Their relationship was still somewhat new back then. They were serious, but hadn't been for very long. Ryker hadn't been at all sure of where it was going, or where he wanted it to go. But at that time he'd really wanted to find out.

So if he loved Jill, that made Mark family. And Ryker was a lot of things, but he was not someone who left family to die.

He just wasn't sure there was anything he could do to keep this particular family alive.

Except...

He cursed, and stopped the truck.

"What's... what's happening?" Jill asked.

Ryker got out of the truck and ran around to the other side. He pulled open the passenger door, and reached in to pull Mark out.

"Jim, no!" Jill yelled. "Please!"

Ryker ignored her and lifted Mark out, then stooped and picked him up, carrying him around to the back of the pickup.

"Get back here and put the tailgate down!" he shouted.

Jill got herself together, and ran around to lower the tailgate.

Ryker placed Mark on it, at a slight angle, with his feet in the bed of the truck. He then fished around until he found the rag he'd been planning to use as a fuse. It was bone dry by now, though it still smelled of gasoline.

Ryker returned to Mark, and Jill was standing beside the tailgate, her hands caressing her brother's forehead.

"Jill, I'm going to need you to be my light." He took the lighter out and lit the rag at one end, and handed the other end to Jill. "Hold it so that I can see his wound."

She nodded and did this.

"Mark, buddy, this is going to hurt. A lot."

Mark nodded.

Ryker took out his knife, and then flicked on the lighter, heating the metal of the knife until he could see a tendril of white smoke curl off of it, the residue of oils and other materials burning away.

"Deep breath, buddy," he said to Mark

Mark huffed a few times, and then as he was exhaling, Ryker plunged the burning hot tip of the knife into this wound.

There was a sizzle, followed by the sickening smell of burning flesh.

And there was screaming. A lot of screaming.

Ryker had a hand on Mark's chest, and the man was so weak from blood loss he was easy enough to hold down. The knife continued to dig into the wound, burning the flesh, until Ryker found what he was probing for.

He twisted the blade, and brought the slug out of Mark's chest.

It dropped with a clink to the tailgate, and Ryker once again began heating the knife blade. When it was hot enough, he pressed it to the wound. More sizzle, more burning flesh, but less screaming.

Mark passed out, which Ryker figured was a blessing and a mercy.

It was the worst kind of triage, as unsanitary as they come. Infection was pretty likely. But the wind was cauterized, the bleeding was stopped, the slug was out. It might give Mark at least a chance of survival.

Ryker slid Mark off of the tailgate, and Jill helped with getting him to the passenger seat. This time Mark was sitting in the middle seat, strapped in place by the lap belt and leaning against Jill as she slammed the door shut.

Ryker started the truck and they began racing along again, though he tried to avoid the roughest patches, as best he could.

"Thank you," Jill said, her voice haunted and quiet. "For not leaving him."

Ryker said nothing. The fact that she knew he'd been thinking it... he wasn't sure what he could say.

Instead, he concentrated on trying to catch up to Faraz. Maybe they could end this. Maybe Mark would survive and they could all get home, and the world would be saved.

It was a lot of maybes, considering the circumstances. But Ryker had made a career out of maybes.

FORTY-THREE

The sun was finally rising, illuminating the road ahead. This was good—this helped them pick up some additional speed.

Ghezna may only have been around three hundred kilometers from Harat, but the drive was long and arduous. They were on their third hour, and by Soban's estimates they were at least another two hours from the city. Faraz had nodded at this estimate, and remained silent. His silence was all the encouragement Soban needed to try to shorten the remainder of the drive. There was a pass, they both knew, that could cut quite a bit of time off of the drive. It was an off-road excursion, and they risked a broken axel or some other trouble. But if they could navigate it safely it would speed things up tremendously.

It was still a ways ahead, however.

Faraz settled in and ran through his agenda, one more time. They would arrive in Ghezna. He would greet one of the security patrols and use the pass phrase. Then he and Soban would be escorted to a facility hidden within the city, where members of Faraz's team would start poring over the data from the hard drive, along with the notes and papers, and studying the prototype itself. Faraz had high hopes that they would have a fully functional weapon within the month. He would encourage his people to beat that estimate by as wide a margin as possible.

The other half of his agenda was more personal.

Once he was in Ghezna, he would send word to the home of his wife's sister. His wife and daughter would be brought to the city immediately, where he would put them up in the nicest hotel he could find. He would give them a few weeks of luxury—and would join them in their enjoyment of it.

He had not seen either of them for months now. He missed them. Especially his daughter. He had not been prepared for exactly how *much* he missed them. But they were his reason for doing this, when all was said and done.

Oh yes, there was service to God. There was loyalty and service to his people. There was his oath to the *Kharif*, and the memory of his uncle. There was the promise to his father. All of those things drove him.

But for Faraz, on a deep and personal level, the real reason for all of this, for enduring months and even years of discomfort and danger, of living in squalor and filth, of risking his life daily—the real reason was his family. If he believed his family would be safer for his having abandoned the *Kharif*, for turning on them and betraying them the same way the American had done with *his* people, Faraz knew deep within his heart that he would do it.

That was a large part of why he'd sent them away. He'd wanted to protect them. But he'd also wanted to remove them as a temptation in his life.

"Faraz," Soban said.

Faraz looked up to see him staring at the rearview mirror, a look of concern wrinkling his brow.

Glancing at the side mirror, Faraz could see a plume of dust rising from the desert road behind them. Someone was on the road, moving in the same direction. And moving *fast*.

"How long have they been behind us?" Faraz asked.

Soban shook his head. "I only just noticed them. I cannot say for sure."

Faraz nodded, and opened the glove compartment, removing the MEUSOC—a .45 ACP pistol liberated from the Americans. He chambered a round, and picked up two spare magazines, placing one in his pocket.

He handed this weapon and the second magazine to Soban, then removed another weapon from the compartment. Soban took it and laid it across his lap, shoved the magazine in his pocket, and resumed his grip on the steering wheel.

"If they overtake us, keep moving. We'll see if they just keep going."

"And if they shoot at us?" Soban asked.

"We shoot back."

They continued to bounce along, both watching their mutual mirrors as the cloud of dust in the distance grew ever closer. They were closing in on the ravine, the shortcut that would get them to Ghezna faster. Faraz didn't want whoever this was to see them veer from the road. If they followed them into that ravine, they might be able to overtake them, to pin them in a place where their escape options were severely limited.

Soon, Faraz could make out the features of a small Toyota pickup.

He held the gun in his right hand, pressed against his thigh. He had made a mistake, he now realized. In the interest of expediency, he had chosen to make the run to Ghezna with as light a load as possible. That meant leaving without an escort, beyond Soban. Faraz had assumed that Harat would be a target for the US military, but had hoped the lone SUV would be able to fly under their radar.

That did not seem to be the case.

That gut feeling was back, and Faraz peered once more at the side mirror.

It is the American, he thought. The lone wolf operative who had killed dozens of *Kharif* by now. Faraz couldn't explain how he knew, he just did.

"Can we pick up speed?"

"I'm trying, Faraz. If we move much faster, I am afraid we may end up doing some damage, slowing ourselves down."

"They will reach us any minute," Faraz said. "The time for caution is over."

Soban nodded. "Yes, Faraz," he said, and jammed the pedal to the floor.

To Faraz's dismay, the SUV did not gain much more speed, and the Toyota was still catching up to them.

It was clear—this was going to come down to a firefight.

But as he looked around, he realized where they were.

Perhaps God is with us after all, he thought.

"Pull into the desert," Faraz said.

"I don't..."

"Do it now!"

Soban turned the wheel, taking a sharp right, and the SUV bounced hard before zooming into the sand of the desert.

"There, that dune!" Faraz said.

The SUV moved toward the foot of the dune, then up, sliding slightly from the loose sand before gaining purchase enough to reach the crest and go over.

"Stop!" Faraz shouted.

Soban did so, and as soon as their motion ceased Faraz stepped out of the SUV, holding the .45 ready, taking cover. Soban joined him in an instant.

"Anything that comes over that dune, we shoot," Faraz said through gritted teeth.

Soban said nothing, but pointed his weapon, waiting.

FORTY-FOUR

Ryker stopped the truck, suddenly.

Mark bobbed forward a bit, still unconscious, but Jill held him in place with her left arm.

"You drive," Ryker said, opening the door and climbing out. He grabbed the M16 from where he'd propped it beside him, wedged between the door frame and the seat. He sprinted around the front of the pickup, briefly meeting Jill before she continued on around and slammed the driver's door shut behind her.

Ryker rolled down the passenger window and closed the door as he positioned himself in the seat. He had the M16 ready. "Go over that dune, but do it from back here. Slow, but be ready to gun it on my word."

Jill said nothing, but put the Toyota in gear and started up the slope of the dune.

It wasn't easy. The sand was as loose as flowing water, and the angle was steep. The truck struggled for traction, but eventually made its way up to the crest.

They moved over the line, coming down on a much less steep incline on the other side.

Up ahead was the SUV.

They fired shots, but the Toyota was far enough away that aiming was a challenge.

"Gun it and get us closer!" Ryker shouted. "Keep us to their left as much as possible!"

Jill did as she was told, and Ryker rose from his seat, leaning out of the window and bracing his right foot under the dash for support. He leveled the M16, and began spraying bullets across the sand, marking his range until rounds starting pinging the SUV.

The two men firing at them ducked for cover, and Ryker pressed that advantage. "Stop the truck!" He shouted.

Jill stopped, and Ryker rolled out of the window and into the sand, regaining his feet and running in a full sprint toward the SUV. The M16 was aimed and ready, and as soon as one of the men ahead of them dared to rise and start firing, Ryker unleashed a chain of rounds into the doors and windows of the SUV. Glass sprayed outward like water droplets, and soon Ryker was close enough to arc around the back of the vehicle.

There was only one man, laying on the ground, bleeding into the sand. He wasn't moving.

The SUV suddenly started up and sped away, using the angle of the dune to its advantage.

Ryker fired, but he was on the opposite side from the driver. He had no clear shot.

He turned and sprinted back to the Toyota. Jill had the presence of mind to start moving again, and Ryker leapt up and into the passenger seat. "Follow him!"

Jill followed, speeding along the sand as fast as the truck could move. It had a slight advantage over the SUV, in terms of 4-wheel drive and engine power. But the SUV had a head start, and the driver seemed to know how to handle the sand and terrain much better. He also seemed to know exactly where he was going.

They were close to a series of stoney hills, up ahead. Ryker knew immediately that the driver of the SUV was heading straight for them, and would likely be able to lose them in there. Or to at least take cover and hold them off for hours.

They followed, and as predicted the SUV turned into a pass between two outcroppings of stone. It disappeared among the rocks, which rose like the jagged remains of a giant's skeleton from the sand of the desert.

The driver knew this terrain far better than Ryker. He knew not only how to navigate it, but where to hide.

They weren't close enough for Ryker to get a decent shot, but he fired anyway, hoping for some luck.

It wasn't with him.

The SUV was gone. Out of sight.

"Slow down," Ryker told Jill. "Going in there is suicide."

Jill slowed, and finally stopped. "Jim… I'm… I'm sorry."

Ryker looked at her, and for the first time realized just how scared she looked.

He shook his head. "You did outstanding. But now I need to you to park this thing and keep your eyes open. Be prepared to go back to the road, if I don't come back within the hour. Ghezna is a couple of hours away, in the direction we were driving. Get Mark there, get to the US embassy. They'll help."

"What about you?" Jill asked.

Ryker took the .45 from his waistband and tossed it to her. "Just in case. But if I'm not back in an hour, I'm not coming back," he said. And with that he stepped out of the Toyota and sprinted into the rocky terrain ahead.

FORTY-FIVE

It was done. All of it. The village of Harat was no more, and the only real regret Malleus had was that he couldn't say the same for the *Kharif*. Or for Faraz.

The drones had spent their loads, there were no more bombs to drop. Their hydrogen fuel cells were finally reaching depletion, and soon they wouldn't be able to generate enough electricity to keep the things aloft. Their programming kicked in, and each drone began making its way back to the mobile base by autopilot.

All but one.

Malleus could override the autopilot, if he chose. And sometimes that was necessary. The objective was to keep these things out of enemy hands, but they could be used kamikaze style, if need be. Or as a delivery system for some other resource, for an operative in the field—their location beacon could be pulled and used by an operative, for example. Sometimes the last of their ordnance was put to better use by someone on the ground, as an improvised explosive device. Though, was it truly an IED, if you literally started with a bomb? Gray areas.

Malleus let all the other drones circle back to the mobile base, where they'd be refueled and reloaded. But he kept one moving out over the desert—the one he'd used to signal Ryker.

He'd been following Faraz's SUV from above. If the drone still had any ordnance onboard, Malleus would have lit the thing up like Burning Man and let it become a dark smudge on the road. All problems solved.

As it was, Malleus was calculating whether the drone could do the job by crashing into the SUV.

Maybe. But it would be tricky, and there was no guarantee it would work. The occupants might survive, and the hard drive might stay intact.

Malleus decided that the drone was better used for reconnaissance. Though that usefulness, too, was on a clock.

Already the drone didn't have enough fuel to get back to base, but that wasn't really a problem. Soon enough it would be in restricted airspace, near the Ghezna city limits. It would be shot down, and the CIA would ultimately release a CYA statement about how a drone had malfunctioned during a training exercise in the area. Their A's would be appropriately C'd. Though they'd be down one $200 million piece of equipment. Not ideal, but hey, accidents happen.

But if Jim Ryker failed to take out that SUV, Malleus intended to use that drone as a last-ditch effort to keep the *Kharif* from getting their hands on a doomsday weapon. A last resort. And, thankfully, it seemed like he might not have to use it.

One advantage of having the drone in flight was that Malleus was able to watch the whole encounter in the desert. He saw the SUV veer off into the sands, followed shortly by the Toyota. He saw Ryker make a commando run on the thing, only for it to make a run of its own into the hills nearby. And as he watched, he saw Ryker going in, all alone and on foot, to hunt down the driver and end all this.

By God, it was the kind of scene action movies were made of.

The trouble was, it was doomed to fail.

Those hills were rough and rugged, but they were also passable. The SUV was already zipping and zig-zagging along. And soon it would pass out of the canyon it was in and back out onto the sand, not a mile from where the road curved back and continued on to Ghezna.

Basically, it ended up being a shortcut. The road had cut around the hills to avoid the rough terrain, but if one was brave enough—or desperate enough—they could cut at least half an hour off of their drive by diverting through that pass.

Ryker, on foot, stood no chance of getting to the SUV. Even at its current snail's pace, it would bounce through the canyon in a few minutes, and be too far ahead for them to catch up again.

And Malleus suspected that Ryker had given Jill Adams instructions to continue on to Ghezna, if he didn't return. She'd still be trailing the SUV, and would likely never realize it was ahead of her.

This was all going bad.

Malleus considered his options. And really there was only one. There only ever had been one.

He tapped in the override and took control of the drone, and watched the screen as the world grew large before erupting into pixels and blackness.

"Your guardian angel just lost his wings, Ryker," Malleus said. "Don't let it go to waste."

FORTY-SIX

The terrain in the canyon wasn't as rough as Ryker had thought it would be, and that made his heart sink. He had hoped he'd be able to overtake the SUV on foot, but the deeper he went the more he worried that he'd just lost them.

He was considering turning back, getting the Toyota and seeing if he could make up for lost time, cutting through here. He was just preparing to turn to do that when he heard a familiar whine and buzz in the air overhead. He looked up in time to see one of the drones, on a rapid descent into the canyon.

Seconds after it passed over, Ryker heard an explosion, followed soon after by a dark plume of smoke rising into the desert sky.

He picked up his pace, sprinting and scrambling over the rocky terrain.

As he got closer he could see that the drone had crashed directly in front of the SUV, blocking its path.

Ryker approached cautiously, the M16 raised and ready. He

was scanning the canyon, left and right, up and down. The driver's door of the SUV stood open, and there was no sign of anyone. The back hatch was also opened, and Ryker peered in to see a metal case, its top raised. Inside was a device that Ryker didn't recognize, sunken into a block of foam cut to fit its shape. Next to that was an empty rectangular slot, roughly the size and shape of a laptop.

The driver must have halted and grabbed the laptop—which must have contained the stolen hard drive and all of the data on the EM weapon. That meant this device must be the prototype.

Ryker spun and scanned the canyon. The driver had to be out there somewhere. And by now he might have gotten to high ground, which meant Ryker could be a sitting duck.

He saw no signs of anyone, and after a moment he sprinted for one wall of the canyon. He had a 50/50 chance of picking the side that would obscure him, if that guy was up there somewhere.

His back pressed against the rough stone, Ryker sighted along the barrel of the M16, scanning the ridge line above. The rifle wasn't great at long shots, but he figured he was in range enough to spray the ridge, if he spotted someone. He might get lucky and get a hit. At the very least he could cover himself enough to run to the other side.

The smoke from the crashed drone was billowing into the canyon now, obscuring Ryker's vision and burning his eyes and nose.

Perfect, Ryker thought. If his vision was obscured, so was the bad guy's.

He leaned the M16 against the rock wall and took off his shirt, and then the T-shirt beneath it. Layers kept the sweat on him, out here, which helped keep him cool. He tore one sleeve from the T-shirt, and pulled this over his face like a gaiter, then quickly redressed.

He was reaching for the M16 when he heard the sound behind him.

Without hesitating he dove, grabbed the M16, and rolled. His enemy fired, missing, but not by much.

Ryker was back on his feet and running. He didn't bother turning to fire—he had no idea how close the guy was, but he currently had the advantage. Ryker's best shot at surviving was up ahead, the growing cloud of black smoke that was filling the canyon.

He raced into it, letting it cover him, zig-zagging to avoid any shots the guy would take.

And he took several. The sound of gunfire echoed from the stones, masking both Ryker's footsteps and those of the guy chasing him.

Ryker angled toward the drone. The fire was hot enough to give him a sunburn, but that could work to his advantage. Once he was close to the wreckage he leapt and rebounded from a large boulder, sliding into a gap in the stone. He crouched here, and waited, watching.

The smoke was trying to trick him with shadow puppets—every billowing bulge looked like someone emerging, and Ryker had to keep hesitating, scanning, determining a response instead of a reaction.

His enemy might be too smart for this play. After all, he had the hard drive and the high ground. He might have decided to circle back to the SUV, and drive right out of this place, doubling back to go the way he'd come. He'd have to drive backwards for a ways—the canyon was too narrow to turn around, but he'd still be moving too fast for Ryker to catch up.

Ryker cursed himself for not considering this, and was just about to work his way back to the SUV when he finally saw a figure in the smoke. The man was crouched and moving slow, sticking close to the canyon wall. There was no shot.

Ryker waited. The heat from the drone was getting unbearable, but he thought it might actually be dying down. There was only so much fuel to burn.

Unfortunately, that meant the smoke would die down as well. And sure enough, as Ryker watched, it was like a fog starting to clear.

The man noticed as well, and slowed, then stopped. He looked as if he was considering his options. His advantage had been catching Ryker by surprise, and having control of the high ground, but Ryker had superior firepower.

Time to press that advantage.

Ryker rose quickly, and started firing immediately. The man jolted back, his advantages spent, and raced toward the SUV.

Ryker trailed him with bullets, tails of dust rising like tiny eruptions at the man's heels. But in a moment the man dove into the SUV and had it started, racing backward down the canyon.

Ryker cursed and chased him, taking more shots, dotting the windshield of the SUV, but not enough to get the kill. The vehicle made one of the tight turns and was out of sight, covered by the rock walls of the canyon

Ryker ran after it, ejecting the magazine for the M16 and popping in a spare. He pushed himself, panting and racing. Praying.

Jill was out there, outside of the canyon. If this guy got out of here before Ryker got to him...

Lungs burning, eyes watering, Ryker yanked the improvised gaiter down around his neck to get more airflow.

And he ran.

FORTY-SEVEN

OUTSIDE OF THE CANYON

Jill saw the drone fly over, followed soon after by the rise of a pillar of thick, black smoke from within the canyon. She had no idea what was happening, but she held her ground. Jim still had almost half an hour left.

Though she really had no intention of racing away when time was up.

"Jill," Mark said beside her, his voice quiet, strained.

"You ok, Marky?" She leaned toward him, put a hand on his forehead like she had anytime he'd gotten sick, when they were kids.

He laughed, and winced. "Marky? You haven't called me that since I was five."

"Maybe sixteen," she frowned.

"A long time," he said, and winced again.

"You've lost a lot of blood," she said.

He nodded. "I'm aware. Where's Jim?"

Jill nodded toward the canyon.

"What's he doing in there?"

"The bad guy drove in there," Jill said.

"And the smoke? Is that the bad guy?"

"One can only hope," Jill replied.

Mark studied the situation for a moment. "How much have I missed?"

"Not enough," she said. "You need to sleep."

Mark was about to reply when he stopped, staring ahead.

Jill turned to see what he was looking at, and gawked. The SUV was racing backward out of the canyon.

They were in a direct line with it, and she could see through the open hatch that the man driving was not Ryker.

"Faraz!" Mark exclaimed. "That's Faraz!"

"The terrorist?"

"The leader of the *Kharif*," Mark said. "And if he still has the laptop, we have to stop him!"

Jill shook her head. She was more concerned with what this meant—that Faraz was rocketing backwards out of the canyon, with Jim nowhere in sight.

But Mark was right.

Without thinking, Jill put the Toyota in gear and jammed her foot onto the pedal. The pickup jumped, the tires spinning in the sand for an instant before gaining enough purchase to rocket them forward.

She realized, belatedly, that she didn't have a seatbelt.

It didn't matter. Mark really was right. They had to stop this.

"Jill!" Mark shouted.

She ignored him, and just as Faraz was finally clearing the edge of the canyon she yanked the wheel and the Toyota spun on the sand, blocking the gap. The SUV ran rear-first into the bed of the pickup, and halted with a crunching racket.

The impact jarred Jill hard, throwing her against the driver's door. She banged her head, and for a moment the world was filled with blackness and stars.

She blinked, and eventually things cleared. With her vision, there also returned sound, and she realized Mark was groaning from his side of the truck.

"Are you ok?"

He straightened, waved her off. "He's... still out there."

She looked, and saw that he was right. Faraz stumbled out of the SUV, then straightened, eyeing the pickup. He raised his hand, and Jill saw the weapon.

She looked down at the seat between her and Mark. The pistol that she'd had there was gone. She leaned forward, trying to see if it had fallen to the floor.

There was the sound of the passenger door opening, and she looked up in time to see Mark stagger out, raising the pistol, taking wobbly aim at Faraz.

"You should have run while you could, American," Faraz said, firing.

Bullets struck the truck's door. Mark didn't move, didn't flinch, but he was not steady. He fired back, and was nearly knocked off of his feet.

Faraz dove, taking cover behind the SUV.

"There's no more running, Faraz," Mark said, his voice sounding strong. But Jill could see the effort it was taking just for him to stand.

"Mark, get back in the truck! We can run for it!"

"No," he said, shaking his head and then firing two more lazily aimed shots into the back glass of the SUV. It shattered, falling inward.

Suddenly Faraz rose, firing rapidly, and despite his protests Mark did dive into the truck. Jill jammed the pedal, but there was a sputter. The engine died, and Jill looked up in dread.

Faraz, smiling, was walking around to the front of the pickup. In a moment, he'd be able to shoot the two of them.

"No!" Mark shouted, rising up and firing the rest of the rounds from the pistol. Each missed, and Faraz never even bothered taking cover.

The clicks of the weapon sounded pathetic and hollow, and eventually Mark let his hand fall. The pistol rattled into the floorboard, and Mark leaned back, huffing.

He turned to Jill.

"I'm... I'm so sorry," he said.

She was about to say something, about to forgive him, about to tell him she loved him. But before she could utter a word he started to growl, and he lurched out of the truck, charging Faraz.

There was only a single shot. Jill watched in horror as Mark stopped, straightened, and then slumped to the ground.

She screamed, and started to crawl across the seat, to try to get to her brother.

She fell out onto the sand, and crawled toward him. And in a moment, she reached him, turned him, cradled him in her lap. She was sobbing as Faraz came to stand over her, the gun pointed at her head.

"Do not mourn. I will send you to him."

She closed her eyes, tears streaming from her tight lids.

And then the shot was fired.

FORTY-EIGHT

She sat in the sand. Her brother in her lap. She felt the impact of something falling next to her.

Jill opened her eyes to see Faraz, face down on the ground.

She looked up, surprised, and saw Jim standing on the hood of the SUV. He was lowering the M16, staring at her, huffing as if he'd just run here from miles away.

He leapt to the ground and sprinted to her, dropping to his knees. He first checked Faraz, felt for a pulse. Then did the same for Mark, though Jill could have told him not to bother.

He looked at her, and she looked back.

There were no words. Nothing he could say. Nothing she could say back.

She sobbed, and he reached for her, pulled her to him, held her face against his chest and let her scream.

After several long moments she finally calmed. She got control of her breath, and then she leaned away, wiping her tears on her sleeve.

Jim rose to his feet, and started searching Faraz. He took the man's gun, and the spare rounds from his pocket. He took some of his personal belongings as well. Then he went to the SUV.

She rose, and turned Mark so that he was laying on his back. She wanted to cover his face, but couldn't find anything she could use.

She looked at Faraz, and then started kicking his corpse, screaming, yelling words she couldn't even hear. All these weeks of huddling under conference tables, fearing she would die soon, fearing that Mark was already dead, and then watching this man murder her brother in cold blood—she screamed and kicked until she was exhausted from it, and then she collapsed back to the sand, sitting with her hand on her brother's forehead. There were no more tears. Just the sound of her own breathing, ragged and uneven.

Jim came around from searching the SUV. He tossed a laptop and a stack of papers into the metal case in the back of the vehicle, then dragged the case out and onto the ground. He slid it across the sand, away from the SUV, away from the pickup.

As Jill watched, he raised the M16 and fired, spraying the contents of the case with hundreds of rounds. He then slung the weapon over his shoulder and marched over to the pickup. He retrieved the gas can from the back, and carried it over to the case. Then he emptied its contents into the case, tossing the can in for good measure. He fished a lighter out of his pocket, flicked it until it was lit, and then tossed it into the case.

The contents went up in flames instantly, and Jim watched it burn for several minutes before walking back to her, apparently satisfied that he'd destroyed the hard drive and the prototype, along with everything else, enough that none of it could never be resurrected.

He walked around to the driver's side of the pickup, and slipped into the seat. He tried to start it, but was met with only a wheezing protest that resulted in nothing. After a few more tries he gave up, put the truck in neutral, and then pushed it back and away.

He came to Jill. "We have to go," he said.

She shook her head, her hand still pressed to Mark's forehead.

Jim knelt, and put his hand on top of hers. "We'll take him with us," he said. "I promise, he will get a good burial. I promise, I'll make sure people know what he did. That he was a hero. Not a... not a traitor."

She looked up and saw that he was serious. He meant it. She almost laughed. She couldn't imagine that *anyone* could get that sort of outcome for Mark. No one.

No one but her, maybe.

One last rescue. One last chance to help her little brother out of a jam. Bigger than getting mall security to overlook his petty crimes. Bigger than convincing some poor knocked up girl to take the money and get on with her life.

She might not be able to get Mark a hero's funeral, but she'd try. Because in his last moments, he gave his life for her. And she would pull every string she'd ever had to make sure he was remembered for that.

And nothing else.

EPILOGUE

After hours on the road, they had finally arrived in Ghezna, and from there Ryker had somehow managed to not only keep anyone from noticing the dead man hidden in the back of the SUV, but he'd gotten them to the American embassy without incident. Once inside, everything became a blur of officials and debriefings and paperwork. They'd stayed there five days before Agent Anonymous walked in.

Chief of Station Michael Malleus, as he finally introduced himself.

Ryker had expected him, though he'd really thought he'd see him much sooner.

Malleus had pulled Ryker into a small, private conference room, and the two now sat across from each other. Ryker, mostly recovered from the ordeal in the desert, sat and watched Malleus closely. After a long moment of silently playing "you go first," Ryker finally decided he didn't care who won this ridiculous game.

"You didn't think I'd make it," he said.

Malleus smirked, and nodded. "That's about the gist of it."

"And Jill. You didn't think she'd make it either."

"Actually, I always intended for her to get out of the FOB. It was dumb luck that Faraz ended up with his hands on her."

"Dumb luck," Ryker sneered. "I should break your neck, right here."

"You could do that," Malleus said. "I mean, damn, Jim—I've got footage of you practically taking out an army all by yourself. I'm betting that if you wanted me dead, no one in this embassy could stop you."

Another stretch of silence. They both knew that Malleus was right. Just as they both knew that Ryker had no intention of killing him.

There'd been more than enough killing.

But more than that, Ryker knew that his only chance at walking out of here a free man was how this conversation went. If he killed Malleus, that would be it. The end.

But it might be the end anyway.

"You got what you wanted," Ryker said. "Hard drive destroyed. Faraz dead. *Kharif* scrambling to put things back together. You have your window. Do this right, and you can maybe fix this screwup with the Katakstan withdrawal. You could actually *help* these people. If that's really what all of this was actually about."

"You know it will always be more complicated than that."

"It always has been," Ryker replied.

"Your country thanks you for your brave and selfless service, yada yada yada," Malleus waved dismissively. "We'll take it from here. You know how this works. There are plans within plans, and most of them aren't going to look anything like you think they should. But on a more genuine note, Jim, I want to tell you... I'm impressed. A lot of people are. We knew you were good. But this was next level. You hit all the objectives, harder than we could have ever hoped."

Ryker didn't want to hear praise. He didn't want anything from this man, except to be finished with him. But he suspected that was one prize Malleus would never offer.

"So what now?" Ryker asked.

Malleus shrugged, then sighed. "That's up to you. We were impressed by your work. This was not an easy assignment. And there are a lot of... *situations* like this. Some more delicate than others."

"But it's up to me," Ryker said, doubtful.

"Mostly," Malleus said. "I mean, you are still technically under contract with the Company. Though you're certainly a special case. The truth is, Jim, I think you have some real potential. But I don't want to waste you on just any assignment. I think you're better suited for a little... side project I have in mind."

"You want to make me an Avenger or something?" Ryker asked.

Malleus smiled. "Something like that. I see you as more of a consultant."

"Consultant?"

Malleus shrugged. "Like I said, sometime we have special circumstances. Special causes. Terrorist cells. Guerrilla armies. Drug cartels. We deal with a lot of dangerous scenarios, and sometimes we need someone who can handle himself, without needing a lot of backup. Or, you know, *any* backup. The kind of thing you've proven you can do."

Ryker shook his head. "I want no part in that."

"No, of course not," Malleus said. "That's why I'll only bring you in when it's absolutely necessary."

"I said..."

"You don't get to choose," Malleus interrupted, his tone hard, icy. "Retirement isn't a thing, in this business. You know that." He was staring at Ryker, his eyes as hard as agates. And then, he softened. Smiled. Laughed. "But listen," he said, suddenly congenial. "It's better for you to work *with* us, than to be forced. And hey, I know that it doesn't exactly make for reliable operatives, when they're being coerced and forced all the time. So how about this—I will drop you off back in the US. I'll even put you back on that old timer's dirt farm, if that's what you want. Avery, right? I'll give you a very significant amount of money, in an account only you can access, and you can live however you like. Though I imagine you'll want to keep moving."

"Why's that?" Ryker asked.

"Because when I need you, I will call. And the work you will do for me will put you in a great deal of danger. And that will make it wiser for you to keep moving, keep your head down. You were living like a vagabond for the past year. That's probably the best plan, going forward."

Ryker didn't like the sound of any of this. But he saw it for what it was.

This was a deal. And an opportunity.

Ryker could go live his life. Or live *a* life, at any rate. And every now and then, every so often, Malleus would turn up, wave him into a helicopter, and drop him in a world of shit, in the name of keeping the country safe.

Not exactly a comfortable life. But Ryker hadn't had much comfort in his life so far anyway, had he? And besides...

Besides...

That boy scout within him, that teenager who had dreamt of serving his country—that kid was still in there. And he still wanted to do whatever he could to make the world a safer place. He still wanted to take down the bad guys.

"Ok," Ryker said. "Count me in."

Malleus grinned, nodded, and stood. "I knew I could count on you. I'll be in touch."

He was about to walk out of the conference room when Ryker turned in his seat. "Malleus."

Malleus turned, curious.

"I have a favor to ask."

"What's that?"

"Mark Adams."

Malleus shook his head. "Jim, we're good, but even we can't raise the dead."

"I want him to get a hero's burial."

Malleus studied Ryker for a moment. "Your girlfriend is already working on that."

"I want her to succeed."

Malleus nodded. "Ok. Done."

"And I don't want any mention of him being the one who turned that weapon over to anyone. That stays away from Jill."

Again Malleus nodded. "Anything else?"

Ryker thought for a moment, then said, "I want my first check to go to Avery Clemmons. For his... *dirt farm*."

Malleus laughed, nodded once more, and then turned and left the room.

Ryker sank back into his seat, considering the devil's bargain he'd just cut. He wasn't sure what would come of it. He'd never know when Malleus would come back around. But he would be ready.

He was the Consultant now.

EPILOGUE

Jill looked around the sterile room. It didn't look like the type of room that should be used for debriefing intelligence assets.

It looked like an interrogation chamber. Hard, empty walls that reflected the harsh lights back to her. Everything around her stainless steel, everything above and below cheap tile and drop ceiling.

She could almost feel the cold emanating from them.

She could almost feel the cold emanating from her as well. She didn't like any of this. It wasn't how this was supposed to go.

"From what I gather, he has no idea," Malleus said. It wasn't a question.

She arched an eyebrow. "From what you gather."

"You have more to add?"

She didn't respond. Instead, she toyed with the mechanical pencil on the table. She noticed that it was metal as well, same as the table itself. She almost laughed. The interior designer must have been a real piece of work. Nothing said modern brutalism like making everything the same color of stainless steel.

"Jill, if there's more you'd like to add —"

Her eyes shot up. "If there was *more to add*, I would have added it." She paused, took a breath. "Best I can tell, he has no idea."

"You didn't betray him, Jill," Malleus said. "This is his job. This is what he does."

"Last I heard his *job* was digging post holes on some dirt farm in Texas." She cocked her head to the side. "*You* swooped in and gave him his old job back. He didn't ask for it."

Malleus chewed the inside of his lip.

She knew she hadn't betrayed Jim. But withholding information from him felt exactly the same. She might as well have lied to his face. Might as well have stabbed Mark — and Jim — in the heart.

No, Jim. I'm just here to find my brother. I'm just here to clean up his mess.

She winced. She knew Jim would figure it out at some point. He was good; he *had* to have been thinking it the entire time he was downrange. And yet he had never asked her the crucial question.

Why was the device in Katakstan in the first place?

She was glad for it, too. She would not have been able to lie to him, not to his face, anyway. She knew that if he ever did ask her that question, she would have come clean.

Because I gave it to them, Jim. All of this was my fault.

"Look, none of this was your intention. I know that — we know that."

She followed Malleus' eyes, trying to discern whether he was telling the truth. She knew it would be impossible — if this guy wanted her to believe he was telling the truth, he would wear that on his face. If he wanted her to think he was lying, his eyes would tell her. As well-trained as Jim and Mark were at concealing their emotions, Malleus was better.

It was his job, after all.

He continued, clearing his throat. "The Company appreciates your cooperation. We understand the complex events that led up to giving the device to Katakstan."

Sure you do, she thought.

"And while we would have preferred that you hadn't, we are past all of that now."

She nodded along, not quite believing this last statement. She knew they would never move past this. The proverbial cat was out of the bag.

She believed there was *never* a reason to withhold information, to keep research close to the chest. Scientific advancement meant just that — it was to be shared with the world, to be studied and enhanced.

But as a *politician*, she knew the exact opposite was true. She should have kept the technology close to her chest, using it as leverage only when there was no better play. She had failed in that regard.

And Mark had paid the ultimate price.

"We'll deposit your payment in the account we have on record —"

"I never agreed to a payment," she snapped. "This wasn't a *job*."

"This *was* a job, Jill. For Jim. For Mark."

"Not for me."

"The Company doesn't see it that way."

"I don't *care* how you see it. I'm not accepting payment for what I did."

Malleus grinned. "I'm not sure we've ever had someone turn down free money."

She winced again. This money was anything but free. It had cost *far* more than whatever measly amount Malleus wanted to buy her off with.

"If we're done here…"

Malleus got the hint. He pushed his chair back — also metal, also rigid and squared, nothing but edges and corners, and stood up. She stayed seated, waiting until he was hovering over his side of the table.

"What now?" she asked.

He chewed his lip again, thinking. "Nothing. At least not yet. This chapter is closed."

She suspected he might say something like this. She hadn't worked directly with the CIA before, but she was no stranger to how they operated. Mark had explained it to her before, Jim had confirmed it. One chapter would close, but there was *always* another one ready to open. The Company never totally burned its assets. Never totally wrote anyone off.

Sure, she had messed up, and she had made amends the best way she knew how. She knew that selling off the technology had been the biggest mistake of her professional life. She could get over that — it had been a calculated risk, one that could have paid off handsomely.

As it turned out, it had also been the biggest mistake of her *personal* life. *That* was a wound that would take far longer to heal.

"I trust you can find your way out?" Malleus asked.

It wasn't hard — this was a single-building facility, a government rental. There was a cheap pre-fab desk inside the front entrance, and a few offices and rooms like this one. Getting lost in here would require losing all five senses at once.

She nodded quickly, then finally stood. She was thinking about Jim, of Mark. Of the massive human cost caused by what she had done. Of *course* she hadn't wanted it to come to this, but she wasn't naïve, either. There were consequences to every action. Her actions had started altruistic, at least in principle. She could forgive herself that. The CIA already had.

But none of that mattered compared to what was going through her mind now.

Jim *was* going to find out. It was inevitable, only a matter of time.

And the thought of that unnerved her. He would find out, at some point.

When he did, could he ever forgive her?

A NOTE FROM KEVIN TUMLINSON

Back in 2015, I was doing a podcast with Nick Thacker (the other guy who's name is on the cover of this book). It was a show aimed at self-published authors, and it was one of the ways Nick and I had gotten to know each other. We'd done the show for about two years, after I'd "bought" him online. I had paid him $200 for author coaching, back when I was thinking of doing that as part of my own business, and wanted to see how it went.

Best two-hundred-bucks I ever spent.

During one of those podcast episodes, now 7 years ago as of this writing, Nick and I were talking about our mutual genres. I was writing mostly science fiction at that point, and doing a little alright. I was starting to have a bit of traction, anyway. Nothing I'd call "success" per se, but I'm not very generous with myself.

But on that episode, Nick dared me to try *his* genre—to write a thriller novel.

I had never written a thriller novel, nor anything resembling one, in my life. I'd read a few—it's a hard genre to avoid, really, if you are an avid reader and love adventure. And I was a big fan of certain types of moves in the genre, especially *Indiana Jones* and franchises like it.

Despite my lack of having ever written in that vein, however, I was confident that I could. I'm kind of arrogant about my writing, honestly. I believe I can write anything. Just my particular form of ego.

So I gave it a shot. And to give myself at least some advantage in starting, I combed through a bunch of what I call my "Thirds." That being the "first third of a novel." The starts and stops of stories I'd begun over the years, but had abandoned for one reason or another. I took around four scenes I'd written to start other novels, mashed them together, cleaned them up, added a bit to them, and bam—I had the Prologue for *The Coelho Medallion*. And the character of Dan Kotler, Archaeologist and FBI Consultant, was born.

By this time, I had read a ton of thriller novels that, I now realize, inspired the crap out of that first Dan Kotler book. Not the least of which was Dan Brown's famous (some might even say infamous) *The Da Vinci Code*. Which, I realized one fateful evening in a hotel room, after a long day of speaking at an author's conference, and upon seeing the film adaptation of that book on HBO, I totally wholesale lifted huge chunks of plot from. But not to the point of plagiarism, at least. And the result of *my* story was very different from the plot of that book or film, by the time the dust settled. But the similarities were there, and pretty clear.

I can proudly say that since then, I've veered wildly from mimicking Brown's books. And the result has been a series that is, arguably, my "life's work." Though I suspect I'll write many more characters and books between now and the time I go to that great Library in the sky, I have a feeling that Dan Kotler will be with me right to the end.

I'm fine with that. Because that character, and those books, have given me the career I always dreamt of, when I was a kid. They opened up for me a world I had been confined to be more fantasy than the actual fantasy novels I was reading. A fairytale. A myth.

But instead... legendary. For me, at least.

And a big part of that legend is thanks to Nick Thacker, for daring me to do something he figured I'd be good at. And I'd like to think I am.

This book is not the first book he and I have co-authored together. But it is the longest, to date. Our first attempt at co-writing was a short set of books called *The Lucid*. And we've both discussed revisiting those, updating them, and adding to them. We probably will at some point.

So, not our first work together. And we did many things outside of writing together, too. We have, for many years now, enjoyed a friendship that borders on brotherhood. And I'm maybe more grateful to Nick for that than for the thriller stuff. By a tiny margin, anyway.

But this book represents a different step forward, I think, than what we've done together to date. It represents, first of all, the first solid, real crossover of our talents that we've had since we both started taking on a bit of notoriety among readers. We each have fans these days, as it turns out. And while that's a kick, there's more to it than just some really pleasant ego stroking.

Our readers have known about our relationship for years. And many of them have asked when we were going to do something together. This represents us saying, "How about now?"

So I hope you enjoyed this book. Because if I have my way, it's just the first. I can't say how many, or how rapidly they'll show up. But this should be a "Book 1." And let's see what Book 2 brings us.

Now, go read Nick's note. His probably contains poop jokes.

Kevin Tumlinson
    10 August 2022
    Liberty Hill, Texas

A NOTE FROM NICK THACKER

Poop.

There, now I've checked that box.

I deny everything Kevin just said. None of it is true — the man writes lies for a living, after all!

...In actuality, every word he wrote in his section is accurate, and I would like to expand on some of the themes he brought up.

First, I will never tire of telling the story of how we met. I was running a nonfiction blog at the time, and sent out to my list a note that I was offering coaching. One coaching call, followed by feedback and ongoing discussion, for only $200! What a steal!

Unfortunately, my audience didn't think of it as much of a steal at all, unless you consider that they probably thought *I* would be stealing from *them* if they were to take me up on the offer.

But there was one soul — one victim — who *did* take me up on it. I got a $200 PayPal payment from a man named Kevin Tumlinson, based at the time in Houston, Texas.

I was ecstatic — this was it! This was my ticket to the top. I was now an official coach; I was now ready to start my Tony Robbins-inspired campaigns of talks, public appearances, and million-copies-sold book launches.

I prepared heavily for that first (and only) coaching call. This guy, like me, was a fiction author! What were the odds? So I decided I would impress him by reading not one, not two, but *all three* of the books in his sci-fi series, Citadel.

It worked. I remember Kevin being genuinely surprised by my knowledge of his fiction, blown away that I had spent the time to read it. (I didn't tell him that I had nothing better to do — of course I was never going to let him know he was the only person who paid me for coaching.)

The call went well, and the follow-up even better.

I got a voicemail from him a few weeks later, saying that we should at some point write something together. He was talking about nonfiction, doing more of this coaching thing. He had more experience than I did in many fields anyway, so this was a natural step — we could combine forces, make even more $200 coaching calls. He would be the Tony to my Robbins.

Of course, I misunderstood that voicemail. While he was talking about teaming up on *nonfiction*, I thought he meant *fiction* instead. My assumption was that he wanted to write a book series with me. I was flattered, and immediately began drafting and outlining the first few scenes of what would become the book series *The Lucid*.

When I told him I was doing this, there was the necessary pause — far more pregnant than I would have liked — and a brief, stuttered acceptance of his new reality... and fate.

I wouldn't say I *coerced* him into it, but I certainly wouldn't say that he agreed jovially.

Nevertheless, we split up the writing duties. I would write the hero, he would write the villain. And we began dashing off the first draft of book 1 of *The Lucid*.

We still haven't finished the series today. It's only been 10 years or so.

While that book's success leaves much to be desired, our relationship does not. And lest you think I am about to devolve into a soliloquy for the love of my brother... well, I am.

Through the process of working through that first book, Kevin Tumlinson became the closest and best friend I have ever had in my adult life. More importantly than friendship, I think, was his support.

When I was struggling with what to do with my fiction career, Kevin was there.

When my fiction career began taking off and I decided to leave the day job I loved to chance it in this new world of creating stories, Kevin was there.

When that decision turned into years of panic attacks and chronic anxiety, Kevin was there.

I have a loving and caring spouse, and I could not do any of this without her. But this little anecdote is about Kevin. Without diminishing the support my wife provides, it's important for me to emphasize that *no one else on the planet* besides Kevin is 'in it' with me in the same way. He's in this world with me — and I'm not sure I could have managed to stay in it without someone like him by my side.

This project was something I've been dreaming about for years. Unlike *The Lucid*, which I feel was sort of a 'happy accident,' *The Backup Plan* was a purposeful, premeditated project. We had to wait for the stars and planets to align in order to get it done, but it's something I've been wanting to do... well, for forever.

I can't wait to see where Jim Ryker ends up next. With Kevin also holding the reins on this series, the I know the answer will not just surprise me — it'll blow me away. I've got so many stories I'd like to tell, and I know Kevin's the same way. Putting those ideas together gets us something like what you've just read, and it's pretty incredible that it's finally here.

Okay, I need to check the word counts to make sure my note's longer than Kevin's (Perfect: beat him by one!)

Nick Thacker

2 September 2022

Woodland Park, Colorado